Follow Lieutenant Julia Todd in the first two books
in the *Murder In Memphis* series:

The Chartreuse Envelope

"...an intricately plotted mystery thriller...sleuthing is engaging...Paavola keeps the action coming and his characters consistently interesting..." — *Kirkus Reviews*

"...well thought out...riveting...couldn't put it down." — Memphis Police Department Colonel Lori Bullard, Precinct Commander, Union Station

They Gotta Sleep Sometime

"...a brisk, engaging whodunit...The plot sizzles as case leads and shady characters smoothly integrate themselves into the author's grand design and rousing conclusion. An assured, soft-boiled sequel..." — *Kirkus Reviews*

Which One Dies Today?

Murder In Memphis

a novel by
James C. Paavola

Facts

Health Insurance Companies: U.S. Senate Testimony

June 24, 2009: Wendell Potter testified before the U.S. Senate Commerce, Science, and Transportation Committee, chaired by Senator Jay Rockefeller (Democrat-West Virginia). Thirteen months earlier he had been the head of public relations for CIGNA, and for Humana before that, two of the nation's largest for-profit providers of health insurance. Potter testified that publicly traded health insurance companies in the U.S. "confuse their customers and dump the sick—all so they can satisfy their Wall Street investors."

State of Health Care in the United States

Remote Area Medical (RAM): a Knoxville-based non-profit program founded in 1985 to provide free medical care to people in third-world countries with particular emphasis on people in notably remote areas with no access to healthcare. The United States has long been touted by the health insurance industry as having the best healthcare in the world. Yet the lack of access to healthcare, or at least to affordable healthcare, in the United States persuaded RAM to provide free services to Americans. RAM has provided free medical/dental services to more than 350,000 patients worldwide. Over half of those services have been provided within the

United States.

UC Atlas of Global Inequality: the United States leads the world in healthcare spending, while U. S. life expectancy is equivalent to that of Cuba, with worldwide rankings of 27th and 28th respectively.

Glossary

Asperger's Syndrome · a developmental disorder falling at the high-functioning end of the Autism Spectrum, characterized by severe deficiencies in the capacity for effective social interaction. It is often accompanied by peculiarities of speech and language, difficulty comprehending the nuances of conversation, good vocabulary, obsessive-compulsive characteristics, anxiety, depression, coordination problems, and an unusual preoccupation with a particular subject.

Pharaoh Health Management Systems · a fictional multistate health insurance company based in Memphis, Tennessee

OPRESSD · the fictional Organization of Patients Refused Essential Services and Sentenced to Death

Spin Doctor or Spinmeister · an individual accomplished in the art of spin—the manipulation and distortion of information to shape the perceptions and beliefs of the public—portraying a client in a positive light, and/or portraying the client's opposition in a negative light.

Spin message(s) · the use of words and short phrases intended to elicit either positive feelings toward one's client, or negative feelings toward the client's opposition (especially fear-related). Underlying the efficacy of a spin message is the fact that *perception,* even when based on fabrication, often *becomes* the public's *reality.*

Spin playbook · an internal publication intended to enhance the potency of a particular spin campaign, emphasizing strategies for consistent and repetitive use of spin messages throughout the information system—media releases, company representatives' interviews, lobbyists' communications, statements from so-called *credible* public interest groups, and public comments by politicians. For the campaign to be effective, all participants must be on the same page, giving the same message(s) repeatedly. When the public hears a message often enough, accurate or inaccurate, they are likely to believe it.

Acknowledgements

I want to express my sincere thanks to my wife, Marilyn, for her encouragement and constructive feedback. To our daughter Shannon Paavola who designed the book cover. To our daughter Nicole and her husband Jerry Penley for their help with the world of internet gaming. And to Bradley Harris who, for the third time, edited my work. To all of you—Thanks so much.

A special thanks goes to Wendell Potter, author of the national bestseller *Deadly Spin, An Insurance Company Insider Speaks Out On How Corporate PR Is Killing Health Care And Deceiving Americans.* (2010, Bloomsbury Press, New York). Wendell graciously provided feedback on my conceptualization of the health insurance industry. The depiction of that industry within this book is my responsibility alone.

Dedication

This book is dedicated to Barney DuBois, an extraordinary newspaper reporter, co-founder of the *Memphis Business Journal*, a renaissance man, a dedicated husband, father, brother, mentor, and boss—a man who touched many lives, a man with many friends.

Barney died at the age of 68, on June 11, 2011 of Amyotrophic Lateral Sclerosis (Lou Gehrig's disease). One of Barney's last professional activities was to assist in the editing of the *Deadly Spin, An Insurance Company Insider Speaks Out On How Corporate PR Is Killing Health Care And Deceiving Americans*—a national bestseller written by Wendell Potter (2010, Bloomsbury Press, New York).

Chapter 1

Fantasy to Reality

3:15 AM Saturday, April 4, 2009... The odor pungent, the smell unmistakable—male, not bathed in days. A gooseneck table lamp shed the only light in the room. Bags that once held nacho-flavored chips and *Twinkies* lay near a small trash can, refusing to stay crumpled. The silver rims of *Red Bull* drink cans reflected light from their scattered positions on the floor. The lamp outlined a figure hunched over a desk, agitated, mumbling.

He recalled his mother telling him how, as a baby, he'd destroy every tower, wall, and pyramid she constructed from blocks. He'd always thrilled watching things blow up in cartoons and movies. The more explosions the better— the bright colors, the loud noises reverberating in his chest. He loved the feeling of power he experienced when playing violent video games, obliterating anything and anyone he desired, virtually. But tonight was different. A giant step from fantasy. He had promised his friend—his only friend. Tonight he would be playing in the real world.

He had prepared for weeks, learning about all sorts of explosives and bombs on the internet. He honed in on car bombs triggered by cell phones, then made cash purchases from different hardware stores—lengths of pipe, wiring, and fertilizer. A Michigan militia website showed him where to buy triggering mechanisms. Discarded cell phones provided the components necessary to link the bomb to a remote cell phone. He practiced mixing various explosive concoctions using colored sand, water, and wires—always blue and white wires. But practicing was one thing. Creating the genuine article was another. He hesitated initially, unsure of his skills, fending off his conscience. Gradually his confidence grew and his focus narrowed. He worked continuously, sleeping when he could no longer hold his eyes open, and then only for an hour or two.

The harmless components came together sooner than he expected. A live bomb. His eyes opened wide, his focus interrupted. Just when he needed all his concentration, his body began to betray him. Jittery hands. Lightheadedness. What began as a physiological response to caffeine, sugar, and sleeplessness morphed into a sense of doom. The bomb could explode anytime. No warning. His anxiety grew, but he had felt anxious before. He automatically began to count—his only way to protect himself—he had to *count to five.*

So close. Three...four...five. All that remained was to connect two wires. He held one in each trembling hand. The task was simple: Attach the wires to the posts and screw them down. For weeks he had drawn on his intelligence, his persistence. But in his current state, this simple task proved beyond him. A blue wire in his right hand, a white in his left. He began to count. One, both wires touched the circuit posts on their respective sides. Two, he crossed the wires, blue over white, to touch the posts on their opposite sides. Three, he uncrossed the wires and again touched the posts on their respective sides. Four, he crossed the wires, white over blue, to touch the posts on their opposite sides. Five, he uncrossed the wires touching the posts he began with.

"No," he growled, pounding a fist on the desk. "Not right."

Sweat stung his eyes. Stains blossomed on his shirt. He squinted to see the bomb clearly, a real bomb. He rubbed his eyes on his sleeve, blinking and straining to refocus. The stinging subsided, but the bomb continued to blur. He took another mouthful of Red Bull, swallowed, then belched loudly. He changed hands, the blue wire in his left and the white wire in his right. *Five,* he told himself. Count to five. Counting became more important than finishing the bomb, more important than finishing the bomb correctly. One... two...

* * *

*4:30 AM Saturday, April 4, 2009...*Two men in hooded sweatshirts slipped in through the garage side door. No flashlights. The lead man inched his way in, his hand feeling for anything solid in front of him. The second man kept a hand on the first man's back.

"Here," the first whispered, dropping to the concrete floor and rolling on his back beside the vehicle. "Give it to me."

The standing man's foot pressed against the other's hip. He gently lifted the pipe bomb from the plastic grocery bag, and lowered it into the first man's hands. The first man shook off a chill, took a deep breath, and eased the bomb onto his stomach. He held it with one hand, and used the heels of his shoes to force himself under the vehicle. The only sound came from the rivets on the back pockets of his jeans as each small push scratched the pavement. Reaching the center, he pulled the device up his body, passing it beside his head. He raised it slowly until he felt the pull of its magnet and heard a metallic click as the bomb attached. The sound of ripping cloth echoed as he tore off pieces of duct tape, just in case the magnet did not hold. His eyes were adjusting to the pitch darkness. The car bomb came into focus, inches from his face. He froze.

"Shit."

"What's wrong?"

"Pull my feet," he whispered loudly. "Get me outta here." His panic increased as the hollow quiet of the tight quarters grew louder.

His companion grabbed both ankles and pulled upward, banging the man's shins.

"Ow! Goddammit! Get me out of here."

The other man changed his grip and struggled backward with shuffling half-steps. The first man's tightly furrowed brow relaxed the instant his face cleared the vehicle. He pulled free and scrambled to his feet. The two men hurried out the door and ran down the driveway, around the corner to their pickup. They yanked opened the doors and threw themselves in. Breathing heavily they searched the neighborhood for movement or sounds. A few minutes passed before they felt confident.

"Okay. Dial it in."

The man in the passenger seat flipped open his cell phone, turning his head further away with each number punched, anticipating a loud explosion.

Nothing.

"Try it again."

He looked hard at his phone, and punched numbers carefully.

Nothing.

"Again!"

His hands trembled as he tried for the third time, slowly, pressing each number, hard.

Nothing.

"Damn. It's not working. You screwed up. What'd you do?" the driver said.

The other man began rocking, wringing his hands.

"Did you take your pill before you built this thing?"

He rocked harder.

"I bet you didn't. You got all caught up in the *fives*. Didn't you?"

No response.

"Shit. Now I've got to go back and get that *thing*. It's probably got your finger prints all over it. Hasn't it?"

"Gloves," he said, rocking. "No prints."

"Okay, okay. You'll just have to do it over. Be ready to go early next week. And this time, take your pill," he said, opening his door.

Chapter 2

On The Mend

Saturday morning, April 4, 2009...getting back to okay. Memphis Police Lieutenant Julia Todd ran to the InsideOut Gym, taking her usual circuitous 4.7-mile route from home. Today she worked the heavy bag, punching and kicking the eighty-pound target. She felt good. Snap...pop, pop, pop...thwap, bam! This was only the second week Julia had been able to work out pain-free since a very angry woman—with a black belt in karate—broke three of her ribs. She had battled back, knocked the assailant unconscious, and cuffed her. But Julia was less successful coping with her convalescence. It had been a painful and frustrating seven weeks, especially without being able to exercise. Finally, she was getting back into shape—pow, pow...thwap, bam, pwoof! She stopped to catch her breath, blotting the sweat from her eyes.

"Looking wicked," said a woman standing inside the doorway. "Haven't seen you hit the bag like that in while. You in one piece now?"

"Hey, Girty," said Julia. "Yup. One piece. A bit sore, but no pain."

"That karate chick still locked up?"

"Still locked up. Locked up for a long, long time."

Julia topped off her workout with free weights and crunches. As usual, she jogged home from the gym, using a more direct 2.4-mile route. She felt stronger, her confidence building.

* * *

Sunday evening, April 5, 2009...for want of a rib. Julia pulled into the parking lot of the *Haven for Seniors* retirement community. She parked well back from the main building. The large complex spread out before her. Four months ago her seventy-seven year-old Aunt Louise told her she wanted to sell her house—the home Julia and her brother Wayne grew up in—and move into a retirement community. Twenty-five years earlier Arizona protective services had removed two young children from their abusive mother and assigned them to the custody of their father's sister Louise. The children thrived in their new home, their new family. Aunt Louise became the nurturing parent they'd never had.

Julia was still warming to the notion of the Haven being Aunt Louise's home. She took a deep breath and left the car carrying her usual contribution to Sunday dinner: a loaf of French bread from *La Baguette* bakery and a bottle of wine from *Buster's Liquors,* today's choice an inexpensive French blend, *La Vieille Ferme.*

* * *

"So, how're you doing, dear?" asked Aunt Louise.

"Better. Much better," said Julia.

"Your ribs have healed?"

"Yes, thankfully. I can breathe without pain. In fact, I can even run without hurting. And last week I went back to the gym—exercises, weights, and hitting the heavy bag. Look. I can even open this bottle of wine. Ta-da! Thank goodness it's a screw cap."

"No pain. Glad to hear it."

"Not now," Julia said, pouring the wine. "Just sore. But this kind of ache feels good."

"I can tell by your posture and your face you feel better. In fact, your attitude is better," said Aunt Louise, smiling. "I've got my little guardian back."

"My *attitude*?" Julia made a face. "Was I all that bad?"

"Let's just say you weren't always easy to live with, dear. Not very tolerant. Snippy, even angry. Sometimes I was walking on eggshells."

"Eggshells. Whoa."

"Maybe that's why Mark hasn't been around lately?"

"Mark? Oh, yeah. Mark." Julia stared into her glass of wine. She looked up. "He stopped talking to you, too?"

"I see him around the Haven as usual. But we don't talk. I figured either I did something really bad, or you two had a falling out."

Julia paused, returning her eyes to her wine. "He was just being Mark. You know—helpful, caring, tolerant. I couldn't take it. I told him I needed my space."

"Think maybe he gave you more than your space?"

"More than my space?"

"Like maybe he crossed you off his list?"

Julia was quiet during dinner, not even small talk. They cleared the table and started the dishes, Aunt Louise washing, Julia drying.

"I messed up, didn't I?" Julia said.

"Can't say. But I do know you two made a great couple," said Aunt Louise. "Getting over your injuries was harder than you expected?"

"Yeah. It's been a bear. It was like my life had been taken away from me. It was just a stupid rib."

"*Three* stupid ribs."

"Yeah. Three stupid ribs."

"Pain can change things."

"I couldn't tie my shoes, reach in my pocket, or even put

on my seatbelt, let alone run and work out. I felt so helpless, so defenseless. How could I protect myself? How could I protect anyone else?"

"You're getting worked up just talking about it."

"Sorry. I thought I was over it."

"You, more than most, should understand how difficult it can be. Your meetings with officers who've had to deal with horrible situations. What do you call them?"

"Critical Incident Stress Debriefings."

"Yes, debriefings. I'm certain you've learned how normal your reactions are."

"I thought I was stronger than other people. I hated feeling so weak, so vulnerable. I felt embarrassed, frustrated. Sometimes flat out furious. Now my body's healed, but my emotions haven't. They're still all screwed up," Julia said as her eyes filled with tears. Aunt Louise wrapped both arms around her.

"You're not a machine, *Miss Perfect*. Give yourself a break." She stroked Julia's hair. "Now if your young man is the psychologist I think he is, he'll understand all of this."

Julia pulled back to look at her aunt. "You think so?"

"Sounds as if you've got some work to do. It's time to use those super people-skills of yours."

Chapter 3

Fire in the Hole

Monday morning, April 6, 2009...it worked. Two cars were parked in the garage, the device attached to the underside of the Mercury Mountaineer. In the kitchen, the Tuttles were finishing breakfast. Robert stuffed the last piece of toast in his mouth and gulped his coffee. He swallowed hard, as he collected his briefcase and filled his thermo coffee cup.

"Remember, there's a soccer game *and* a basketball game tonight. I'll be late," he said, leaning in to kiss his wife Shelly.

"I'll have dinner waiting," she said.

He walked through the kitchen door into the garage. Tuttle slid behind the steering wheel and punched the garage door opener. As the door rolled up, he started the car—

BOOM!

The explosion rocked the neighborhood.

* * *

The two men were pumped, breathing hard, as they watched from their parked car.

"It worked," said one, eyes wide.

"Damn," said his partner. "I never dreamed it'd be that big. I'm not so sure I can—"

"Don't even go there," the first man interrupted, glaring. "They're the murderers. They'll keep killing until someone stops them. We're in this till the end. No backing out.

You promised."

* * *

*Monday morning, making the scene…*Julia was enjoying getting back to her old self, her routine, her life. She finished her morning run and chugged a glass of water. She showered, toweled off, and dressed. She shook her head doggy style, and her short brown hair fell into place. Julia rarely wore make-up or perfume. Today would be no exception. She dressed and stood in front of the mirror. Her uniform was crisply pressed, the brass shiny, and her shirt buttons lined up with her belt buckle. She finger-combed her hair, took one last look.

Julia's morning habit was to ease into the work day by way of the neighborhood coffee shop, the *Deliberate Literate*. It was her practice to sit and read the *Commercial Appeal*, eating her *Cup of Gold* nutrition bar, and drinking the specialty coffee of the day. She had just unwrapped her nutrition bar when BOOM! She heard the sound with her whole body.

"What the…" Julia was the first one out the door. Everyone followed.

People emptied establishments up and down Union Avenue. Some pointed to the northeast, where a cloud of smoke was rising. Julia ran to her car and jumped in. She flipped on the siren and lights, and gunned it onto Union Avenue, whipping in and out of traffic. She pulled herself over the top of her steering wheel, straining to see the smoke. She took a left on Cooper, then a right on Court, grabbing her two-way.

"Dispatch! House in flames on Court, west side of East Parkway. Roll fire trucks, ambulance."

The tones sounded and big doors shuddered open. Firefighters raced to don their gear and board the vehicles. Fire trucks noisily pulled out of nearby stations on Union Avenue

21

and East Parkway Boulevard, horns and sirens blaring, picking up speed.

Julia screeched to a stop in front of the Tuttles' home. The garage and a portion of the house were engulfed in flames. She grabbed the car's small fire extinguisher and raced to the garage. She thought she could see the outline of a person's head in one of the cars, but the heat from the flames kept her back. She turned left and sprinted to the front door. Locked. She smashed the small window with the fire extinguisher, straining to see in. A key protruded from the deadbolt. She stretched, sticking her arm in up to the shoulder—just out of reach. She jumped, forcing herself in further, and grabbed the key. The lock clicked open. She yanked her arm out and burst into the living room, yelling, "Fire! Fire! The house is on fire! Anyone here? Memphis police! Anyone here?"

Thick black smoke hung halfway down the wall. Julia crouched, the fingertips of one hand brushing the floor. She moved from the living room down the hall to the kitchen. The outline of a body lying near the refrigerator came into view—a woman, her dress on fire. Nearby lay the internal door to the garage, burning. Julia pulled the pin on her fire extinguisher and sprayed enough to quell the flames on the dress and door. Fire truck sirens blared, then cut off. She moved to the woman, felt her carotid artery and found a pulse. She tried to get her conscious. The woman moaned.

"Ma'am! Where are you hurt?" Julia yelled. "Ma'am! Where are you hurt? Can you stand?'

"Wha hapon?" the woman mumbled, her eyes not focusing.

"An explosion. Can you stand?"

"Think so," the woman said. But she didn't seem to know how to do it. Julia struggled to help the woman to her feet as two firefighters ran in.

"Give her to us," one yelled through his mask. "You need to get outta here. Too much smoke." Julia felt a strong hand on her back, pushing. She heard the other firefighter yell to the woman, "Anyone else in the house?"

"Hubun…gara." The woman looked where the door used to be, and she began screaming,

"Bobby! Bobby!"

"Any children?" asked the firefighter.

"Skoo bud. Bobby!" the woman called out, then collapsed.

Julia held her arm across her mouth and nose, her eyes burning. Crouching even lower to avoid the drooping smoke, she tried to get to the door without taking a breath. But it was too far. She inhaled caustic smoke and doubled over, coughing uncontrollably. Julia dropped to one knee, feeling lightheaded. She summoned her strength for a final push, and stumbled through the door, escaping in a large cloud of smoke. Julia stopped when she felt the cool outside air on her face. She drew in a breath but doubled over again, coughing. A paramedic passed her, running to meet the firefighters, and yelled to her partner to bring the stretcher.

"Lieutenant. You okay?"

Julia looked upward, her eyes watery and stinging.

A large African American man held both of her forearms. "You're bleeding," said Sergeant Johnnie Tagger. "And your hair's sparking." He pinched a clump of her smoldering hair.

"Thanks, Tag," she coughed. She shook her head and rubbed her hair frantically. "Must have cut my arm on the glass."

"It's dripping out at a pretty good clip, and you need some oxygen. Let's find our own paramedic." He pulled her to him, supporting her as they worked their way toward the street.

"What about the person in the car?"

"I drove in right behind the fire trucks and saw you going in the front door. Those two firefighters jumped off the truck as it pulled up. They were hauling ass, beat me up the sidewalk. Smoke was too thick. I held back. I don't know any more than that. But I'm certain anyone in that car is cooked."

* * *

Julia sat hunched on the rear bumper of an ambulance, breathing into an oxygen mask.

"Hey, Lieutenant," said an older African-American man in firefighting gear.

"Morning, Chief Johnson," Julia said through the mask. "We need to stop meeting like this."

"My boys tell me you were the one who made the call. Got us here early enough to knock it down before it destroyed the neighbors' houses. No doubt you also saved the woman's life." Julia managed a tight lipped smile. "I'd say that was a good day's work."

"Just happened to be in the neighborhood," she said.

"Lucky for all of us. How's the arm?"

Julia lifted the oxygen mask. "Technically I think they said it was *just a flesh wound.* I've had worse."

"So I understand from my little sister Teresa. Say, if she gives you any trouble, you know where to find me."

"You kidding? Teresa's the glue of Union Station. We couldn't function without her."

"That's what she tells me. I figured it was just BS."

Julia pulled the oxygen mask to her face and took several deep breathes, then removed it. "This was an awfully big explosion, Chief. Any idea what caused it?"

"It clearly started in the garage. We're still waiting on things to cool off."

Julia grabbed two more breaths of oxygen. "Can't help but think about the man over in Wynne, Arkansas who was blown up in his car last month," she said.

"Yeah. I know. I really don't want to be dealing with terrorists."

"I guess when you're the person getting blown up, it doesn't matter whether it was a terrorist planted the bomb or a copycat murderer."

"You'll know soon as we know."

* * *

Tagger walked up with his partner, Sergeant Anthony Marino. Though a good six feet tall, he looked short next to Tagger.

"How ya doin, Lieutenant?" Marino asked.

"Better, now I can breathe without the oxygen mask," she said, coughing. She returned the mask to her face, and took several breaths.

"We checked with the neighbors. Nobody heard or saw anything," said Marino.

"I'm going back to get my coffee," Julia said. "Maybe they'll warm it up for me. Then I'll head on to Union Station. Leave a few officers. Treat it like a crime scene, till we know different. And just in case we're dealing with a murder, assign someone to watch the Mrs. while she's in the hospital. May be a good idea to track down a relative who can take care of the children. We'll talk about this later."

* * *

Julia drove the half-mile back to the *Deliberate Literate*. She felt exhausted. Her body ached as she swung her feet to the pavement. She waited for the pain to come from her ribs. None came. She felt as though she'd taken a spin in a cement mixer—stiff, sore, disoriented. She moved slowly into the shop.

The owner walked up quickly. "You look like you've had a full morning," Millie said. "And you smell like barbeque, after the pig caught fire."

"Sorry about that," Julia said, trying unsuccessfully to smell it. "I suppose I have had a full morning."

"I don't mean to be out of line, but you might want to go to the restroom and clean up a little. I think you'd feel better."

Julia was confused by Millie's comments. She looked at the soot on her uniform and shoes, then her hands. "Thanks. That's probably a good idea."

She walked to the restroom. When she turned on the light and looked into the mirror she did a double take. "Holy shit," she said out loud. Not only do I feel like I've been in a cement mixer, she thought, but I look like it. Julia brushed at her pants, then her shirt. She couldn't see any improvement. She saw the place where Tagger had pinched out her burning locks. What remained of those hairs was sticking out straight, like she'd stuck her finger in an electrical outlet. Shaking her head didn't help, nor did finger combing. Julia stared. Eventually she washed her face and hands, and returned to the counter.

"Well, at least your face looks better," said Millie. "I'm sure your nutrition bar and a fresh coffee will help." She walked Julia to her table, pulled out a napkin-wrapped *Cup of Gold*, and sat it beside a steaming cup of coffee. Julia reached in her pocket. "No charge, Lieutenant. You never had the opportunity to finish these the first time. Too busy saving the neighborhood."

Julia sat slowly, out of breath and staring at her table top. Eventually she grabbed the nutrition bar and chewed mechanically. The food and the coffee helped. Julia didn't look any different, but she felt better. She waved a thank you to Millie as she left the shop. She drove home to shower, change clothes, and start her day all over.

Chapter 4

Pieces to the Puzzle

*Monday morning...*Julia arrived at the Union Station precinct house, looking sharp, feeling better.

"Morning, Lieutenant," said Teresa Johnson, the Union Station secretary.

"Morning, Teresa," said Julia. "I thought Monday was your day off."

"Got a phone call. Thought maybe I could help."

"Thanks. Say, just had a chat with your big brother."

"The policeman or the fireman?"

"Chief Marvin Quincy Johnson of the MFD."

"Marvin was at the explosion?"

"Yup. He told me be sure and keep an eye on you."

"And you said?"

"It's a full time job."

Julia walked down the hall to her office. Teresa followed.

"You look a whole lot better than Marino described. You go home and clean up?" Teresa said.

"You ought to be a detective," said Julia. "Good contacts, good observation, and good intuition."

"Thank you, ma'am. I'm afraid I cheated a little. I called Millie at the *Deliberate Literate* to check on you. She said she thought you might go home."

"What is this? You got the secret numbers and names of

everyone I know?"

"Not *everyone*. Only the important ones. Speaking of which, I haven't heard anything from Dr. Blue Eyes lately. What's up with that?"

"Miss Johnson, please confine your nose to your own business."

"Yes ma'am. By the way, the sergeants and I have talked about having a welcome home party."

"For who?"

"I think that's for *whom*."

"Okay. For whom?"

"For the return of our former lieutenant."

"What former lieutenant?"

"The *old* Lieutenant Julia Todd, of course. Glad you're feeling better," Teresa said as she turned toward the door.

"You been talking to my Aunt Louise again?"

"No, ma'am. Just being a good observer," Teresa said, smiling as she left.

* * *

Tagger filled the doorway.

"Is now a good time, Lieutenant?" he asked.

"Yeah, come on in," said Julia.

Tagger walked in first, Marino following. They took seats.

"Thanks for taking care of me this morning, Tag," she said.

"You were the one doing all the heavy lifting," Tagger said.

Julia forced a smile. "I still haven't heard from Chief Johnson yet," she said.

"The guys were going through the garage but stopped, moon-walked out of there, put away their tools, and called ATF," said Marino. "Said it looked like some type of bomb."

"Damn," said Julia. "I was hoping for a gas leak."

"That would be two car bombings inside a month," said Tagger.

"The guy in Arkansas is still alive—really messed up, but alive," Marino said. "From what I hear, ATF is leaning toward the attack being a personal vendetta, rather than a terrorist."

"Think that bomber had anything to do with this?" asked Tagger.

"He'd have to be doing it from behind bars," said Julia. "But he may have started something."

"I don't like the Midsouth becoming the new Middle East," said Tagger. "I want to nail this dude, now."

"Or dudette," said Marino.

"So how to proceed?" asked Julia. "We know the Arson and Explosives guys from ATF are going to be all over this. Maybe even the same agents who worked the Wynne bombing. I want to cooperate with them, but I don't want to be cooperated out of house and home."

"We're with you, Lieutenant," said Marino. "It's kinda like when we worked with the FBI on the hedge fund killings last year."

"That kind of cooperation's pretty rare," said Tagger.

"Right on both counts," said Julia. "I think we should make some preliminary assumptions about splitting duties. Let's assume this is a plain old murder rather than a terrorist attack. We'll investigate it like any other murder. We'll defer to ATF to investigate the bomb, where it came from, who might have made it, and whether the maker is a terrorist."

"Sounds reasonable," said Marino. "We'll start checking on Robert Tuttle. Interview his friends, relatives, co-workers. See if he made any enemies."

"Where'd he work?" asked Julia.

"White Station High School," Marino said. "He was an assistant principal, in charge of student discipline."

* * *

*The lay of the land...*Marino wanted a cop-to-cop talk before walking into the school. He called Kendrick Willis, the Memphis Police Officer assigned to White Station High School as part of the cooperative arrangement between the Memphis City Schools and the MPD.

"Yes, Sergeant," said Willis. "The news about Tuttle is out. Folks are pretty freaked."

"Any ideas on possible suspects?" asked Marino.

"I don't know of anyone who'd want to kill him, but—"

"But what?"

"There's one White Station student we've just gone round and round with. He threatened to blow up some classmates who've been harassing him. Normally a student who makes threats like that is suspended, maybe even expelled."

"Normally?"

"In this case there's a major issue because he's a special education student."

"And that's an issue because…?"

"Can't say I'm an expert in special ed law, but I can tell you what I think I know. This student has been threatening to blow people up almost since his first days in special education, at age five or six. Turns out there's some kind of regulation that a special ed student can't be suspended from school if their misbehavior is related to their diagnosed problem. It's kind of special ed's version of being declared innocent by reason of insanity. You know—like he can't help it. Like it's not really his fault. Least that's what it seems like to me. The upshot for this kid is that attorneys have been battling one another. A special ed administrative judge ruled in the kid's favor. He's back at school."

"Can you pull his file?"

"No can do. Special ed laws are pretty strict. We'd need a subpoena or a court order. In fact, the law stops the principal and teachers from even talking to any non-school person about the kid. On top of which this kid's father is rather intense. He's not going to let anyone talk to his kid without him and his attorney present."

"I'll get the court order," said Marino. I have a meeting with the principal, right after school. Meet me in her office at two-thirty."

* * *

*The bureaucracy catch-twenty-two-step...*White Station High Principal Margaret Seymour invited the two policemen into her office. She shook their hands, took a seat behind her big circa 1950s wooden desk.

"Thanks for meeting with me," said Marino.

"So sad," said Seymour. "So very sad. The word went through the school like wildfire."

"Can you think of anyone who might want to see Mr. Tuttle dead?" asked Marino. "Anyone mad at him?"

"Bobby was well-liked by students, parents, *and* faculty. He was in charge of student discipline, but was known for being fair and respectful," said Seymour.

"You must have some gang-bangers here. Every school does," said Marino.

"We work hard to stay on top of that stuff," said Seymour. "There have been some stare-downs and posturing between members of the Vice Lords and one of the apartment posses. They're some of our bus riders. Every so often things get a bit hairy at one of the bus stops. Bobby's been working on that. I thought things were getting better."

"Speaking of threats," Marino said.

Seymour looked at Willis. "Not sure this is relevant, Sergeant," she said. "But there is one student we've recently dealt with for making threats—bomb threats."

"And...?" Marino encouraged.

"You know, after the school shootings across the river in

Jonesboro, and the next year at Columbine, all school districts in the country cracked down on students who make threats," said Seymour. "Memphis City Schools' procedure is for these students to be suspended, and for our mental health team to evaluate them and give us a best guess as to how dangerous they think the kid is. Afterwards, an administrative decision is made regarding the student's status—expulsion, assignment to an alternative school, or return to the assigned school."

"I know there's a point somewhere," Marino said.

"Yeah, sorry," said Seymour. "I was just trying to give a sense of the context."

"The context of what?" asked Marino.

"One of our twelfth graders threatened to blow up some students who were harassing him."

"And?"

"And I can't discuss his case without written authorization," said Seymour.

"Allow me," said Marino handing her a court order for a copy of the records, and allowing Memphis City Schools staff to discuss the student.

Seymour read the court order. "I see you came prepared, Sergeant," she said. "I and any of my staff will be happy to discuss Charlie Barrington with you. However, it *will* take a while to get a copy of Charlie's file. Given recent legal events, it's being held at the administrative offices on Avery. The board attorney has put some extra restrictions on it. I'll send the court order to him."

"Okay, just so it doesn't take long," said Marino. "What about Charlie?"

"Charlie is a student with Asperger's Syndrome," said Seymour. "He's been special ed his entire school career. Currently he's being mainstreamed in the regular classroom.

That means he takes regular education classes with regular students. Charlie is very smart. Academics are not his problem area."

"He just wants to blow people up," Marino said.

"According to his file, he's been talking about blowing people up since kindergarten," said Seymour. "But there's no record of him so much as hitting another student."

"What triggered *this* threat?" Marino asked.

"Charlie, like so many persons with Asperger's, has problems with obsessive-compulsive disorder. The number five is very important to him. Charlie has to do things *five* times and he always carries *five* pencils or pens in his shirt pocket. A classmate took one of his pencils. Charlie freaked. Some boys played keep away with it. Charlie threatened to blow them up."

"So Charlie was suspended for committing the *second foul?*" said Marino.

"Something like that," said Seymour. "Bobby handled the investigation and disciplinary actions, suspending Charlie for making the threat, and suspending his classmates under our anti-bullying policies."

"The other students back in school?" asked Marino.

"Yes, but only after everything went ballistic," said Seymour. "Parents were enraged. Each side wanting the other side expelled and sent to Siberia. Charlie's father threatened everyone with legal action, absolutely unable to see anyone else's perspective. His attorney was cut from the same cloth. The parents of the harassing boys also threatened to sue, and decided to try the case in the media. Everyone was incensed, and that sells air time and newspapers. I've had calls from several of our elected Board of Education Commissioners, as well as other politicians from here to DC, telling me what to do. Of course by federal education law, school personnel are forbidden from discussing any disciplinary issues. So we fuel the circus by being unable to discuss this with the public, including politicians."

"Charlie's back in school, too?" Marino asked.

"That's correct, but only after hours of meetings with attorneys from all sides, and hours of required manifestation hearings, and one big due process hearing with a judge."

"What's a manifestation hearing?"

"Special education law says no one can interfere with a special ed student's right to an educational placement when the offending behavior is deemed a manifestation of their handicapping condition. Charlie's condition includes an obsession with blowing people up. That's a documented part of his handicap, his disability. And so threatening to blow up his classmates was clearly expected. Because of this, the special education law says he cannot be held responsible for his actions. In this case that meant Charlie had to be returned to all his regular education classes."

"I don't get it," said Marino. "That sounds as if the law says it's okay for him to blow other students up."

"I understand that interpretation," said Seymour. "All I can say is that the federal law takes a slightly different perspective in protecting Charlie's right to an education. In fact, it was Charlie's attorney who argued that the responsibility for keeping Charlie from blowing up other people fell squarely on the shoulders of the Memphis City Schools. She argued the school system had to wand him daily for weapons, and hire an 'ex-Marine'—her words—to accompany Charlie everywhere he went on school-related business."

"So what have you done?" Marino asked.

"We wand him every day for weapons, but we don't think we need an ex-Marine body guard," said Seymour.

"This is way beyond my capacity to understand," said

Marino. "I'd like to talk to the boy."

"I'm afraid that can only happen after your attorney talks to the board attorney who talks to the father's attorney," said Seymour. "Then...maybe."

* * *

*A hello from the past...*Julia was reading through case files stacked on her desk. Her phone buzzed.

"Lieutenant, ATF on line one," said Teresa. Julia punched the blinking light.

"Lieutenant Todd," she said.

"This is Special Agent Werner Powers. I'm with the Arson and Explosives section of the ATF."

"I've been expecting a call."

"Let me begin by telling you that FBI Special Agent Masterson says hello. Says he worked with you last summer. Nothing but good things to say about you and your team. Course, he also said Memphis was too damn hot."

"Masterson? Nice surprise. He still in New York?"

"Yup. Irascible as ever. If you can work with him, you can work with anyone. In fact that's why I'm calling. I want to sit down with you and talk about this morning's bombing."

"My team's out of pocket at the moment, but we can set something up here at Union Station for—say, four-thirty?"

"Four-thirty it is. See you then."

* * *

She has a name... Tagger drove to the Elvis Presley Memorial Trauma Unit of the Regional Medical Center at Memphis, known as the *MED*. He found the officer who had been assigned protection detail. She stood as he approached, surprised at his size. She spoke first.

"Sergeant," she said. "I'm Officer Shawna Franklin."

"Officer Franklin," he acknowledged. "Bring me up to speed."

"The woman has been processed through the trauma unit."

"The woman has a name, Officer Franklin," he said.

"Yes, Sergeant. Er, Shelly Tuttle has been processed through the trauma unit. The trauma team stabilized her and is waiting on test results."

"Is Mrs. Tuttle conscious?"

"Yes."

"Can we talk to her?" asked Tagger.

"The doctor said I—I mean you—could talk to her in ten minutes," Franklin said.

Tagger looked at her expectantly.

"Oh, her name," she said, pulling a notepad from her pocket. "Dr. Bella Torruilla, Sergeant."

"Officer Franklin, have you had any experience talking to people who've lost family members?"

"No, Sergeant. Only those who've been victimized."

"Your first lesson is to know the names of the family members you'll be talking to. For your second lesson, I want you with me when we go in."

The door opened and a small Hispanic woman in green scrubs backed through, still talking to someone inside the room.

"Dr. Torruilla?" asked Tagger, walking to meet her. "I'm Sergeant Tagger. What can you tell us about Mrs. Tuttle's condition?"

"Sergeant," Torruilla said, raising her chin to look up at him. "Mrs. Tuttle's doing remarkably well for what she's gone through. The force of the explosion threw her into something, perhaps the wall. She has a broken nose, missing two front teeth, lots of bruising, probably broken ear drums, some first and second degree burns, and most serious of all is the head trauma. We're watching her closely for internal bleeding, especially in the brain."

"I was at the scene, and saw her being carried out. She really took a shot."

"I understand her husband didn't make it."

"Far as we know, he was the one in the SUV where the explosion occurred. Burned beyond recognition. We're waiting on the coroner's determination. Has she said anything about her husband?"

"Not that I've heard. She's been in and out of consciousness. I thought she was coming out of it earlier. But I'm afraid she went under again. I don't know what to tell you."

"Officer Franklin has been assigned to stay with her. She will follow her wherever she goes, even to the x-ray machine."

"I don't understand," said Torruilla. "Do you think someone did this deliberately? Do you think my patient is in danger? Are *we* in danger?"

Franklin's eyes widened.

"This is just a routine precaution," Tagger said. "I'm sure everything will be fine. Please let Officer Franklin know as soon as Mrs. Tuttle is able to speak. We need to ask her some questions."

"I understand her family is in the waiting room," Torruilla said.

"Thanks," Tagger said. "I'll talk to them, make sure someone is watching her children."

"Were they in the explosion too?" Torruilla asked.

"No. They'd already boarded their school busses. They might not even know yet."

Torruilla left. Tagger turned to Franklin, who was noticeably bothered by the thought of a bomber coming after Tuttle.

"This is serious shit, Franklin. You gotta know the names of all the people involved in a case, and you absolutely must show respect for family members by using their names. Understand?"

She nodded.

"Call me the minute Mrs. Tuttle can talk."

"Yes, Sergeant."

"I want you to treat this as an attempted murder. Someone may be trying to kill Mrs. Tuttle. Don't let that happen."

"No, Sergeant."

Chapter 5

"I Don't Know" Is On Second

4:30 PM Monday...getting beyond turf issues. Tagger and Marino were already seated in the conference room. Julia walked in with a white man wearing an ATF baseball cap, and carrying an energy drink, *Zico* coconut water. He appeared to be in his forties, hair military style—high and tight. He was about Julia's height, five-seven or five-eight, and outweighed her by seventy pounds. He was built like an Olympic weight lifter, his shirt not big enough to hold him in. The two sergeants stood for introductions.

"Masterson told me about you guys, too," said Special Agent Powers. "He neglected to tell me how big you were Sergeant Tagger. I can see now how the two of you crushed that martial arts dude last year."

"What'd he say about me?" Marino asked.

Powers turned to him. Marino looked so much like his Italian friends, his size, his dark hair, his demeanor. Powers considered his words. "And I can see why Masterson kept talking about how smart you were,"

Tagger burst out laughing, reached over and patted Marino's stomach.

"What was it he called you? Oh, yeah. 'the professor'," said Powers.

"Don't be fooled," said Tagger. "His stomach is licensed as

a lethal weapon in four states." Marino's face was red, but he was mostly laughing.

"Okay, gentlemen. We've got business," said Julia. "I'm hoping we're here to figure out how to coordinate our efforts so we can find the bad guys and stop the bombings. And we can do that if we do what each of us does best, without any turf wars or stepping on each other's skirts."

"I like all those words," said Powers. "And I have to say my friend Masterson's endorsement of you really kicks up the trust factor."

"So, put that into words I can understand," said Marino.

"We've already started our investigation with the explosive device. It seemed like you guys were giving us lots of room to work," said Powers. "Can I assume that you've focused your investigation elsewhere?"

"Let's say we're looking to work together with the ATF," Julia said. "We need your expertise with the bomb. Working a murder investigation is what we do well, especially one in our own backyard. You need us for that. This case may have something to do with terrorism, but we're approaching it like it's plain old murder. We're hoping we can do this cooperatively."

"I can live with that," said Powers. "We'll keep touching base."

"That's not exactly what I had in mind," Julia said. "I want regular meetings. No more than fifteen minutes, unless we agree to extend the time. We'll keep one another in the loop—ask questions, get answers, and agree upon next steps. Sometimes MPD can help you. Sometimes ATF can help us. At all times we'll keep focused on finding the bad guys and protecting citizens, not on who gets the credit."

Powers sat back. "Damn, Lieutenant," he said. "I think I'm really going to like working with you guys. Can we count this as the first meeting? And can we agree to keep going until we've brought each other up to speed?"

"Agreed," said Tagger and Marino in unison.

"Ain't life grand?" Julia said.

*　*　*

"The person in the bombed-out SUV is a white male," Tagger began. "We're assuming him to be the home owner, Robert Tuttle, age thirty-seven. We're still waiting on confirmation from the coroner. Mrs. Shelly Tuttle was in the kitchen at the time of the explosion, right next to the garage. She was severely injured in the blast, but she's still alive."

Julia looked at Powers.

"I didn't have the lead, but I've been working the car bombing in Wynne," said Powers. "A well-known community leader was killed when a bomb was placed under his car and detonated. I'm sure you know Arkansas is one of the states with a sizable population of heavily armed, anti-government militia. Our primary suspect has ties with a militia group and reportedly with Tony Alamo."

"Tony Alamo?" asked Marino. "That the Christian cult guy who's been charged with child molesting?"

"Child molesting, tax evasion, polygamy, child pornography, and child abuse," said Powers. "His home base is just outside of Fort Smith, Arkansas. He's heavy into spewing anti-Catholic, anti-government propaganda."

"The victim Catholic?" asked Tagger.

"No. Jewish," Powers said. "The various wings of the Arkansas militias tend to have a white separatist philosophy, including anti-Jewish—especially the neo-Nazis and racist skinheads."

"So it was a hate crime?" asked Marino.

Powers shrugged. "Possibly...American terrorists as opposed to foreign terrorists. The interconnections across these groups are amazing—weapons, training, propaganda, and recruitment. We have a number of undercover agents working their system."

"Sounds like we're at war," said Marino.

"All protected by the Second Amendment," Tagger said.

"Shortly after the Wynne car bomb we picked up a guy at a gun show on the west side of the state, the Fort Smith area, trying to buy explosives to build a car bomb. Said he had some unfinished business with a cop."

"How about the two car bombs?" Julia asked. "Any similarities?"

"The two bombs are totally different," said Powers. "Except for the remote detonation component, the Wynne bomb didn't require any expertise. We're still keeping this quiet, but I'll tell you it involved grenades."

"Something any militia group probably has plenty of," said Tagger.

"The bomb fragments we recovered from the Tuttle bombing indicate something from one of the standard build-a-pipe-bomb websites," Powers said. "Materials and explosive components are readily available from any hardware store. The signature was neat, clean. The device effective."

"So, we've probably got a copycat murderer," said Julia.

"Feels that way, but I can't say for sure," said Powers. "We're making the rounds in the hardware stores. What've you guys uncovered?"

"Marino and I interviewed the onlookers at the scene, and did a walk-through in the neighborhood, talking to every-one we found home," Tagger said. "No one saw or heard anything before the explosion. Nobody suspicious. Not even a car that shouldn't have been there."

"We got the same response," said Powers. We're going back this evening to catch folks we missed."

"I was at the hospital," Tagger said. "Mrs. Tuttle is really messed up. As of a few hours ago, she hadn't regained consciousness for any appreciable period. Doctor's concerned about possible internal bleeding, especially in the brain."

"Mrs. Tuttle talked to me in their kitchen," said Julia.

"You were the officer who went into that burning house and pulled her out?" Powers asked.

"Guilty," said Julia. "She was unconscious when I found her, but I roused her. She told the firefighters her husband was in the garage and her kids had taken the school bus. Then she passed out."

"We assigned an officer on protection detail at the MED just in case Mrs. Tuttle is a target," Tagger said. "I talked to her sister. She'd already made arrangements for the kids."

"Professor?" said Julia.

"Mr. Tuttle was an assistant principal at White Station High School, in charge of student discipline," Marino said. "The principal painted him in glowing colors. Said she didn't know anyone who'd want to kill him. But it turns out Tuttle was involved in two recent situations worth pursuing—a conflict between youth gangs, and the suspension of a student who had threatened to blow up some of his classmates."

"Sounds promising," Powers said. "Especially that part about the kid threatening to blow people up."

"Haven't had time to follow up on the gangs," Marino said. "But the school's police officer's arranging a big get-together. And I only dipped my big toe into the bureaucratic swamp of dueling laws. In this case, criminal law versus federal special education law. Tuttle suspended the kid for threatening to blow up his classmates, but he's back at school. The kid's attorney ate the school board attorney's lunch. The board's still smarting, not very enthusiastic about cooperating with us. Lieutenant, I think our next step will be to give our attorney a heads-up before we bring the kid in for questioning. He'll have his father and attorney in tow."

"Special Agent Powers," said Julia. "I'd like to go back to the house so you could walk me through the scene and fill me in on the bomb."

"No problem," Powers said. "Let's do it now."

"We all have things to do," she said. "Let's meet back here at eight-thirty Friday morning to compare notes. Agreed?"

"Agreed."

* * *

*Reliving the rescue...*Julia was not prepared for her visceral reaction when she pulled up to the Tuttle house. The pungent smell of smoke hung in the air. She winced when she opened her car door. Her nostrils stung, her eyes watered, and she started coughing. She was immediately transported to the kitchen, one day earlier. Her face felt cool as she began to sweat. Julia held tight to the car door, getting her bearings, clearing her throat. She forced herself to look where the kitchen had been—no window, no walls, a partial ceiling. The second floor dipped at the corner, near the garage. She reached up and found where her hair was missing. She steadied herself and walked to the house. No need to go through the front door this time. She stepped directly into the kitchen. The internal garage door still lay on the floor. She looked up into the room on the second floor. Julia felt danger, a feeling she could not allow herself to feel yesterday. "Jesus," she said softly.

"Always different coming back," said Powers.

Julia was startled. She had not heard him walk up. "What?" she said. "Oh. Yeah. Things are different. Worse than I remembered."

"You don't want to think about it too much. It'll mess with your head."

"I suppose it would." Julia felt the need to retrace her steps exiting through the front door. She composed herself as she joined Powers. He walked her into the taped-off area. "How on earth do you find pieces of an exploded bomb?" she asked.

"You have to know what you're looking for," he said. "First you identify the blast pattern, rope it off, and work your way to the center, inspecting everything. It's kind of like archaeology—collecting things, dusting larger pieces with tiny brushes, filtering the small pieces through a screen."

"And you get enough pieces to determine what the original looked like?"

"As much as possible. We also look at the scope and pattern of the explosion to determine the type and size of the charge. That gives us an idea of the bomb's contents."

"And you're sure these two bombs were not made by the same person?"

"They're two different devices. But that doesn't mean they weren't planted by the same person or the same group."

"Yeah. I was wondering about that."

"We'd need some tie between the victims," said Powers. "I'm not seeing it. The Wynne victim was Jewish and lived and worked in a small town on the other side of the Mississippi River. Tuttle was an assistant principal, Southern Baptist I think, who lived and worked in Memphis."

"And you've been monitoring these suspects for several weeks."

"True. But the group may be bigger than we've imagined."
They considered that for a while.

"Thanks for the walk-through. I'm heading back to the station. See you Friday, unless something significant pops before then."

Chapter 6

Learning the Ropes

11: 20 AM Tuesday…she's conscious. Tagger received word Shelly Tuttle was conscious. He drove to the MED.

"Officer Franklin," Tagger said as he got closer. "Thanks for the call. What do we know?"

"Morning, Sergeant Tagger," she said. "I know I was relieved by Officer Jenks, and I relieved Officer Burk. I know Dr. Torruilla was relieved by Dr. Solomon Momariste. I know that Shelly Tuttle's sister, Jacqueline Forest, came to visit her, even though she was not yet conscious."

"Impressive," he said. Franklin smiled. "How about Mrs. Tuttle?"

"She regained consciousness a few minutes before I called you. Dr. Torruilla told me she had a good night, the tests came back negative, and her vital signs were looking good. She says we can have five minutes. No more."

"Does she know about her husband?"

"Dr. Torruilla said Mrs. Tuttle asked about him. She told her he'd been killed. She didn't tell her that he'd been murdered."

"Okay. Ready for lesson two?"

"Yes, Sergeant."

He knocked. A nurse opened the door. "Is this a good time to talk to Mrs. Tuttle?" Tagger asked.

"Dr. Torruilla told me you'd be coming," she said. "I'll give you some privacy. Just push the call button if you need us."

They approached the patient. "Mrs. Tuttle, I'm Sergeant Tagger. This is Officer Franklin. We're very sorry for your loss."

Mrs. Tuttle began crying. She turned her head. Tagger got Franklin's attention and nodded to the box of tissues. Franklin pulled a few, walked around the bed, and handed them to her. Franklin looked over at Tagger. He nodded.

"Ma'am," said Franklin. "Can you tell us anything about that morning?"

Tuttle's crying subsided.

"There was nothing unusual," Tuttle said. "The kids left for the bus stop, and Bobby and I finished breakfast. He was running late. He kissed me goodbye and left for work. The next thing I knew, a woman was yelling at me, asking me if I could stand up." She paused. "Could that be right?"

"Yes ma'am," said Tagger. "My boss, Lieutenant Todd, found you. The firefighters were right behind her. They're the ones who carried you out."

Tuttle gasped, and covered her mouth. "Are you sure?" she asked.

"I was there," said Tagger. "I watched them bring you out. I know it was horrible."

Tuttle cried. Franklin began to speak, but stopped when she saw Tagger's subtle hand signal. They waited for Tuttle to compose herself.

"The doctor told me there was an explosion," said Tuttle. "Was it a gas leak?"

"Actually," said Tagger, "it was a bomb, attached to the underside of the car."

Tuttle's eyes widened with fear. "A bomb?" she whispered. "Who'd do such a thing? Why Bobby?"

"We were hoping you could help us answer those questions," Tagger said. "Can you think of any reason anyone would want to murder Bobby?"

"Murder Bobby?" Tuttle said. "Everyone loved him. He was a great husband, a great father, and the people at White Station were always giving him awards." She began crying again. "A car bomb? Does this have anything to do with the Arkansas car bombing?"

"We're looking into that," said Tagger. "But so far, they don't appear to be related. Have you or your husband received any threats—phone calls, emails, letters?"

"Threats?" Tuttle said. "No. Who'd want to do that?" She began crying again, but stopped, her eyes opened wide. "My children." Tagger looked at Franklin.

"Your sister Jacqueline has been watching them," said Franklin. "She's been here to visit. She said she'll be coming back this afternoon."

Tuttle relaxed, blew her nose.

"If you think of anything, please let Officer Franklin know," said Tagger. "Again. We're sorry for your loss, and for all the pain you're going through." Tagger and Franklin left the room.

"Sergeant?" said Franklin. "Thanks for letting me come with you. I'm not sure I'm going to get it out of my head anytime soon."

"That's lesson number three," he said. "Aside from being attacked or shooting someone, it has to be one of the most stressful things you'll do as a cop. And Franklin?"

"Yes, Sergeant."

"You'll *never* get it out of your head."

* * *

*Working the system...*Marino and Willis sat across from one another at a table outside of La Baguette bakery on Poplar, across the parking lot from the main library. They were eating their way through a bag of day-old pastries, washing them down with coffee.

"I need help getting through all this confidentiality crap," said Marino. "I need information on those two gangs Seymour talked about yesterday, the vice lords and some posse."

"The posse is probably the Lil Bro Posse, out of the Lebrow apartments in Orange Mound," said Willis.

"Kids gets bussed to White Station from the Mound?"

"White Station's boundaries are still influenced by the old federal court bussing plan."

"How do I get names, dates, and places?"

"I run into it every day working in the schools," said Willis, reaching for the last pastry. "It's a zoo. You can't get a court order without a name, and you can't get a name without a court order. Heck, for years the *only* information about youth gangs in the city of Memphis was maintained by the city schools' Pupil Services Center, where they process student suspensions. A federal court order from the sixties or seventies made it illegal for law enforcement to spy on groups of people who had no apparent connection to crime. You know, in the sixties, the FBI took everyone's pictures and started case files on people involved in the 'I Am a Man' marches here in Memphis, the anti-Vietnam War rallies, and the like. The federal court held that monitoring and infiltrating groups of any kind could only be done when there was obvious criminal activity, and even then it was tough to get approval. One result was that no one in the MPD kept up with youth gangs."

"The records, Willis."

"Yeah. Like I was saying, Pupil Services keeps records on all school suspensions. I've heard there are some twelve thousand each year. In Judge Turner's heyday a formal agreement was made between Juvenile Court and the Memphis City Schools. Each one has access to the other's daily list of names. And then the youth gangs got going in the late eighties. Till the early nineties the only identifying or tracking of these kids was done through the Pupil Services Center. A similar type of sharing agreement was extended to the MPD Metro Gang Unit. So, if a student has been suspended and processed through the Pupil Services Center we can get that information through Juvenile Court, or in the case of gang involvement, the Metro Gang Unit."

"Why didn't you just tell me this in the first place?"

"I wasn't through with my pastries. You're buying, right?"

Chapter 7

The Alibi

Wednesday Morning...an interrogation to remember. Assistant
Attorney General Robert H. Diggs insisted on being present
at the initial interrogation of Charlie Barrington, at least on
the other side of the one-way glass. Julia and Marino sat on
one side of the table. Charlie sat across from them, rocking
forward and back, fidgeting, eyes staring at the middle of the
table. He was flanked by his father Lindsey Barrington and
attorney Lucy Collins.

"Thank you for coming in Mr. Barrington, Charlie,"
said Julia

"Like we had a choice," Barrington said, looking at what
Julia thought was her left ear. "I'm sick of this harassment.
Charlie did nothing wrong. He has rights. I'm going to
have your badges. And I'm going to own that damn school
board when I'm through. They had no right talking to you
about Charlie."

"Yes, sir," Julia said. "We just wanted to ask Charlie
some questions."

"What kind of questions?" asked Collins.

"Charlie has rights," Barrington repeated, face red,
lips pursed.

"We're investigating the murder of Robert Tuttle,"
said Julia.

"Tuttle had no right suspending Charlie," said Barrington. "It was a violation of federal law. We proved it before a judge."

"As you no doubt know by now, Mr. Tuttle was killed when a bomb exploded under his car," said Julia. Charlie rocked faster, smaller.

"And you took Charlie's recent suspension, added in the fact that Tuttle illegally suspended him, and came up with the brilliant conclusion that Charlie had to have been involved in his death?" Collins said, looking incredulous.

"Charlie, I'm Lieutenant Todd. Do you know why you're here?"

"Hello, Lieutenant. Over here. It's me, Charlie's attorney. He doesn't need to be answering your questions. Talk to me."

"Well, *me*," Julia said. "How about for starters you fill us in on Charlie's whereabouts on the morning of April sixth, this past Monday. We know he wasn't in school."

"Charlie was home, sick," Collins said.

"And who can corroborate that?" asked Julia.

Barrington reached down into a large catalog-style leather case. He extracted a hefty three-ring notebook, and opened it on the table, flipping to the back pages. He unfolded an oversize sheet of paper, touched the page with his index finger, then turned the notebook around, guiding it to Julia. It was a color-coded spreadsheet, dated April 6, 2009 with TIME heading the first column, broken into fifteen-minute intervals. The next columns had a variety of headings: SLEEP, CLEANING, DRESSING, BREAKFAST, TRAVEL, DESK ARRANGEMENT, WORK, BREAK, TELEPHONE, and others. Barrington reached across the table and again touched the spreadsheet with his finger. Julia noted the column, TELEPHONE. She followed the column down to see, "Charlie" written in every hour on the quarter hour.

"I don't get it," said Julia.

"Really?" Collins said. "It's pretty self-explanatory, Lieutenant. Mr. Barrington maintains precise records of his activities for each day, in fifteen minute increments. He's showing you that he had regular telephone conversations with Charlie throughout Monday, April 6, 2009."

"You're telling me this is Charlie's alibi for Monday morning?" Julia said, raising her eyebrows.

"Precisely," said Collins.

"And how did Mr. Barrington know Charlie was speaking to him while on a phone in their home?" Julia asked.

"Because the phone in the Barrington home has a unique electronic signature," said Collins.

"And of course there's no way to fabricate that signature, or to forward calls through the home phone from any other phone." Julia said.

"Mr. Barrington is a computer expert, employed by the U. S. government to track telephonic and online terrorist chatter. If anyone can tell which phone was used, he's the one."

Julia sat back, took time to look at each of the three people sitting across from her, then began clapping. "Bravo," she said. "In all my years as a police officer I've never heard such a cock-and-bull story. I may have to frame a photo copy of this spreadsheet and hang it on my wall."

"Lieutenant, I believe this interview is over," said Collins. She stood and motioned to Barrington and Charlie. Barrington reached for his notebook, turned it around slowly, meticulously refolded the spreadsheet, closed the notebook, and carefully slid it back into its slot in his carrying case.

The three walked out.

Chapter 8

I'm Tougher than That

Wednesday late morning...meddling, thank goodness. Julia was googling *bomb making,* and getting scared. Any fool with an issue can put one of these together, she thought. Julia jumped when her phone buzzed.

"Yes, Teresa," she answered.

"Your Aunt Louise is on line one, Lieutenant."

Julia pushed the button. "This is a surprise. What's going on?"

"I know I'm meddling, dear," Aunt Louise said. "But I wanted to let you know that I talked to Mark this morning."

No response.

"You still there?"

"Still here."

"The part I wanted to tell you was that he was the same old Mark—friendly, respectful, chatty. He seems to be doing just fine."

"And you're telling me this because...?"

"I've been thinking about our conversation Sunday. I didn't want to leave you with the impression Mark was ignoring me, because of you."

"And that's supposed to make me feel better, how?"

"I'm not sure at the moment. But four minutes ago it seemed as if it would be something you'd like to hear."

"I'm not feeling better."

"Oh, dear."

"Goodbye, Aunt Louise."

"Goodbye, dear."

Julia hung up, and started doodling. How can Mark be doing fine without me? she thought. Maybe I need to call him and...and what? Tell him I'm sorry, I was an idiot, there's no excuse for my behavior, I want to see him?...I can't handle this right now. I need something to eat, maybe a nachos bell grande from Taco Bell. Maybe two.

* * *

*Asking for help...*Julia's stomach was doing flip-flops. The nachos were not agreeing with her. She thought about the White Station student, and picked up the phone.

"Hello. This is Dr. Proctor."

"Tonya, this is Julia. Got a second?"

"For you, of course. We need to schedule a debriefing?"

"Not unless it's for me."

"Why? Is this about the bombing?"

"Kinda. I guess I have a two-part question."

"Fire away."

"We're looking at potential suspects. We've found a high school senior who recently threatened to blow up his classmates."

"That's not good. What's your question?"

"Turns out the kid has Asperger's, and he's been talking about blowing people up since kindergarten, but he's never done anything violent."

"People with this syndrome often have obsessions and compulsive routines. Is he on medication?"

"We don't know. We haven't been able to secure a copy of his file."

"You want to know if he's capable of carrying out

his threat."

"Yes. And I want to know how to talk to him, if his father and attorney ever give me the chance."

"There's quite a range in their skills and behaviors, but they tend to be intelligent, sometimes very intelligent. Their common weakness involves an inability to understand and respond to social cues. Kids with Asperger's get picked on and harassed frequently by their classmates, for being different. They typically want to have friends, but their lack of social skills often turns off other kids. But just like any kid they get their feelings hurt, they get angry. Sometimes they strike out. I guess the pivotal question in this case is *means.* Does this boy have the means to make a bomb? The intelligence? The materials? The knowhow?"

"He's in regular education classes, is reported to be extremely smart, and loves violent video games. ATF tells us the materials and chemicals of this bomb can be purchased at any hardware store. And as for the knowhow, I've been, excuse the pun, blown away by all the build-a-bomb sites on the internet."

"Just from what you're telling me, I don't think you can rule him out."

"The father is a piece of work. He never looked me in the eye this morning. He kept on the same message ad nauseam, and there was no physical or visual contact between him and his son."

"That's not surprising. Research shows a genetic predisposition for the majority of Asperger's cases, often linked with the father. Sounds as if these two share a lot of the same characteristics. I bet he has a job that doesn't require him to interact often with people, one involving a lot of detailed, repetitious work."

"Bingo. He works for the government looking for

communications between terrorists, by phone or computer. And you should see the boatload of daily spread sheets he carried into the interrogation, each with the entire day broken into fifteen minutes increments."

"Of course the interrogation had to be highly stressful, as it would be for anyone. So neither the boy nor his father would be at their best. I'd assume both are perfectly capable of listening and following directions. Otherwise they'd never have been successful in school and business. You might have better luck working through the boy's favorite teacher—a less threatening person in a less threatening setting."

"Thanks. Good idea."

"And part two of your question?"

"You probably heard that right after the car bomb exploded, a crazy person ran into the burning building and almost got herself killed."

"That crazy person was you?"

"Fraid so."

"And now you're having episodes of anxiety? Feeling jumpy? Unable to concentrate? Second guessing your instincts? Feeling ineffective?"

"I can see why you're a psychologist."

"Julia, we've worked lots of debriefings together. You know how helpful they can be. Why didn't you call me? Wait. Don't tell me. You thought you were too tough for this to affect you."

"Now you sound like Aunt Louise."

"Being friends, it'd be better if you were debriefed by someone else. I'll call Dr. Notting about seeing you tomorrow. You should expect to hear from him shortly."

"Thanks, Tonya. I'll look for his call."

* * *

Wednesday afternoon...a turn for the worse. Tagger's phone rang.

"Sergeant, this is Officer Shawna Franklin."

"Yes, Franklin. What's going on?"

"It's Mrs. Tuttle, Sergeant. She's lapsed into a coma."

"Damn...Fill me in."

"Dr. Torruilla said it happened right after her kids came to see her. She's afraid she's hemorrhaging in her brain. She was on her way to surgery."

"You know her chances?"

"No, Sergeant. The docs didn't say anything."

"Stay with her, Franklin. Keep me posted."

"Yes, Sergeant."

* * *

*A team player...*Julia flipped through a case file. Her phone buzzed.

"Lieutenant. Special Agent Powers on line two," said Teresa.

Julia punched the flashing button. "Todd."

"Lieutenant, this is Powers. We may have something for you."

"Good. Whatchagot?"

"Last night we followed up on the remaining houses for possible witnesses. One of our agents talked to a Linda McCall who told us she remembered seeing a stranger walking through the neighborhood the week before. Described him as white, bearded, medium long hair, about five-foot-ten, and slender. Judged him to be in his thirties."

"Where was he walking?"

"According to McCall, he walked in front of the Tuttle house several times."

"Anything else?"

"Yeah. He was missing fingers on his right hand."

"How about *we* follow up on this lead?"

"Thought you'd never ask. I'm betting you guys can do a better job tracking him in your own precinct than we can."

"Give me Ms. McCall's address and phone number. And thanks."

* * *

Wednesday evening...sounds, smells, and fear. Julia fell asleep almost immediately. Dream sleep came faster than usual. She was in her car, her window down. The smell of smoke gagged her. Flames licked fiercely through the billowing smoke to her left. Burning wood cracked loudly, like gun shots. She forced her car door open, and immediately began choking. She could see a person, a man, inside a car flailing his arms, slapping at his flaming hair, screaming for help. Julia felt the intense heat of the flames, and was overcome with fear. She turned away from the burning man and ran, but couldn't outrun the sound of his cries. She stumbled, falling on the front porch steps. More smoke poured over her from under the door. She stood and smashed through the glass of the door with her fist. Blood gushed from her arm. The door swung open. More smoke. More coughing. She dropped to the floor and crawled in the darkness until she bumped into something—a woman, lying face down. When she turned the woman over she found herself staring at a mangled *Julia Todd*, bloody face, busted out teeth, broken nose, and hair burning. Julia lost her breath, as if she'd been punched in the stomach. She felt out of control, unable to breathe.

The next second she was wide awake, fists clenched, heart racing, straining to see in the dark. She felt blood dripping down her face and into her eyes. She reached wildly for the lamp, hit it with the back of her hand, knocking it to the floor. In one motion she pulled the covers off, swung her legs over the side of her bed. Her feet hit the floor and she stood, seeking her balance. Her legs felt heavy, but she did her best to hurry to the bathroom. She had to know. She flipped the wall switch and leaned in to the mirror. Staring back at her was a pale frightened woman, hair in disarray, sweating profusely.

Chapter 9

The Other Side of the Table

Thursday, morning...getting nowhere fast. Julia felt frustrated by her inability to get back to sleep. Her mind at full throttle, refusing to pull back. I tried all my usual tricks, she thought—relaxation, pacing through every room in the house, warm milk, music—nothing worked. The more she tried to calm down, the more thoughts ricocheted inside her head, spawning other thoughts—all generating more anxiety. What's happening to me? Is this what it feels like to go crazy? Julia's anxiety grew as thoughts about the morning's scheduled debriefing joined the mix. She had teamed up with Tonya to facilitate a dozen debriefings for other officers who had been in potentially traumatizing situations. But this would be her first time to be on the receiving end of this process. What's Dr. Notting going to find out? she thought. What's he going to think of me? Am I going crazy?

Julia had never been a person who could just sit. She pulled on her running clothes and laced up her shoes. She knew better than to attempt a full workout, so she shortened her run, going directly to the InsideOut Gym and returning home. She switched to autopilot, showering and dressing. She double checked to make sure she hadn't forgotten anything, armed her alarm system, and hoped she would feel better once she had her *Deliberate Literate* coffee.

* * *

"Morning, Lieutenant," said Millie.

Julia offered a small wave.

"Bad night, huh? Grab a seat. I'll bring you your coffee. Biscotti's on me."

* * *

8:00 AM Thursday…the debriefing. Julia drove east on Poplar Avenue. Traffic was heavy in the oncoming lanes, carrying people from the suburbs to offices and shops in the city. Twenty-five minutes later she was taking the elevator to the third floor.

"Thank you for arranging to see me at this early hour, especially on such short notice," said Julia.

"It's not a problem," said Dr. Larry Notting, smiling. "Besides, short notice is the only way we respond to the needs of officers for a debriefing. Can't plan these things."

"I've never been on this side before," Julia said.

"But you've been on *this* side enough times to know what a debriefing is, and what to expect," said Notting. "Remember, this is *your* debriefing, your time. I'm here only to walk you through the process."

Julia forced a smile and nodded.

"We can skip all the explanations of what the stress debriefings are for, and how they work. Let's move right to the part where you tell me what you recall the morning of the car bombing. How did you learn about the explosion?"

"I was about to drink my coffee at the *Deliberate Literate*, on Union, just up the street from Union Station?" He nodded. "I heard an explosion, and rushed outside."

"Okay, let's back up a bit. When you heard the explosion, what was going through your head?"

"It was so loud, I thought people must be hurt. I needed to find out where it was, what the situation was, and how I could help."

"I know we don't always discuss feelings this early in a debriefing, but you understand what our goals are. So, describe your feelings when you heard the explosion."

"I was energized, like firefighters when the tone goes off in the station. I wanted to get there. I wanted to be a part of helping."

"Were you fearful, even a little bit?"

"Only for the people who might be hurt."

He gestured for Julia to continue.

"I hurried outside hoping to see something. Several people were coming out of shops, a few pointed at the thick black smoke. I got in my car and went to investigate."

"Did you just casually drive over, or were you going with lights and siren?"

"I punched it. Even cut across traffic at a no-left-turn on Cooper. I lost sight of the smoke because of the buildings, and was leaning into my windshield to find it. The house was just north of Madison and east. I called it in."

"And your feelings?"

"The same, but I was more intense at that point. I saw no other first responders. I hadn't thought about it, but I was getting nervous."

"About...?"

"It was all going to be on me. As the first person on the scene I would have to do something, and do it right. Someone could live or die because of what I did or didn't do."

"That's a lot of pressure."

"Yeah. But I tried to use the pressure to help me make good decisions. Doing nothing would be unacceptable."

"To whom?"

"To me and to anyone in need of my help."

"Has anyone ever told you how high you set the standards

for yourself?"

"Only my Aunt Louise. She raised me."

"What does she say?"

"Depends. When she's getting on my case she tells me I'm not a machine, or calls me, 'Miss Perfect'. When she's proud of me she calls me her 'little guardian'."

"I think I'd like your Aunt Louise."

Julia smiled.

"Okay, you've called it in…"

"As I drove up I could see flames coming primarily from the garage. I reached over and grabbed a fire extinguisher and ran to the garage. The heat from the fire was unreal. The garage door had been blown off. I could see two cars, both on fire. But the car on the left was ripped up like it'd been in a bad accident, and I could see the outline of a head in the driver's seat."

"What were you thinking?

"I was thinking there was no way I could get near the fire, let alone get to the person in the car. Too hot. And I was thinking there was nothing for me to do there. I needed to check inside the house."

"Where did that idea come from?"

"I don't know. Maybe because there were two cars, or because the garage was attached to the house. Maybe because I thought I just had to know."

"And your feelings?"

"I was feeling frustrated at not being able to help the person in the car. And I was afraid if I waited any longer I wouldn't be able to help whoever might be inside the house."

"So, you're still using the pressure to drive you in your goal of helping someone?"

Julia nodded.

Notting gestured for her to continue.

"The closest entrance was the front door. I ran there. It was locked. I broke out the glass with my fire extinguisher and looked inside. The key was in the deadbolt, as it so often is. I tried, but couldn't reach it. I jumped, got it on the second try, turned it, and went into the house. The smoke was thick, hanging about five feet above the floor, just like in the training films. I squatted and began moving into the house, shouting all the way."

"Feelings?"

"I was getting scared, both for anyone who might be in there, and for me. I knew I didn't have much time. I just focused on checking as many rooms as I could before I'd have to get the hell out of there."

"How long before you found Mrs. Tuttle?"

"It felt like forever, going in crouched like that, but it was probably no more than fifteen, twenty seconds. The smoke was dropping, maybe four feet, but I could see better because there were flames in the kitchen. That's when I heard the fire trucks. The inside door to the garage had been blown off and it was lying beside Mrs. Tuttle, burning. That's probably what smacked her in the face. Her dress had caught fire. I turned the extinguisher on her, then on the door. I checked her carotid, found a pulse. I didn't know how badly she was hurt, but I knew I had to move her. I kept yelling. Finally she answered. I got her part way to her feet. But the smoke was all over us. Thank goodness that's when the firefighters came in. They grabbed her and ushered the two of us outside."

"And how were you feeling during this time?"

"I was focused on the task at hand. No place for feelings. But when I helped her up, I felt weak for the first time. I really don't remember much after the firefighters came in."

"And when you got outside and got some oxygen, how'd

you feel?"

"I just stayed in a kind of daze, coughing hard, trying to get air. Starting with those firefighters, people were helping me. Sergeant Tagger, one of my team, took care of me as soon as I made it through the door. My arm was bleeding and my hair was burning. He put out the fire in my hair with his bare hand, and walked me to a paramedic who gave me oxygen and bandaged my arm. At some point I left, and the owner of the coffee shop took care of me. It was a while before I was thinking clearly again."

"And now?"

"Tonya probably told you about my being jumpy and not being able to concentrate." He nodded. "And last night I had this horrible dream that *I* was the woman on the floor in the burning house."

"And it scared you. You thought you could have died in that house, didn't you?"

"Yes."

"You know from your experience in facilitating debriefings that all of this is absolutely normal—the anxiety, the lack of concentration, the dream, and the sleeplessness. Just because it hasn't happened to you before, doesn't mean it's not normal for you. And it doesn't mean you're weak. You're Aunt is right. You're *not* a machine."

"But—"

"No buts," he interrupted, smiling. "At least not yet. First, I have to say that what you did is so honest-to-god brave I've got goose bumps."

"Come on."

"I've debriefed enough firefighters to know that strange things happen when the brain is deprived of oxygen by smoke. Of course, you can die if you stay in the smoke long enough. At some point before that happens, reality can get distorted. Let me try some thoughts on you. Tell me if they feel right."

Julia nodded.

"You strike me as a person who strives to be in control."

Julia smiled, embarrassed.

"Being in control during an emergency is a process of continually weighing the pros and cons of changing information. That includes assessing your ability to meet the challenge at any given point. As I listened to you, I heard a person who did precisely that. On top of which you were able to use stressors to motivate yourself, to push you harder."

"Okay so far."

"Would you acknowledge that a person is likely to die when they run into a burning building?"

Julia nodded.

"And this belief is not new. You believed it before you stopped drinking your coffee that morning, right?"

Julia smiled, tightlipped.

"Would you also acknowledge that if a person makes it out of a burning building, there will be evidence of close calls, like a cut arm, or singed hair, or a hacking cough?"

"Agreed."

"So at issue here, it seems to me, is not so much a fear that you almost died. Rather, it is a fear of being out of control in a life-and-death situation."

Julia said nothing. She was trying to make sense of this. Trying hard to understand what Notting said.

"What was different after you tried to get Mrs. Tuttle to her feet? I would suggest that as the lack of oxygen took its toll on you, you lost access to vital information. You no longer had all your physical, mental, and emotional skills. You no longer were in a position to make informed decisions, let alone good decisions. Others had to help you. That's what's scared you. You were no longer in control. You don't want to experience that feeling again."

Now it was Julia who felt goose bumps. The interior light bulb was glowing.

"But as I see it, it was *your* earlier action that guaranteed help would arrive. You called it in. The fire trucks were on their way. The irony is that even though you'd lost control, everything unfolded the way you drew it up. It was your plan. Your decisiveness. Your timing was perfect, as was the fire-fighters'. You had a major role in the final act of this play, even though you were not fully conscious. And you *both* survived."

Tears flowed. Julia could feel Dr. Notting was on target. It was not so much the fear of dying. It was the fear of dying without a fight.

Notting handed her a box of tissues. Julia cried harder.

Chapter 10

Sanctuary

10:05 AM Thursday...rode hard and put up wet. Julia had gone to the debriefing session sleep-deprived and anxious. She walked out spent, nothing left. God, she thought. I feel like a bowl of jello. But not the trembling, anxious kind. It just feels as if I have no strength to keep myself upright, no bones left. I've been reduced to a glob of jello, with just the quivering to tell the world I'm alive. Julia punched in the numbers on her iPhone.

"Hello."

"Aunt Louise, it's me, Julia. I'm kinda in your neighborhood. Can I come by and get something to eat?"

"Of course, dear. Is something wrong?"

"Nothing's wrong. Everything's going to be all right."

* * *

Louise waited in the Haven lobby, concerned. The automatic doors opened. Julia walked slowly. Her posture and every step advertising exhaustion.

"Over here, dear," Aunt Louise said as Julia cleared the front door. "I'm signing you in." She dropped the pen as Julia approached. They held a long embrace. Louise studied Julia's face for clues.

"Are you hurt?" Aunt Louise asked.

"No, ma'am."

"Something happen at the station?"

"No, ma'am."

"You look exhausted."

"Yes, ma'am."

"Let's go up to my apartment. I've fixed a nice brunch. Your favorite, tuna fish sandwiches, potato chips, and lemonade."

They walked to the elevator, arm in arm. Julia needed food, but she really craved the nurturing and affirming embrace of her Aunt Louise.

Julia stared in silence, took small bites, and chewed slowly. It was as if she was too tired to move her jaws. Aunt Louise struggled to remain patient, quiet. Julia pushed back from the table after finishing only half of her sandwich, and moved to the couch.

"Could you call Teresa?" Julia asked. "Tell her I won't be coming in right away. I just want to lie down for a minute."

"Of course, dear," Aunt Louise said. But Julia never heard. She was already asleep.

Chapter 11

The Students

Thursday morning...getting on the same page. Two high school seniors huddled in the corner of the lunchroom.

"Keep your voice down, Charlie," JR said. "You had to go to 201 Poplar? And be questioned by the cops? Jesus!"

"We went to 201 Poplar," said Charlie.

"Jail? You were in jail?"

"No. There are other parts connected to the jail—courts, and police offices, and sheriff's offices, and lawyers."

"Who went with you?"

"We went to 201 Pop—"

"I know. I heard you the first two times." JR touched Charlie's wringing hands to cue him to relax. Charlie's rocking calmed as well. "Was your dad with you?"

"Yeah."

"Shh. Keep it down. Did your lawyer go?"

"Yeah," Charlie whispered loudly.

"What'd you tell the police?"

"Charlie said nothing."

"Oh, God. They suspect you made the bomb. You sure you didn't say anything?"

"Charlie said nothing."

"The other kids have been talking. Everybody's sure you blew up Mr. Tuttle."

* * *

Thursday afternoon…the gang's all here. Marino's phone rang.

"Sergeant, this is Willis. We had the sit-down with the gang-bangers. I thought you'd want to know."

"You know I do. Were all seven of the boys there?"

"Actually, Mrs. Seymour heard about three girls who've been involved in this recent clash. Seymour, one of her assistant principals, and I sat around a table with ten kids."

"Sooo?"

"Turns out the big gang rivalry's nothing more than Memphis's version of Westside Story."

"What? You mean they were singing and dancing?"

"Not that part. I mean that one of the boys from the Lil Bro Posse was getting it on with one of the girls from the Vice Lords. And everyone else was all pissed off about it."

"Anyone threatening to blow anyone up?" asked Marino.

"Lots of threats about who was going to blow who *away*," said Willis. "But nothing about blowing anyone *up*."

"Any talk about getting Tuttle?"

"Nada. In fact, just like Seymour said, they were all down with Tuttle. Said he was always respectful, never dissed any of 'em."

"He was, like, an honorary member of *both* gangs?"

"Just about," said Willis. "They even offered to help find the guy who killed him."

"Seriously?"

"Not only that, they got to talking about ole Charlie being *that* guy. Said he was always acting weird and talking crazy."

"Oh, damn," Marino said.

"Yeah. We had to do some fast talking on that one."

"What did you say?"

"I told them the police already checked him out, there was no reason to think it was him."

"Did they buy it?'

"Seemed to," Willis said.

"That brings us back to Charlie."

Chapter 12

Back In the Groove

5:10 PM Thursday...sleeping beauty. Julia stirred.

Aunt Louise looked up from her book. "Hey, dear. Welcome back to the world."

Julia squinted, trying to get her eyes to focus. "Aunt Louise. What are you doing here?"

"I live here, dear. Remember?"

"Live here?" Julia looked around the room, the light in her eyes returning. "Oh, yeah."

"You have a good sleep?" Aunt Louise asked.

"Sleep?" Julia swung her feet to the floor. "What time is it?" she said, trying to get her watch into focus.

"A little past five."

"I've been out for...six hours?"

"About that. You must've been really tired."

"Didn't sleep last night."

"You want something to drink?"

"The station. I need to get to Union Station," Julia said, standing.

"No you don't. Teresa and I talked. They're not expecting you till the morning."

"Oh."

"How about some decaf tea?"

"Okay. And some of your ginger snaps. But I need to go

to the bathroom first."

Louise went to the kitchen.

"Oh, no," Julia said, loudly.

Louise cringed. "What's wrong?" she called.

"Nothing. I just saw my pillow hair. It may never straighten out."

Louise put her hand on her chest, took a deep breath, and smiled. Julia came out of the bathroom, attacking her hair with a towel.

"What in the world?" said Aunt Louise.

"I threw some water on my head in the sink, to get the kinks out of my hair."

Aunt Louise shook her head. "Come get your tea while it's hot."

"Thanks," Julia said, feeling more awake.

"Teresa told me what you did. I had no idea you were involved in that bombing incident."

Julia felt like a little kid who just got caught doing something wrong. "I meant to tell you," was all she could think to say.

"You saved that woman," Aunt Louise said. "But you could have been killed."

"Yeah."

"That why you haven't been able to sleep?"

"Yeah."

"You didn't think you could talk to me?" Aunt Louise said, surprised by her anger.

"I'm sorry. I haven't been myself."

"I didn't mean it that way."

"I know."

"I just realized that this must've happened right before I called you yesterday to tell you about Mark. How insensitive of me."

"That's okay."

"Are you going to talk to anyone? You know—are you going to one of those debriefing things?"

"I went this morning. That's another reason I was so spent. The reason I had to be with you. I had to be where I felt safe, safe enough to sleep."

Tears flowed down Aunt Louise's cheeks. She moved to the other side of the table to hug Julia. "I'm sorry you had to go through all that," said Aunt Louise. "No good deed goes unpunished."

"I think there was some stuff left over from the three ribs as well. It all kinda ganged up on me. The psychologist I saw this morning was wonderful. Remind me to thank Tonya for her referral."

"But he exhausted you?"

"There wasn't much left in my tank when I went to see him. Didn't take much more to drain it. Except in this case it was a good thing 'cause he helped me know how to get through this."

"Anything you care to talk about?"

"Maybe another time. Let me work this out first."

"I'm here for you."

"I know."

"You hungry?"

"I will be pretty soon."

"What are you up for? I can fix something here. We can go to a restaurant. Or we can eat downstairs."

"Actually, it might be good to get some air. Either a restaurant or here at the Haven."

* * *

*The hushpuppy four...*The sounds and smells of the Haven dining room were inviting. Julia and Louise walked in.

"Hey, y'all. Over here," called a woman.

Julia talked through a small smile, "If it isn't the hush-puppy four."

Aunt Louise stifled a laugh. They had met these four residents last fall, in the midst of a discussion concerning the facility's propensity for preparing all foods fried. They shared a look.

"Why not?" said Julia.

"Louise and, er..." said Joyce.

"Julia," Beatrice said.

"That's right," Julia said. "And you're Joyce, Beatrice, Shirley, and, don't tell me...Lawrence."

"Good memory," Beatrice said. "C'mon and join us."

"You still on a diet?" said Shirley.

"Diet?" said Julia.

"Yeah. You know. The last time you joined us, you only ate jello," said Joyce.

"That's right. I'd forgotten," said Beatrice. "Only jello."

"Something about not fitting into your clothes," said Shirley.

"Oh, my God," Julia said. "That was right after eating all those Christmas goodies. And I needed to be able to get into my clothes for—"

"For your post-holiday party," finished Aunt Louise.

Julia had just remembered she'd needed to get into her dress clothes because she had a date with Dr. Mark Sanders. Their first date. Closing her mouth, she looked at Aunt Louise, thanking her with her eyes.

"And how are you, Lawrence?" Aunt Louise said quickly changing the subject.

"He's been a little down," said Shirley.

"Nah," Lawrence said. "I'm doin' okay."

"The constabulary put the kibosh on his trips to Walgreen's," Beatrice said.

Aunt Louise asked, "You mean the Walgreen's run you always made for the—"

"Shh. Not so loud," interrupted Joyce. "There are spies all around us."

"My gracious," Aunt Louise said.

Joyce leaned in, motioning for the others to get closer. She said quietly, "Not long after we last saw you two, the director—"

"Geraldine Jacobson," Beatrice said.

"Yes, Jacobson," said Joyce. "She posted a notice that off-campus trips for condoms and stimulating lubricants would no longer be tolerated."

"Yeah," Shirley said. "The notice said there were already plenty of approved choices available at the nurse's station."

"Two, I think," Joyce said.

"And the notice also said the police were investigating the rumor that some residents were bringing in black market drugs for men," Beatrice said.

Aunt Louise looked lost.

"You've seen all those TV commercials," Joyce said. "Viagra, Cialis?"

"With those warnings about seeking medical help after four hours?" said Beatrice, smiling.

"Surely you've seen those ads with the couple sitting naked in side-by-side bathtubs," Shirley said.

"Doing Lord knows what," Joyce said.

"They put bathtubs just about anywhere," said Beatrice.

"Oh," said Aunt Louise, trying to maintain her composure. "I haven't seen either the notice or the commercials. But I'll look for them."

Julia was smiling. She had forgotten how much she enjoyed being with this little group, each one finishing the others' thoughts. And how embarrassing was this topic of sex after seventy for Aunt Louise.

"Anyway," said Shirley. "Lawrence lost his status as the go-to guy."

"But we keep cheering him up," said Beatrice, blushing at the pun.

"Must be a real bummer, Lawrence," Julia said.

"Just cause they say I can't doesn't mean I won't," Lawrence said.

His three female friends snickered like adolescents.

* * *

Aunt Louise walked Julia to the Haven's front door.

"I haven't seen your running buddies, Beth and Dell."

"Oh, poor Beth. Her grandchild is having serious medical problems, and the health insurance company just dropped him, saying he was costing the company too much money. Now the family is up against it. Beth flew down to be with them. Dell insisted on going with her."

"I'm so sorry. What a terrible situation. How old's the kid?"

"Six, I believe. May not be able to finish first grade. I remember when you could depend on companies. Not now. They take your money, but then when you need them, they drop you like a hot potato."

Chapter 13

Eye Witness?

*6:30 PM Thursday...*Tagger drove slowly past the Tuttle home, pulling into the driveway four doors down. He walked to the porch and rang the doorbell. A curtain moved.

"Sergeant Tagger, ma'am. I called?"

"Yes, Sergeant," Linda McCall said, holding the door for him. "Come in."

Tagger judged McCall to be in her sixties. Short gray curly hair, small rectangular dark-rimmed glasses. She was dressed in a white blouse and an ankle-length skirt. She held herself erect and stood far enough away to look him in the eye without having to strain her neck. It gave her a haughty look.

"I'll tell you what I told the other officer. I saw this man walking our neighborhood. He just walked up and down the street. I don't know where he came from or where he went. He's probably living in those vacant buildings over yonder, the empty French Quarter Hotel, or in the abandoned parts of Overton Square."

"I want to double check his description."

"Like I told him—white, thin, unshaven, medium long hair, and missing fingers on the right hand."

"What was he wearing?"

"Khakis, dark jacket..."

"Shoes? Hat?"

"Tennis shoes, maybe. No hat."

"Was he carrying anything?"

"Yes. A cane or a long stick. I guess I thought it was something to keep the dogs away."

"You were close enough to see he was missing fingers?"

"A car pulled up right in front of my house. He waved. I could see clearly. Only a thumb and little finger. I remember thinking how ugly it looked."

"And what about this car that pulled up? Did you recognize it?"

"Never saw it before."

"Color, make, model?"

"It was dark, but I think it was black, dirty. A small SUV."

"About what time?"

"My grandfather clock had just chimed eight-thirty."

"Anything special about the car? Maybe a bumper sticker?"

"Didn't see any."

"Any chance you caught the tag number?"

"Nope. I was watching the man. He was right in front of my house, big as you please."

"How about the driver?"

"Can't say."

"Man, woman? Old, young? White, black?"

"Well, let's see. A man I would think. Not old. Not young. Black."

"Did the man and the driver seem to know each other?"

"Don't know. I couldn't hear anything, but they were talking to each other."

Tagger gave her his card, thanked her, and left. He drove the neighborhood before heading home.

Chapter 14

That's More Like It

Friday morning…a new day. Julia rolled over and found the clock—five-thirty. She rolled back on her pillow, and took inventory. I feel okay, she thought. Not tired. Not anxious. She checked her arm. Seems to be healing. She sat up and swung her legs over the side. This is a good day for a full run and a workout, she thought.

* * *

The first leg of the run had felt good. She passed her card under the InsideOut reader, and saw her picture pop up on the screen. She grabbed a towel. She felt good on the weights, but decided not to overdo it. The *bosu-ball* routine forced her to concentrate, as she completed exercises while standing on the half-ball. It was affirming to have her sense of balance back. She made the return run home with equal energy.

Julia took her time in the shower, reacquainting herself with the muscles in each part of her body as she lathered up. She grabbed her stomach with both hands, and shook her head. But overall she felt strong, confident. She was starting to feel like the old Julia. She toweled off, and shook her hair into place. No pillow hair today. She dressed, and left for the *Deliberate Literate.*

"Now that's more like it, Lieutenant," said Millie. "You

look like a real person today."

"Thanks, Millie. And thanks for taking care of me."

* * *

Julia pulled on to Union Avenue for the short quarter-mile trip to the Union Station Precinct.

"Morning, Lieutenant," said Teresa. "You look bright-eyed and bushy-tailed this morning."

"Hey, Teresa," Julia said. "Yup. Feeling good this morning." Julia went to her office and began work on a crime board.

Known & Unknown

- car bomb exploded—not like bomb in Wynne, AR
- may/not be same person/group
- no tie between Wynne vic & Tuttle
- one man killed: Robert Tuttle, coroner confirmed
- one woman injured: wife Shelly Tuttle, hospitalized, uncons
- H.S. student bombing threats: Charlie Barrington, Sp Ed
- gang members clashing: VLs & Lil Bro Posse
- one stranger walking the streets: cauc, missing fingers on rt. hand
- small, dark SUV: male driver, AA

* * *

8:30 AM Friday...the team plus one. Tagger and Marino walked into the conference room, coffees in hand. A few minutes later Powers came in, wearing his cap and carrying a bottle of *Zico.*

"Morning, gentlemen," said Julia. "We'll try to keep this meeting to fifteen minutes." The men nodded. "Let's go down the crime board. Special Agent Powers?"

"I think those first three things are still accurate. We haven't found anything more about the Memphis bomb," said Powers. "We're still not ruling out the possibility that both bombs were constructed by persons from the same group or terrorist cell, American or otherwise.

"And the Wynne bomber?" Marino asked.

"The task force is collecting evidence and the D.A. is building a case for the grand jury on our suspected bomber," Powers said. "But it's still going to be a while. You can imagine how she's playing this pretty close to the vest. But it looks as if our suspect wasn't acting alone. Getting back to Memphis, there's nothing I can see that connects the Arkansas bombing and the assistant principal."

"I'm assuming you have a good profile of the Wynne victim," Marino said. "You know, the people and organizations he was associated with, maybe a history of gambling, criminal record, or out-of-town travel. Any chance we could get a copy of that?"

"Let me see what I can do," said Powers. Julia raised her eyebrows and cocked her head. "Let me rephrase that. I'll get you a copy."

"We received the coroner's findings," said Julia. "Blunt force trauma, broken neck, and fourth degree burns—all consistent with an explosion. Dental records confirm the victim as Robert Tuttle. Tag?"

"Mrs. Tuttle is having a rough time, in and out of consciousness," said Tagger. "She was operated on for a brain hemorrhage. As of this morning, she's still not conscious. We have officers stationed at her room twenty-four-seven. No indication of any interest from strangers."

"You ever get a chance to talk to her?" asked Powers.

"Yeah. Maybe five minutes," said Tagger. "We were the ones to tell her that her husband had been murdered. She was pretty shook up. Said she didn't believe anyone would want to kill him."

"Not sure where we're going with White Station students who might have a score to settle with Tuttle," said Marino. "The gang-bangers, Vice Lords and the Lil Bro Posse—they all seem to actually like Tuttle. Even offered to help find his killer. Of course their top suspect is Charlie Barrington."

"That the kid who threatened to blown people up?" asked Powers.

"That's the one," Marino said. "The Lieutenant and I had the opportunity to meet him, along with his father and his attorney. Not a very social bunch. Charlie seemed plenty scared, never said a word."

"Turns out he wasn't at school Monday," said Julia. "And his only alibi is a handwritten log his father keeps of Charlie phoning in every hour."

"What a crock," said Powers.

"We still don't have a copy of the school board's records," said Marino. "We need to light a fire under someone."

Julia nodded.

"Anything on that guy with the missing fingers?" asked Powers.

"I talked to Mrs. McCall," said Tagger. "She pretty much told me the same story you had, except she added that the guy was talking to someone in a small black SUV. She was guessing an African American male. I drove around the neighborhood but didn't see anything."

"Okay," Julia said. "Assignments."

"I'll stay in touch with Mrs. Tuttle, start questioning family members," said Tagger. "And I'll be driving the neighborhood in the evenings to see if I can spot the guy with missing fingers and the SUV."

"I'll question more faculty members at the school," said Marino. "See what I can dig up."

"Professor, how about you get with Special Agent Powers,"

Julia said. "See what he can teach you about homemade bombs. And while you're there, you can pick up that list he's going to get for us." Powers put up his hands in mock surrender, smiling. "I'm going to meet with our assistant A.G. Diggs to see how we need to proceed with Charlie. Let's touch base again next Tuesday at eight-thirty."

* * *

Friday late morning... Teresa wheeled in a cart of files.

"Teresa," Julia said loudly. "Here I thought it was going to be a slow paperwork day."

"I consider it an important part of my job description to make sure our officers always have plenty to do," said Teresa, piling the files on Julia's desk. "You know the public thinks y'all just sit around eating doughnuts and drinking coffee. Wait till they find out how much time y'all spend in the bathroom getting rid of it."

"Maybe your brother was correct. I really do need to keep a close eye on you. Maybe a referral?"

"I have a date tonight," Teresa said.

"That explains it. Anyone I know? I may have to warn him about what he's going to be in for."

"You don't have to get all uppity, just because I'm going to be with your ex."

"My ex?"

"Yeah. Dr. Blue Eyes."

"Mark? Mark Sanders?" Julia felt her stomach lurch, as if she were in a plane that hit an air pocket. She felt the warm, red blotch growing up her neck. She covered it with her hand.

"Yup. I figured since he hasn't been calling you it's a clear sign that he's available."

"Teresa, I—"

"Okay, okay. I'm actually going to be one of about twenty

people on this 'date'."

"What *are* you going on about?"

"You know my granddaddy has Alzheimer's," Teresa said, turning serious. Julia nodded. "It's been so hard on my family. Granddaddy's doctor recommended we go to one of Dr. Sanders' respite groups, over at the Haven. I'm meeting my brother and his wife there tonight."

"I've heard nothing but good things about Dr. Sanders' work with families," Julia said. "I'm sure it'll be well worth your time."

Teresa gave a hopeful smile, and wheeled out the cart.

Julia felt an emptiness, a place Mark used to fill. He's the best thing that ever happened to me, she thought. It didn't happen right away, she remembered. I kept him at a distance, but there were all these *signs*. We just kept running into one another unexpectedly. And people seemed to be pushing us together—Tonya, Aunt Louise, and her friends at the Haven. And I felt myself falling in love with him. But then came the broken ribs. The stupid three broken ribs. They just wouldn't heal. They turned my life upside down. They... what was it Dr. Notting said? It was all about my need to be in control. I felt useless, helpless, worthless. I was no good to myself, and I felt I no longer deserved to be with Mark. He was still Mark—fun, upbeat, supportive, caring, understanding—damn I miss him. I'd been confident enough to stand toe to toe with him before. But no longer. My God, how could I live up to his ideal of me? I didn't deserve to be with him? So I pushed him away before he decided to leave me. Julia's eyes welled up. She hurried to her office door and closed it.

* * *

Julia felt frustrated. The morning had turned into a personal disaster. She could not reconcile her current state with the fact that she had felt great earlier in the morning. My legs felt great on the run, she thought. My balance was good doing exercises, and I felt strong. My attitude was upbeat. I thought I'd left all that emotional garbage behind. I thought I was over it. Then just the mention of Mark's name, and all the shit came flooding back—the self-doubt, the lack of self-control, feeling worthless. And now this sense of loss. What's happening to me?

She grabbed her cell.

"Doctor Proctor," she answered.

"Tonya, it's Julia. You have some time?"

Chapter 15

Gearing Up

Friday morning...

"Jesus, Mary, and Joseph," said Marino under his breath.

"You praying again?" Tagger asked. "You know as a government employee, that's not allowed."

Marino shot him a look. "You have any idea how many websites there are detailing the construction of bombs?"

"I bet there's more small black SUVs registered in Shelby County."

"Powers gave me a few sites to check out before we get together. I'm not sure why the Lieutenant wanted me to learn this crap."

"Because she needs to have someone keep tabs on the ATF guys," Tagger said. "You know, be able to ask the right questions, and know when we're being jacked around."

"There's that," said Marino.

"Whoever this bomber is, he's dead serious. It feels like Iraq or Afghanistan."

"You have to think Tuttle really pissed somebody off."

"Think the kid's good for it?"

"He's got motive, smarts, and a history of being infatuated with blowing people up. Probably he's played every video game on the *too-violent-for-kids* list. Hell, he probably knows how to make the damn bombs."

"You said he's never acted out any of his threats?" Tagger said.

"There's always a first time."

"How about the suspect they're working on over in Arkansas?"

"The A.G.'s not sharing any information with us."

"That's probably another reason the lieutenant wanted you to chum around with Powers."

"Yeah. We'll see how all that works out. Any hits on the SUV?"

"I've got about forty or fifty with addresses in the midtown and downtown zip codes. It's a start."

"Tag, you think there's going to be a third bomb?"

"I hope not. But then I'd've said there wouldn't have been a first one."

* * *

*Friday afternoon...*Tagger's phone rang.

"Sergeant, this is Franklin. Dr. Torruilla just told me that Mrs. Tuttle is showing signs of coming out of the coma."

"Good news. She say when we can talk to her?"

"She's being cautious. Says maybe tomorrow morning."

"Keep me posted."

"Sergeant?"

"Yes."

"I won't be on duty tomorrow, but I want to be here. Is that okay?"

"Of course. I'd be disappointed if you didn't."

"Thanks. I'll see you tomorrow."

* * *

Friday evening...the bond of the margarita. The waitress brought frozen margaritas and took their orders.

"Masterson told me about this place," said Powers. "Said that Molly's La Casita had one of the best margaritas he'd ever had."

"I like 'em," said Marino. "You go by Werner?"

"People who know me call me Chip."

"Why Chip?"

"Before I had my plastic surgery and got all pretty, I used to have a chip in my front tooth. Nothing dramatic. When I was ten I saw a guy in a movie open a beer bottle with his teeth. I tried it on a bottle of Coke." Marino winced. "After my Hummer took an IED in Iraq, I had to have my face put back together. I told them to fix my tooth while they were at it."

"Damn."

"How about you? What name you go by?"

"Tony. Just Tony. No Story to go with it. No Coke bottle. No IED."

"Well, Tony," Powers said raising his glass. "Here's to our new partnership."

Marino raised his glass in reply.

* * *

Friday evening...the hood. Tagger patrolled the neighborhood around the Tuttle house. He started small, broadened his sweep, and retraced his route. No men fitting the stranger's description. No small black SUVs. He turned on Poplar Avenue. A small black SUV was heading west, in the right hand lane. He pulled in behind. He could see two children in the back, one in a car seat. He couldn't determine their race. A woman was driving. She appeared to be white. He took note of the license. Tagger drove through the larger parking lots in the area—Overton Square, Ike's, Playhouse on the Square, and Walgreen's. No hits.

* * *

Friday evening...it's all about timing.

"It's too soon," he said. "The cops are all over this."

"The timing is perfect," his friend said. "They won't expect us to act again this fast. We're not going to be anywhere near the last one. And besides, they have no idea we're coming. We go *this* weekend."

Chapter 16

First I Decide

3:17 AM Saturday...courage. Julia hadn't slept much, her brain popcorning all night. Feeling-laden words raced inside her head—attributes from others, attributes from herself. She worked to balance negative qualities with positive qualities. But mostly it turned into negative self-talk. It's not going to get better until I decide to get off my butt and take action, she thought. That simple choice gave her a focus. She pulled the covers back, slid her feet into her slippers. Julia began to walk through her house, every room. The physical action of walking energized her, increased her resolve. The more focused she became, the faster she walked until her pace matched the intensity in her head. She replayed the insights and encouragement from Dr. Notting and Tonya. I don't have to fix it right away, she thought. I just have to believe I can get through this.

Chapter 17

Jarvis

Saturday morning...an odd kid. Marino walked into Union Station.

"Morning, Sergeant," said Teresa. "Welcome to the weekend warriors."

"Morning," said Marino. "I forgot you work flex hours. I need to be on the computer for a while."

"There's coffee," she said.

"Thanks."

Marino heard unusual noises as he passed a conference room. He looked in. An African American boy, not much more than twelve, was playing a video game. He walked over to him.

"You look kinda young to be a cop," he said. "You undercover?"

"What?" the boy said. "I'm not under any covers."

"No, I mean are you working as an undercover cop?" said Marino.

"Under what covers?" the boy asked.

This isn't going anywhere, thought Marino. "Are you here with anyone?"

"You," the boy said.

"I mean did someone bring you here?"

"Aunt Teresa."

"What's your name, son?"

"Jarvis Johnson."

"I'm Sergeant Marino," he said, sticking out his hand. Jarvis hesitated, but extended his without touching Marino's. Marino moved to grasp his limp hand.

"See you later," said Marino.

Jarvis had already returned to his video game. Marino walked back to Teresa's desk.

* * *

"I just met a kid who says you're his aunt," said Marino.

"He's my brother's kid," said Teresa. "You know Raiford."

"Sure. Worked with him in the south precinct back in the day. You babysitting?"

"Kinda. Raiford wanted to visit our granddaddy in the nursing home today. He's got Alzheimer's. His wife's pulling a two-day at the firehouse. He wasn't sure how Jarvis would handle the visit. So he asked if I could keep an eye on him till he picked him up. I don't want him to be any trouble. He wasn't doing anything wrong, was he?"

"No, no. He just seemed different. He was so intensely involved in his video game. I suppose that's why he kind of *geed* when I *hawed*."

"He kinda of what?"

"We didn't seem to be on the same page. My grandfather used to have a horse and wagon. He'd yell 'Gee' when he wanted her to turn right, and 'Haw' to turn left."

"I get it. Well, that's not really so far off. Jarvis has *some* problems, but he's doing much better now. He still gets all caught up in the literal meaning of word. And he's really into shoot-'em-up video games."

"So I heard. I'll keep half an eye on him if you'd like."

"Thanks. Yeah. I'd like that." Marino turned to walk away. "Sergeant?"

"Yeah," he said turning back.

She dropped her voice. "Jarvis has Asperger's."

"Asperger's?"

"Yeah. He's really improved over the last three, four years. He used to have some bodacious meltdowns. But I haven't heard of a single one for quite a while now. He's very smart, especially with computers and science, but he's not so good at being social with folk."

"You mean he doesn't play well with others," he said, smiling.

"It's really sad. Raif says Jarvis wants to have friends, but he doesn't know how to do it. The kids at school make fun of him and push him around. He reads tons of books. Even memorizes them. But he can't read people, and he's not so hot at being able to see things from another person's point of view. I'm sure you noticed he talks loud, bit of a mono-tone. But he'll do what you tell him. Just don't expect him to look you in the eye."

"Got it."

"Raif has set up a schedule so he has to change what he's doing every twenty or thirty minutes. Jarvis seems to like the structure, as artificial as it is. I set my watch to buzz for each change. I'll take him a snack in a few minutes, and make sure he moves to the next activity."

"I'll check on him every so often."

"Thanks, Sergeant."

Chapter 18

A Turn of Events

Saturday afternoon…a double take. A small group huddled outside Shelly Tuttle's room. Tagger recognized Dr. Torruilla and Officer Franklin.

"Sergeant," said Torruilla. "This is our neurosurgeon, Dr. Foruke." They shook hands.

"And this is Officer Norse," said Franklin. "He's on protection detail this weekend."

Tagger nodded.

"I was just saying Dr. Foruke and I are very pleased with Mrs. Tuttle's improvement," said Torruilla. "We still need to watch her closely, especially the next two or three days."

"We can talk to her?" asked Tagger.

"Yes. Just be alert to any changes in her—breathing, pains, coherence," Torruilla said. "And let us know if you see anything."

Tagger nodded to Franklin. They walked into Tuttle's room. "Mrs. Tuttle, remember us? I'm Sergeant Tagger and this is Officer Franklin."

"I remember," she said.

"Dr. Torruilla says you're doing much better. She and Dr. Foruke are pleased with your progress," said Tagger.

Tuttle managed a polite smile.

"We wanted to ask you some more questions about the

bombing," Tagger said. Her face became expressionless. He chose to continue. "This may seem repetitious, but could you take us back to that Monday morning?"

Tuttle inhaled slowly. "I fed the children and got them off to the bus stop like I do every school day," she said softly. "Bobby had to leave earlier than usual, and he was running late. Said he didn't have time for breakfast. Just grabbed a piece of toast and he poured coffee in his travelling cup. He was still chewing on the toast when he kissed me goodbye, then he walked into the garage."

She paused, looking toward the end of the bed. Franklin touched Tuttle's hand. She looked up. "The next part runs together. I think I was on the floor before I heard the loud noise, but I can't be sure. Then the woman—your lieutenant you said—was yelling, asking me if I was hurt. It seems as if a lot of hands grabbed me."

Tagger looked at Franklin.

"Do you remember any other noises before the explosion?" Franklin asked.

"You mean like the garage door?" Franklin nodded. "Let's see," said Tuttle. "The garage door rolled up, and I heard the car door slam. That's all I remember."

"Did you hear the car start?" asked Tagger.

"I'm not sure."

"When your husband got in his car—"

"Oh," Tuttle cut him off. "He wasn't in his car. He was in my car."

"Your car?" he asked.

"Yes. He had a special school thing. He needed the SUV to carry a bunch of stuff. I was going to take his Taurus."

* * *

Tagger pulled his cell phone as he left Tuttle's room. "Lieutenant, this is Johnnie. You sitting down?"

Chapter 19

A Beginning

5:00 PM Saturday, April 11, 2009...first things first. Julia listed the positive attitudes she needed to adopt, and the tactics for coping with setbacks, then made her indispensable to-do list. She had no doubts about her top priority, and had given herself a deadline of five o'clock. Julia had been sitting in her beanbag chair since four, gathering courage. Her cell phone lay in her lap, keeping clear of her sweaty palms. Just before the hour, she dried her hands on her upper shirt sleeves, opened her cell, and punched in a single number. The phone rang five times. Not voice mail, she hoped. *Please* not voice mail.

"Yes," he answered.

"Mark?" Julia said cautiously.

"Yeah."

"I want to apologize."

"For what?"

"For how I treated you. You didn't deserve any of it. I was a bitch. It's inexcusable, I know. And I understand if you..."

Silence.

"Mark? Say something. Please."

"What do you want me to say?"

"Anything."

"Like how much you hurt me? Or, how pissed off

I've been?"
    "I know I hurt you, and you have every—"
    "You're damn right I do."
    "Please forgive me. I want to see you."
    "I can't trust you."
    "Let me earn back your trust."
    Silence.
    "At least let me call you again. We need to talk."
    "*We* don't."
    "All right. *I* need to talk."
    Silence.
    "Please."

Chapter 20

Next!

Sunday, late afternoon…jerks are made, not born. Internist Dr. Craig Lyndale pulled into his three-car garage in Collierville, east of Memphis, just north of the Mississippi state line. He grimaced at the irritating sound of the lawn crew—the riding lawnmower, gas-powered edger, gas-powered leaf blower. He checked his watch. They'd damn well better be done and gone in the next forty-five minutes, he thought. He opened the trunk of his BMW Gran Turismo, and hoisted his bag of golf clubs and pull cart. He rolled them across the spotless floor to the opposite corner, clicked the garage door closer, and went inside to shower and dress. His guest would be arriving within the hour. He stopped to check the temperature of the hot tub.

Lyndale had an ideal job with perfect hours for a physician, and an ample base salary supplemented by generous bonuses. He was forced to pay alimony and maintenance for wife number one and his two children. But he soon learned the value of prenuptial agreements. So when wives number two and three left him, his money stayed. His guest tonight could be wife number four, if she played her cards right.

* * *

A lawn crew finished the front yard of Lyndale's property, and moved to the expansive backyard. An old black pickup truck parked at the curb. Two men got out and walked to the side door of the garage. They were dressed in workmen's clothes, wide-brimmed sun hats, and gloves. One carried a rake and a black garbage bag, the other a push broom and dust pan. The first man tried the door—locked. He took out a credit card and forced the latch back. They entered. As expected, the security system had not yet been armed. The other man reached carefully into the garbage bag, lifted out a pipe bomb, and set it gently on the concrete. The first man dropped to his knees, rolled to his back, and slid under the BMW. The other man handed the bomb to him. He heard the metallic click as the magnet grabbed hold, and then the strips of duct tape being torn from the roll.

They returned to the pickup, and drove away.

Chapter 21

Catch Him If You Can

6:30 AM *Monday, April 13, 2009...professionals they ain't.* The two men parked in a field under an expanse of power lines, far enough away to avoid being seen in the immediate neighborhood, but close enough to observe a sliver of the garage door through the binoculars. Lyndale was a creature of habit. From previous surveillance they knew he always left his house between 6:25 and 6:35.

"There it goes," said the man behind the wheel. "The garage door is almost up. Call it in."

The man in the passenger seat opened his cell phone and punched in the numbers...6, 3, 9, 4.

"Hey, nothing's happening. You hit the right numbers?" asked the driver.

He tried again. Still nothing. He inspected his phone. "No signal," said the second man.

"There's no damn signal." He began shaking the phone violently, hitting it on the palm of his hand.

"Try mine," the driver said, tossing his cell as he kept an eye on the garage.

He opened the phone. The reception symbol kept changing—half a bar, no bar. He held it out the window. Still no signal. "Yours is dead, too. What the hell do we do now?"

"The bomb could go off any time from the shaking of the

car," said the driver.

"More people dead."

"Can't help that now. If it blows, it blows. Least he'll be taken care of."

"What if it doesn't explode?"

"Shut up, damn it. Let me think. We know where he's going. We'll get ahead of him, and meet him at his office."

* * *

Lyndale's route to the office was mostly expressway. He drove erratically, speeding, cutting in and out of traffic. He narrowly missed a large pothole when he pulled back into the left lane. The old pickup matched his every move. The difference was that the big BMW provided a smooth, quiet ride, while the two men in the pickup bounced around wildly. Lyndale was catching up to them.

"Go faster. Get us out of here. It's just duct tape. The bomb's held on with duct tape. He's going to blow up right beside us."

"I can't go any faster. There's cars everywhere. Nowhere to go."

"Pull off the highway!"

They watched from the side of the road as the BMW went airborne after speeding through a large trough in the road. They both dropped down, their heads colliding. Three seconds without a blast. They peeked over the dashboard to see the BMW veering in and out of lanes. The pickup squeezed back into traffic.

"We've got to catch him before he leaves his car."

Both cars took the I-240 loop, getting off on Union Avenue in the medical district, and driving into downtown Memphis. By the time the pickup pulled within sight of Lyndale's office building, they saw the entrance door closing behind him. The BMW sat in a handicap parking spot near the entrance.

"What do we do now?"

"We catch the son of a bitch when he comes out."

Chapter 22

Not Good, But Better

Monday morning...following the list. Julia sat at her desk feeling upbeat, determined. She was committed to getting back in charge of herself. The two most important items on her to-do list were repairing her relationship with Mark and solving the Tuttle case. She compartmentalized, put Mark on hold, and focused on the bombing. First on her agenda was this morning's meeting with Tagger and Marino.

* * *

"Take it from the beginning, Tag," she said.

"Shelly Tuttle regained consciousness Saturday," said Tagger. "We were there—"

"Who's *we?*" interrupted Marino.

"Officer Shawna Franklin. She's been handling the day watch at the hospital," Tagger said. "May I continue?"

Marino waved him on with his coffee cup. Julia rolled her eyes, but it felt good to be back in sync with her team.

"We just ran over the same questions we'd asked last week. But Tuttle was more alert. Like I told y'all Saturday, their schedule had changed. Shelly was the one who usually left the house first, but she didn't have to go to work that day. Robert needed extra cargo space, so he was taking *Shelly's* SUV."

"Did she realize what she was telling you?" asked Julia.

"That she was the target?"

"Not at first. But her eyes got big and her blood pressure monitor went off," Tagger said. "Doc threw us out. I tried again yesterday, but the doctor left strict instructions we were not allowed to see her. Franklin's there this morning. She knows to keep her eyes peeled and to call whenever we get the go-ahead to talk to Tuttle."

"Where does that put us with Charlie?" asked Marino.

"We still can't say Robert Tuttle was not the target," said Julia. "Maybe both the Tuttles were marks."

"We really need to broaden our scope," Tagger said.

"I was going to talk to one of Charlie's teachers this afternoon," Marino said. "Sounds like I need to keep that appointment."

"I talked to Diggs. He promised to light a fire under the school board's attorney about giving us Charlie's records," said Julia. "I filled Powers in right after your call, Tag. Speaking of Powers, you getting anything from him, Professor?"

"Nothing new on the bomb or the bomber," Marino said. "I've been reviewing those websites he gave me. Bomb building instructions are everywhere. And as long as you're not talking about a nuclear bomb or a dirty bomb, you can get the components from Home Depot. If you approach the militia guys just right, I bet they'll even talk you through the steps. It's scary shit."

"What do you think about Powers?" asked Julia.

"Seems to be a likable guy," Marino said. "Turns out he did a couple of tours in Iraq, with a bomb squad. His Hummer got taken out by an IED. He was pretty messed up. Said he had a lot of facial surgery. Doesn't hear too well, almost blind in one eye."

"Damn," said Tagger.

"Must have had an awfully good plastic surgeon," said Julia.

"Yeah," said Marino. "His nickname is Chip, because he had a chipped front tooth. Said they fixed his tooth when they reconstructed his face."

"So you like him?" Julia asked.

"He's all right," said Marino. "Still, he plays for the feds. Time will tell if he'll play on our team as well."

"Okay, let's clarify assignments," Julia said.

Chapter 23

An Official Hello

Monday morning...keeping the boss apprised.
Teresa buzzed in. "It's the boss," she said. "Line one."

"Morning, Major Williams."

"Morning, Lieutenant. Where are we on the bombing?"

"ATF says the bomb was constructed differently from—"

"I know all that. What's new?"

"Mrs. Tuttle regained consciousness. Turns out Mr. Tuttle was taking *her* car to work last Monday."

"*Her* car?"

"Yes, sir. She had a medical relapse when she realized she might have been the target. Doctor hasn't allowed us to speak to her since."

"And...?"

"We've had officers on security detail twenty-four-seven since the bombing."

"I'm looking at the budget sheet now," he said. "I'll have to shut this down soon."

"I understand, sir."

"Any other leads?"

"A man was seen walking the street in front of the Tuttle house. We have a loose description."

"I understand you ran into the burning house and pulled the Mrs. out."

"Well, yes. I ran in. But the firefighters pulled her out."

"Well done, Lieutenant. Have you had a debriefing?

"Yes, sir. I'm doing fine."

"Glad to hear it."

"Thank you, sir."

"Lieutenant."

"Sir?"

"I don't need to tell you how much pressure is coming on this one. You need to wrap this up, and fast. And we sure as hell don't want another one."

Chapter 24

Asperger's 101

Monday afternoon…if you can read this, thank an effective teacher. The bell sounded, and chaos broke loose for four minutes. A woman walked into the school office. She was directed to one of the assistant principals' office. A police officer stood to greet her.

"I'm Sergeant Marino."

"Nelly Patterson."

"I'm investigating the murder of Robert Tuttle."

"I can't stop crying," she said, raising her closed hand to her sternum. "Bobby was a good man. It's such a loss to the school and the students."

"And a loss for you?"

"Of course. I'm the lead teacher for the special education students. Bobby and I worked together on all their discipline problems."

"So you knew him pretty well."

"I guess so."

"You have any idea who might want to kill him?"

"I can't imagine anyone who'd want do such a thing."

"Tell me about Charlie Barrington."

"I can't talk about students."

"I have a signed court order. Mrs. Seymour has it."

"You think Charlie killed Bobby?"

"Do you?"

"No."

"No?"

"Charlie has been threatening to blow people up since he was a little guy. But he's never so much as taken a swing at anyone. It's just his way of protecting himself."

"Protecting himself?"

"Like most kids with Asperger's, he catches a lot of grief from other students. He's not good at sticking up for himself, physically. And he's not good in a verbal exchange. So he does the only thing he thinks will help. He threatens to blow them up. Nobody believes he'll do it. And it's never been an issue till all the school shootings around the country began. Now parents go ballistic when they hear about Charlie sounding off. A lot of parents have been opposed to having students like Charlie mainstreamed into regular classes. Heck, lots of regular education teachers object to it. So when anything happens with one of my kids, people just jump in with both feet."

"Does he play those violent video games?"

"What kid doesn't?"

"But aren't some kids more susceptible to those messages than others? Like maybe, Charlie?"

"Some are. I just don't think Charlie is one of them. If memory serves, Charlie has been into the games with lots of explosions. I'm guessing the *Saints Row* series. Came out two or three years ago. Seems I remember him talking about having played the old *Battlefield 1942.*" She smiled. "That's the year my parents were married. Of course they didn't have computers back then. The game came out in the early 2000s."

"Do you happen to know whether Charlie has gone on the websites that describe how to make a bomb?"

"Goodness, no. I certainly hope not."

"What about all that teasing and harassing from the other students. Aren't there school policies about that?"

"Absolutely. It comes under our bullying policy. Hard core bullying is easy to see, especially the physical assaults, and destruction of property, even cyber threats. But most of the bullying falls at the more subtle end—teasing, spreading lies, taunting, ostracizing. That goes on all the time. And parents can get just as riled up if their child is the target of this level of bullying as if it had been a physical assault."

"Don't the teachers enforce the anti-bullying policies?"

"Look, teaching has never been easy, but trying to keep up with all the laws and regulations coming down from Washington has only made it worse. Then of course, Nashville and our school board pile on their own regulations to make them look more conscientious. The result is a school board policy manual so heavy you can't even pick it up."

"So they don't enforce the policies because they can't lift them?" Marino asked.

Patterson smiled. "Sorry. I guess I got a little worked up about the bureaucracy," she said.

"We have a large percentage of really talented teachers. No teacher can be effective if she doesn't have good classroom management."

"Management?"

"The skill to handle a classroom to make learning possible. Really effective teachers know that you can't have optimal teaching and learning without good classroom management."

"So teachers who don't have good *management*—they allow bullying and threats?"

"Not quite. But it's true they certainly have much more of it, and a lot less learning going on."

"How are teachers handling Charlie?"

"Actually, I'm rather proud of that. Here in our school we have developed a buddy system."

"Involving teachers?"

"Students," she said, shaking her head. "And it works especially well with children who have Asperger's. It's not like they don't want to have friends—they do. It's that they don't know how. They don't understand the rules of conversation, which is ninety percent non-verbal. These kids can be incredibly literal, they can have difficulty reading facial expressions, and they often focus exclusively on their own agendas. Kind of like a two year-old—it's all about *me*."

"So you buddy up kids who have Asperger's?"

"No," she said, laughing. "We pair a regular education student and a student with Asperger's. We train the buddy about Asperger's Syndrome. Then we put them together and have them discuss a topic, and play a game under our supervision."

"And the buddy is okay with this?"

"Oh, my, yes. It's a popular activity for students who are collecting community service credits, as well as for those who are thinking about teaching as a career."

"And the child with Asperger's?"

"They're delighted to have a friend. Not only that, but the buddy tends to stick up for him."

"Charlie has a buddy?"

"Yes. JR. A great kid. When Charlie gets nervous or upset, JR is one of the few people who can calm him down. Charlie will wring his hands, and rock or pace. JR cues him by putting his hands on Charlie's hands, and Charlie takes the cue and calms down. We had to work with the two of them so that Charlie would tolerate JR touching him, and JR has learned how to do it subtly."

"I take it JR wasn't in the room when the harassment and the threats took place."

"Unfortunately, no."

"One last question. That thing about being *literal*, could these kids have trouble understanding a word like, *undercover?*"

"Very good, Sergeant. They could indeed. A typical example teachers run into is when they ask to *see* a child's paper. It's not uncommon for the child to ignore the request because the teacher is obviously already *looking* at the paper. What the teacher wanted was for the child to hand over his paper. And if the teacher doesn't understand the dynamics of what is happening, she may think he's being insubordinate."

Chapter 25

Digging a Little Deeper

Monday afternoon, April 13, 2009...one tearful onion skin at a time. Tagger drove to the MED.

"Sergeant Tagger," said Franklin.

"Officer Franklin," Tagger said, nodding. "Thanks for the call. Bring me up to speed."

"Dr. Torruilla said Mrs. Tuttle was doing much better. Said we could talk to her." Franklin turned and knocked. She opened the door and peeked in, making eye contact with Mrs. Tuttle. "All right if we come in?"

Tuttle nodded.

"We hope you're feeling better, Mrs. Tuttle," Tagger said.

"Better physically. But I can't get Bobby out of my mind. It should have been me."

"Why do you say that?" Tagger asked.

"Because it was my car. Because I was the one who always left the house first."

"You said before that you couldn't think of anyone who'd want to harm your husband," said Tagger. "Is there anyone who'd want to harm you?"

"I don't think so. I get along with everyone. I'm even given high marks on my annual evaluations for being the nicest one in our office and the most considerate to the public."

"Where do you work?" asked Franklin.

"Pharaoh Health Management Systems."

"Pharaoh? Like the huge statue downtown in front of the pyramid?" said Franklin.

Tuttle nodded.

"That's based in Memphis, right?" Tagger said.

"Yes. The main office is out east on Poplar, near Massey. I work in the downtown office—Policy Review."

"What do you do there?" Franklin asked.

"I'm a secretary. My main job is to answer the phone. I do a little typing. But the phones are my primary responsibility, and they ring constantly. They're ringing when I open the office door at six-thirty, and they're ringing when I walk out of the building at three-thirty."

"You can't think of anyone who's been angry with you?" asked Franklin.

"No one."

* * *

"Sergeant, family members have been waiting to see Mrs. Tuttle pretty much every day since she arrived," said Franklin. "They just haven't been able to see her much. I mention it because it might be easier to ask them questions here, instead of chasing them around."

"Good idea," said Tagger. "Tell me what the visiting rules are so I'll have an answer for them."

"As I understand it, Mrs. Tuttle's allowed no more than two visitors at a time. But her kids have carte blanche to come whenever."

"I'll compare notes with you later about any information we pick up." Tagger walked to the waiting area. He recognized Tuttle's sister, Jacquelyn Forest.

"Sergeant. How is she?" asked Forest.

"She's better. Her physical condition has improved, but she's pretty beaten down emotionally."

"Can we see her?"

"My understanding is that visitors will be allowed shortly. Can I ask you a few questions?"

"Okay."

"You know the explosion was caused by a bomb, right?"

Forest nodded, her face contorting, eyes sad.

"Did you know the car that was blown up was your sister's?"

Her eyes widened and her mouth dropped open. "What are you saying? Do you think the bomb was meant for Shelly?" The sadness in her eyes turned to fear.

"It's possible."

"Does Shelly know this?"

"She's the one who told *us*."

Silence as Forest struggled to understand.

"Can you think of anyone who might want to hurt your sister?"

"Shelly? Come on. She's disgustingly nice. It's a disease with her. Everyone likes Shelly. Heck everyone liked Bobby. They could win couple of the year honors, if there were such a thing."

"Are there other family members I could talk to?"

"None that live here."

"How about friends?"

"Lots of friends."

"Could you give me the names and phone numbers of some of their best friends?"

"Some of Shelly's friends are right there," Forest said, pointing to the other side of the waiting room. "I'd be happy to give you other names, Sergeant. But I want to see my sister first."

"Not a problem," Tagger said, handing her his card. "Please call me when you get a chance."

Chapter 26

In the Garden

Monday afternoon...going backdoor. Julia drove east on Union Avenue, following the curve eastward where the street became Walnut Grove Road, then out past Mendenhall. She followed the side streets into a well-maintained neighborhood shaded by hundreds of mature trees. She pulled into the drive of a large two-story gray house with white trim. A woman waited for her at the front door, standing tall, chin up. She was wearing jeans, a loose-fitting button-down shirt hanging past her waist, and holding a large-brimmed hat. Julia judged her to be in her mid-to late fifties.

"Mrs. Barrington? I'm Lieutenant Todd."

"I'm not sure I should be talking to you. I don't think Lindsey would approve," Barrington said, her eyes darting from side to side.

"As I said on the phone, I just want to ask you a few questions."

"Lindsey wouldn't want you to be in our house," Barrington said, pausing. "All the neighbors are watching. There's a bench in the back garden," she said as she walked past Julia, around the side of the house. She opened the gate to the backyard, revealing a colorful display of azaleas, dogwoods, crepe myrtles, and cherry blossom trees, interspersed with a variety of flowers, a meandering path, and a water fountain.

"This is lovely," Julia said. "Did you do this?"

"The garden is my joy," Barrington said slowly as she sat on the bench, keeping her eyes on her creation. "This is where I can be at peace." Barrington's posture changed, back rounded, shoulders sloped forward. She held her hands in her lap, fingers touching. Her gaze was distant. Julia saw fatigue, sadness, maybe depression.

"I can see why. This is a place I could escape to," Julia said. "I do."

"Tell me a little about your family."

"My family?"

"Yes. How many children do you have? How long have you been married?"

"Oh, there's only one. He's Lindsey's boy, Charlie. We've been married…ten years, now."

"So you married when Charlie was about eight?"

Barrington nodded.

"What was Charlie like then?"

"God, I was so foolish, so full of myself. I thought I could fix him. Or at the very least, find a facility for him…"

Julia waited.

"How old do you think I am?"

"That's a loaded question," Julia said.

"Forty-four. I'm forty-four, but I look ten years older. Charlie…Charlie sucked the years out of me with his meltdowns and his constant problems at school. And the embarrassment—people stare, point. Life with him has been a never-ending battle. It's only been this last year or so he's kind of leveled off. He rarely threatens to blow me up anymore. And thank God, he stays in his room all the time. Sometimes he won't even come out for dinner."

"Sounds like a challenge."

"I had a career, a successful career. I was a top IT specialist. I never came across a problem I couldn't fix, or at least write a work-around for...That's how I met Lindsey. I was upgrading the computer system in his office. He was so smart. He could make that machine sing. We connected— one geek to another. When he told me about his divorce and about Charlie, well, I just knew I could fix it...I was wrong. I was stupid."

"But Charlie is better?"

"Yes. But it's too late. Too late for me. I have nothing but my garden."

"And your husband?"

"He left me with Charlie, and buried himself in his work. He works twelve- to sixteen-hour days, even on weekends. He's driven, absolutely driven. His compulsiveness has taken over."

"And yet, you haven't left."

"Where would I go? Who'd want me? My mind is mush, a pile of mush. My computer skills are ten years old—ancient in today's technology. Charlie has taken years off my life. Lindsey has never fulfilled his promise to be there for me. All I have is my garden."

"You said Charlie used to threaten you. Did he ever hit you?"

"Not Charlie. He'd get all blustery, yelling and carrying on. But he never hit me."

"Mrs. Barrington, were you here last Monday? The day Charlie stayed home from school."

"Last Monday?" She paused. "I suppose I was here, working in my garden."

"Do you remember Charlie being sick?"

"Sick?" she said, shaking her head. "No."

"Your husband showed me a spreadsheet with timelines."

"Fifteen-minute breaks, right? Lindsey has always been obsessed with the number fifteen. Everything has to be fifteen. We were married on June fifteenth at fifteen-hundred hours for God's sakes. I used to think it was cute."

"He had fifteen-minute entries of Charlie calling him from the house all day on Monday. He said he was checking on him because he was sick."

"He used to do that with me. If he was bothered about something, he'd have me call him every fifteen minutes. It was like a cyber water-drop torture. He just had to have it recorded."

"He said he can tell if the call originated from your home phone."

"Oh, I'm certain that's true. He's exceptionally good with things like that."

"I'm confused. Is there any chance Charlie was home all day Monday, but you never saw him?"

"It's *possible.* Charlie stays in his room a lot. If I don't see him, I assume he's at school or in his room. And I don't go looking for him."

* * *

Julia sat in her car. These kids with Asperger's must exhaust their parents, she thought. I'm drained just hearing about it. How the hell do they cope? One of Aunt Louise's favorite quotes from Plato popped into her head. *Be kind to all you meet, for they are fighting a harder battle.*

Chapter 27

Dr. Craig Lyndale

3:15 PM Monday afternoon...looking for leads. Tagger had interviewed three friends of Mrs. Tuttle's in the waiting room. They were all shocked to hear about the possibility that Shelly may have been the target. No one could think of a single person who would have wanted to kill either of them. Since he was in the medical center, he thought he would drive the short distance to Tuttle's office building. He took the elevator to the ground floor.

* * *

3:28 PM Monday...patience. An old pickup was parked on a downtown street within sight of the Pharaoh Health Management Systems' building entrance, time on the meter. No binoculars needed. A small, black SUV sat empty in an uncovered city parking lot across the street.

"I still have three bars," said the man in the passenger seat of the pickup, looking at his phone.

"Me too," said the driver.

They watched an elderly man slowly plopping a walker, step by step in front of him, working his way to the insurance company's front door.

"Come on, come on, damn it," said the driver.

The door opened. Lyndale came out. He sidestepped the old man, making no attempt to hold the door for him. The man turned and said something. Lyndale did not acknowledge him. A woman appeared at the door, offering assistance to the man. Lyndale reached for the handle of his car door, stopped, grabbed the phone on his belt. He talked for less than a minute, then slid into the driver's seat and closed the door.

"Now," the driver yelled in a loud whisper. The other man carefully punched in the code...6, 3, 9, 4.

BOOM!

Lyndale's car exploded. The alarms of cars around him went off. Red and yellow flames licked the air above the car's engine. Smoke billowed.

"Let's get the hell out of here," said the passenger.

"No. We have to wait," said the driver, touching his arm. "We don't want to draw any attention to ourselves."

* * *

Tagger had driven west on Madison, behind the *AutoZone* baseball stadium. He turned at Third Street and looked for a Pharaoh company sign. Nothing. He slowed, reading off the street numbers. He decided to pull into a small parking lot enclosed within a cyclone fence, only a handful of cars. A man with a walker entered the building. The driver of one of the cars closed his door. Tagger had just turned into the driveway when he felt stunned by a huge explosion. His cruiser was assailed with debris, and his view through the windshield changed to smoke and flame. He slammed on his brakes.

"Jesus!" Tagger said. The BMW in front of him had just blown up. His pulse raced. He gasped for air. "Somebody's in that car."

In one motion Tagger clicked off his seat belt, threw open the door, rolled out of the car, and began running. He had observed this kind of scene before, but never this close. A woman opened the office door and stepped out.

"Fire extinguisher!" Tagger yelled, running toward her. "I need a fire extinguisher! Call 911!"

The woman turned back to the office. Seconds later she appeared, her arms wrapped around a large extinguisher. Tagger took the tank in one hand, pulling the pin as he ran to the BMW. He heard the wind being sucked in by the flames, and felt the crunch of broken glass with each step. The heat and smoke were intense. He held his breath, waiting until he was within two feet before squeezing the lever, concentrating the contents around the passenger. He heard sirens. The passenger was not moving. But Tagger managed to keep the flames at bay.

* * *

"Where the hell'd that cop come from?" demanded the driver. He better not screw this up. Lyndale better be dead."

"Let's go, let's go," said the passenger.

"Not yet."

* * *

As usual in the downtown area, several fire trucks were dispatched in the first response. This time there were three. Firefighters unloaded like ants swarming from a nest. They yelled for Tagger to get out the way. Two teams focused on the fire. A third team pulled Lyndale from the car.

"He's still alive!" one yelled, waving for the paramedics.

They put a neck brace on Lyndale, covered some of his burns loosely with sterile gauze, rolled him on a board, and lifted him to a stretcher. The ambulance raced back to the Elvis Presley Memorial Trauma Center at the MED, where Tagger had just come from. He leaned against the wall, still holding the fire extinguisher.

"Sergeant," said a paramedic. "I need to take a look at you." He took the extinguisher, set it on the blacktop, grasped

Tagger's bicep and wrist, and walked him to the ambulance.

* * *

Julia was near Union Station when she heard the blast. She felt it in her chest, then a rush of fear. She sucked in short, quick breaths, her ears ringing. Julia pulled to the curb. Was that real? she thought. Or I am I having some kind of flashback?

The radio squelched. She heard pieces. "...explosion downtown...possible bomb...officer on the scene...paramedics attending..."

Officer hurt? she thought. This is real. Her head cleared, her focus returned. She flipped on the lights and siren, and raced the four miles downtown.

* * *

The area was jammed with first responders and their vehicles, as well as dozens of police officers and visitors from the nearby Justice Complex at 201 Poplar. An officer was directing traffic. Julia went as far as the cruiser could go, got out, and ran through the vehicles, her hand on her bouncing Glock. She jogged through a small group.

"Where's the hurt officer?" she shouted.

Two men pointed to an ambulance parked outside the cyclone fence. Julia's heart raced. She rounded the ambulance and was shocked to find Tagger. Her stomach knotted. He was sitting on the back of the ambulance holding an oxygen mask to his face. His hands were bandaged, part of his hair burned. Still running, Julia hopped on the back of the ambulance beside Tagger, bumping into him. He looked up, surprised. She put her arm around his shoulders.

"My turn," he said.

"You okay?" she asked, her face radiating concern.

Tagger held up his loosely bandaged left hand. His right hand also bandaged, held the mask.

"I couldn't believe it," Julia said. "I heard the explosion, but I thought I was just reliving last week. You sure you're all right?" she asked wiping her eyes on her sleeve.

"*I* didn't run into a burning building, Lieutenant," Tagger said, coughing.

"Well maybe not a burning building," said the paramedic. "But you were close enough to that burning car to toast marshmallows. And if you hadn't been there, the man would be dead for sure."

"What the hell's going on, Tag?" Julia said.

* * *

"All right," said the driver. "Let's ease out of here nice and slow-like."

"You think he's dead?" asked the other man.

"I sure as hell hope so. But if he's not, that's two they've interfered with. I'm getting really pissed at the MPD."

Chapter 28

Follow-Up

Monday...basic police work. Julia assigned an officer to take Tagger to the ER for an evaluation, despite his objections. Other officers monitored the crime scene. Julia alerted them to expect a visit from ATF agents. Marino joined her as they questioned Pharaoh's Policy Review employees. Two nurses and eight clerical staff were housed in the small unmarked building with their medical director, Dr. Lyndale. Marino talked to the clerical staff in the main room, where they had pulled chairs from their cubicles. Julia talked to the nurses.

"Just what do you do here?" asked Julia

"Subscribers undergo certain medical procedures and then expect Pharaoh to pay for it," said Donna Allen. "We review their insurance policy to see if they qualify for reimbursement."

"Sometimes subscribers make requests for reimbursement of procedures *before* they occur," said Francine Dilworth. "We tell them whether or not their policy would cover such expenses."

"Walk me through this," said Julia. "Say I call the office. What would happen? Who would I talk to?"

"You first have to talk to *Virtual Amy,*" said Allen.

Julia's face contorted.

"Virtual Amy is the voice on the answering system. You

know—Dial one for English. Dial two for questions about your policy. Dial three for questions about your bill. Dial four for a review of coverage for a current medical condition. Dial five to check the status of prior requests. And, if you know the extension of your party, you may dial that number now."

"Okay, so I punch two. Who answers the phone?" asked Julia.

"Amy," said Dilworth. "She's going to ask you to identify the company through which you have your policy, by selecting the corresponding number. Then she's going to ask you to punch in your policy number. The system displays the data on a computer screen, ranked in the order in which the call is received, and you are placed on hold."

Julia felt her frustration rising. She understood the emotional state of the customer by the time they actually talked to a human being.

Chapter 29

The Head Shed

Monday evening...touching base with the boss. Marino and Julia finished their questioning shortly after six o'clock. Powers and his ATF team were working the scene. Julia confirmed their scheduled meeting in the morning with Powers, and walked the short distance to MPD headquarters at 201 Poplar Avenue.

"You don't look so good, Lieutenant," said Major Williams.

"I feel better than I look. One of our men almost died because of another car bomb," said Julia.

"So I understand. Sergeant Tagger, right?"

Julia nodded.

"However, I also understand, like you, his actions were heroic. He, too, may have saved the victim's life."

"I haven't heard," said Julia. "How's Dr. Lyndale doing?"

"Critical condition. Touch and go. How's Tagger?"

"A lot like me," Julia smiled. "His hair's singed and his arms are bandaged. He's at the Methodist ER now getting checked out."

"You're going to have to start your own support group."

"Good one, sir. I just don't want any more members."

"Indeed."

"Sir?" Julia hesitated. "Tagger had just learned that Mrs. Tuttle worked at Pharaoh Health Management Systems. He drove down there to ask some routine questions."

"And another employee gets blown away right in his face. What's the motive?"

"Sergeant Marino and I questioned the staff at Pharaoh's Policy Review office. It's the place where people call to get answers about their health insurance coverage."

"Sounds like someone didn't like the answer they got."

"Special Agent Powers from ATF is still at the scene with his team. We began meeting with him last week to coordinate our investigations."

"Don't let those folks do an end run on you."

"No, sir. Officers canvassed the area and have been picking up copies of surveillance DVDs from the businesses."

"This is that *second* bomb we didn't want, Lieutenant. It's awfully brazen, coming so soon on the heels of the first one. There may be a third bomb in the works. I don't have to tell you to tie this up ASAP."

* * *

Monday evening…taking stock. Julia stopped at the Wendy's drive-thru and bought a chicken salad and fries. She sat at her kitchen table, eating slowly, calming herself. The day had been draining. She felt as if she had experienced the depths of depression with Mrs. Barrington, the powerful emotions of a trauma-related flashback when the bomb exploded, fear for Tagger's well-being, and the frustration of Virtual Amy.

Not long after eating the last fry she donned her favorite lie-around clothes—a holey Dallas Cowboy short-sleeve sweatshirt and baggy cotton sweatpants. After a few stretches she folded herself into the Lotus position, and took a long cleansing breath, centering herself. She considered the events of the day. She visualized herself bouncing back from the day's intense emotions, and regaining her self-confidence.

Julia envisioned tomorrow's morning meeting at Union

Station. She felt confident, assured, focused. Tomorrow would be a *better* day—they would be taking their first steps toward stopping another bomb, another mutilated soul, another dead person.

Chapter 30

Revamping the Crime Board

8:30 AM Tuesday...comparing notes. A heavy quiet dominated the Union Station conference room. Only the sounds of papers shuffling, coffee slurping, and squeaking leather belts.

"Before we get involved in other things, I want to acknowledge the heroic effort of Sergeant Tagger," said Julia, raising her cup of police-issue coffee.

"Just trying to keep up with the boss," Tagger said, smiling meekly.

"Doesn't mean it's my turn next, does it?" asked Marino.

"I thought I'd seen it all in Iraq," said Powers. "But you guys can hang with the best."

Julia paused. "The stakes have doubled in just a week," she said.

"Maybe tripled," said Powers. "Depending on where the Arkansas bombing falls."

"Let's update our crime board, and go from there," said Julia. "Professor, tell us what you learned about Charlie."

"Not much," said Marino. "His special education teacher likes him, and doesn't believe he would carry out his threats. She said he's part of a buddy program. A regular education kid kind of mentors him, helps him socially, goes to bat for him when he's harassed. Says he's probably Charlie's only friend."

"I talked to Charlie's stepmother," said Julia. "She didn't know anything about Charlie being sick last Monday. They don't have a great relationship. It's quite possible he was in his room, and she never bothered to check on him. Speaking of alibis, it'd be good to know where he was yesterday afternoon. Tag, you had a full day..."

"We finally got approval to talk to Mrs. Tuttle yesterday afternoon," Tagger said. "The only new thing she told us was her place of employment. That's why I was downtown. I'd just pulled into the parking lot when the bomb exploded."

"As for the bomb," said Powers, "it's another internet special, essentially the same as the Tuttle bomb. The blast pattern looks as if there was a little less punch in this bomb, but the same explosives. The BMW seems to have been more solidly built, so the destruction wasn't as great."

"I couldn't tell the difference," Tagger said.

The group fell quiet. Powers broke the silence. "Did the doc make it?"

"As of eight this morning he was still listed in critical condition and comatose," Marino said.

"The professor and I questioned the staff from the Pharaoh Policy Review office," Julia said. "It seems this place reviews all requests for health insurance policy holders, or as they say, subscribers, who want to be reimbursed for a particular medical procedure, or who want permission for the insurance company to cover some future procedure. I got the distinct feeling that this office was a source of a lot of bad news."

"Me too, Lieutenant," Marino said. "I questioned the clerical staff. They talk to subscribers on the phone all day long. They said many subscribers were very unhappy, some desperate. I asked if any of them made threatening comments.

They said every one of them gets threatened—often. When I asked about Dr. Lyndale, they all shut up. I think it'd be good to talk to them individually."

"Yeah, same with the two nurses," Julia said. "One intimidated the other."

"Surveillance DVDs have been coming in from the downtown area," said Marino. "We'll have a lot of video to watch."

"We've got things to do," Julia said. "Let's meet again on Friday morning." They got up to leave.

"Tag, can I have a minute?"

He sat.

"Just listening to you this morning gave me chills," she said. "I've seen all the dings and scrapes on your car. One minute earlier and you'd have been part of that explosion."

"Yeah," he said. "I've thought about that. Like I said, I'm just trying to keep up with you, Lieutenant."

"This ain't a contest I want to be a part of," she said. "I want both of us to stay in one piece. Anyway, I called Dr. Proctor about setting up a debriefing for you. You've done this before."

Tag shrugged. "Been to a few."

"I had a session last week. It helped me a lot."

"It's always been a good thing. I'll look for the call," he said. "And, Lieutenant? Thanks for being there. I really appreciate it."

"Get out of here before we get all mushy."

Chapter 31

Back to the MED

Tuesday morning...fore! Tagger needed more information about Pharaoh's Policy Review office. His best contact was Shelly Tuttle. He rounded the corner and saw Franklin sitting outside Tuttle's hospital room.

"Sergeant, you're hurt," said Franklin, looking at his bandaged hands.

"Got a little too close to the flame," Tagger said.

"We heard that bomb blew up right in front of you."

"A little too close for comfort."

"My God. If that happened to me I'd still be sitting in the car with my fingers locked on the steering wheel, and my pants soaking wet," said Franklin.

Tagger smiled.

"I'm glad you're okay," she said. "I mean, not badly hurt."

"Thanks," he said. "We need to talk to Mrs. Tuttle."

"Something new come up?"

"Yeah. We need to know about the place where she works."

"The nurse came out ten minutes ago. I think it's a good time. I'll peek in on her." Franklin knocked and opened the door. She motioned to Tagger.

"Morning Mrs. Tuttle," said Tagger, walking to the bed.

"Morning, Sergeant," Tuttle said. "You've been hurt."

"It's nothing," said Tagger. "Have you heard any of

the news?"

"No. Something happen?"

Tagger hesitated. "There's been another car bombing," he said.

Tuttle sucked in a deep breath as she snapped to a sitting position, eyes wide.

"In the parking lot of your office building," said Tagger.

"Who?"

"Dr. Lyndale."

"Dr. Lyndale? Is he…?"

"He's in critical condition, just down the hall. Nobody else was hurt." Franklin started to say something, but Tagger stopped her with a look. "The doctors don't know if he'll make it."

"Lord, Jesus. What's happening?" Tuttle said. Then her eyes flashed. "This means I *was* the target. Oh God. Someone *is* trying to kill me. Who's doing this? What did I ever do to them?"

"We think it has something to do with your office, and your dealings with policy holders," said Tagger. "Tell us about your job. What are your responsibilities?" She plopped back on her pillow. "Mrs. Tuttle?" Tagger said gently.

She looked at him. "I'm the *sand trap*."

"Sand trap?" asked Franklin. She hadn't meant to say anything. It just popped out.

"Dr. Lyndale is an avid golfer. He uses a lot of golf terms. When a call is handled totally by Virtual Amy, he calls it a *hole-in-one*, even if the caller merely hung up."

Franklin's eyebrows knitted.

"The voice on the automated answering system," whispered Tagger.

"It's the job of the front line clerical person to respond to specific policy or billing questions. When the caller is stopped there it's called a *Tiger T,* or just *T,* short for a Tiger Woods T-shot. And if the caller demands to speak to someone else, it's a *dogleg,* a big bend in the fairway. Those dogleg calls came to me and Madison, in the sand trap. It's our job to schmooze everything and defuse the caller, as if his ball were stuck in the sand."

"So you deal with callers who are frustrated, maybe feel they're getting the runaround?" said Tagger.

"For the most part. But I usually give them an answer they can live with, except when it involves a specific medical question. But even then, I'm always nice."

"And when it involves a medical question?" Tagger asked.

"I pass the caller on to one of the nurses. They're qualified to rule on those questions. They're the *course officials.* Their job is to handle as many of the medical questions as possible by themselves. And when they can't hold the line, they pass the caller to Dr. Lyndale. He refers to himself as *the Big Dog,* the name for the number-one wood driver. And of course, when he leaves the office he's always going to *the nineteenth hole.*"

Franklin made a face. "The golf thing's kinda cute," she said. "But a little creepy."

"You got that right," Tuttle said. "Dr. Lyndale has no respect for the subscribers. He's all about shutting them down. He's always telling us that our raises and bonuses depend on how much money we save the company. In fact, we collect that data on every caller with a medical issue. Each medical procedure has an estimated cost."

"Are you saying the purpose of the Policy Review office is to refuse to cover procedures people have already paid for?" asked Franklin.

"Sounds terrible when you put it like that," Tuttle said. "But in some ways I suppose that's our unwritten mission."

"Any reason the office is located away from the main offices?" asked Franklin

"They try to keep the *problem* subscribers away from the muckety-mucks," Tuttle said. "There's no signage on our building, and our address has never been published. I didn't think about it before, but I suppose the anonymity is a security precaution."

"Looks like someone found out," said Tagger. "Can you think of any policy holders who could be responsible for these bombings?" asked Tagger. "Someone who had it in for both of you?"

"No one," Tuttle said. "I've always tried to be nice."

Chapter 32

The Way the Cookie Crumbles

Tuesday morning...divide and conquer. The intercom buzzed.
"Lieutenant, a Mrs. Dilworth to see you," said Teresa.

Julia walked out to greet her. "Mrs. Dilworth. Thanks for coming in. Walk with me to the conference room."

"Did something else happen? Am I...am I in danger?" asked Dilworth, stopping, then catching up.

"That's what we're trying to find out. I think you can help us."

"Help you? But I don't—"

"Coffee?"

"No, no coffee. Thank you."

"Pharaoh close the office today?"

"Yes. Probably'll stay closed tomorrow as well. They need to find replacements for Dr. Lyndale and...and for Shelly."

"I understand the nature of the requests to your office means a lot of policy holders get frustrated," Julia said. Dilworth nodded slowly. "You must have received a few threats yourself."

Dilworth looked down.

"Mrs. Dilworth?"

"We're not, not supposed to talk about it."

"About what?"

"Death committees."

"Death committees?"

"That's what they call us."

"Who?"

"OPRESSD."

"Oppressed? I don't understand."

"The Organization of Patients Refused Essential Services and Sentenced to Death."

"That's a mouthful. What is it? *Who* is it?"

"It's a group of subscribers who have family members who've been denied coverage. Some have died. They blame the company."

"Tell me more."

"They say we're a death committee, deciding who will live and who will die. They blame us for not covering medical procedures that are life-saving."

"You *do* that?"

"Well, yeah...sometimes."

Julia said nothing, gesturing for her to continue.

"Let's say you bought a policy for general health care, but you found out you had to have a root canal. So you call us to see if Pharaoh will cover some or all of it. Well, if you don't have a dental rider on your policy, the answer would clearly be no."

"Sounds logical. So what's the big deal?"

"Let's say your doctor thinks you need a transplant. That can be very expensive, from a quarter to a half-million dollars."

Julia raised her eyebrows. "Really?"

"It's *very* expensive," Dilworth said. "Many Pharaoh policies cover a large portion of the cost of transplants. But it isn't fair to expect Pharaoh to pay when a transplant *isn't* absolutely necessary. Donna and I review a lot of requests like this. We look at medical reports, alongside the patient's history. We evaluate the credentials of the medical professionals making the request. We say *no*, when we think the medical condition is not serious enough, or we think the potential for the patient surviving the procedure is too low. People get upset. Physicians send horrible letters and emails. Sometimes folks get the media involved, telling them our company is terrible, and that we're only in it for the money. When the pressure gets too great, Donna and I send it to Dr. Lyndale. As medical director, he makes the final decision."

"What happens when you say yes?"

"Oh, we...we're not allowed to say yes. If we support any request, we, we have to send it to Dr. Lyndale for final determination."

"How often does Dr. Lyndale agree with your recommendation to support a request?"

"Not...not very often."

"So even when the subscriber meets all the criteria, they frequently get turned down by Dr. Lyndale?" Dilworth nodded. "Why do you think he does that?"

"He says he's protecting the company."

"But...?"

"But his bonuses are calculated as a percentage of the money the company saves from not approving the coverage."

Chapter 33

Closer Inspection

Tuesday afternoon....one frame at a time. Marino sat at a conference table with a box of DVD surveillance discs, an enlarged map of the north half of downtown Memphis, a big cork board, and colored pencils. The map was dotted with colored pins, each corresponding to the location of a surveillance camera. The Pharaoh Policy Review office building and parking lot had been shaded in red. Using green, he colored a clear line of sight from the BMW to what he considered the best camera angle. It was narrow, extending southeast for only two blocks. He began viewing the DVDs from cameras having coverage of any portion of the green shaded area beginning at 3:22 PM, ten minutes before the explosion.

The first DVD was dead on, looking northwest from the furthest point in the green area. The camera swung slightly from side to side. The entrance and BMW were clear, even as the picture moved to its outer extremes. People walked the sidewalks, but no one appeared to be looking at the parking lot. He saw Tagger's car slow and pull into the driveway. Then the explosion. Marino jerked back. He hadn't expected it to be that big. He saw chunks of the BMW rain over the parking lot, and on Tagger's cruiser. He watched as Tagger piled out of the car seconds after the blast. The entire event had been captured. Marino blew out a deep breath, then replayed the DVD. This time he looked at everything except the explosion. He was interested in anyone moving away from the scene, on foot or by car. He saw three different people pull cell phones, presumably dialing 911. But no one was leaving. He repeated his viewing with each of the DVDs focused on the green area.

* * *

Tuesday afternoon…didn't see that one coming. Nurse Allen sat across from Julia, blowing her nose, eyes red, makeup streaked.

"Mrs. Allen—"

"Miss," she interrupted.

"*Miss* Allen. Looks like you're having a difficult time?"

"Wouldn't you? Somebody blew up my boss. A bomb under his car. Right next to mine."

"It's scary."

"Damn right it's scary. You obviously don't have a clue."

"Why don't you clue me in? You have any idea who might have done this?"

"I told you yesterday—no. I do not."

"I thought maybe after some time had gone by you might have remembered something."

Allen blew her nose again.

"Tell me about Dr. Lyndale."

"What about him?"

"Has he been an easy man to work for?"

"He's a wonderful man. He works hard. He protects the company."

"A wonderful man?"

"Yes."

"Do you know him outside the office?"

"So what if I do?"

"No matter. It's just that every piece of information we can gather will help us find out who did this."

"I heard y'all think the bomb was attached to the car at his home."

"I don't know where you heard that. But it makes sense. We've looked at the Pharaoh surveillance DVD. No one tampered with the doctor's car while it sat in the parking lot."

"Well? Do you think it could have been attached at his home?"

"As I said, it makes sense. Sounds as if that would be important to you."

"I'm sure that sniveling Francine already told you."

"Told me what?"

"Don't play dumb. She walked in on us at the Christmas party."

"Just to be clear—no, she didn't tell me. But now that you have, I'd like to hear more."

"You get your jollies hearing about sex?"

"Not *this* afternoon. Why are you so interested in whether the bomb was planted at his home?"

"Duhh. I was there."

"Monday morning?"

"Sunday evening. And yes, I spent the night. My car was parked in the garage, next to Craig's. We got in our cars at the same time yesterday morning. Craig started his up and zoomed out right away, like he always does. I had a phone call. He stopped down the block when I didn't come out. He closed the garage door after I backed out, and we drove to the office."

"So, if the bomb had exploded in his garage that morning—"

"I'd have been blown to kingdom come. What a dumb question."

"There any chance you talk to your policy holders like you talk to me?"

"What are you trying to say?"

"Probably nothing. It just seems to me that your attitude and your mouth could really piss *some* people off."

* * *

*Tuesday afternoon...*The man walked hurriedly from the MED. He pulled his cell.

"He's still alive," he said. "Damn it to hell. These cops are really pissin' me off."

"How do you know he's alive?"

"I checked information. They told me Lyndale was still in critical condition, but Tuttle is receiving visitors. We've gone to all this trouble for nothing. I want someone *dead.*"

Chapter 34

Not Too Big To Feel

Tuesday evening...his tipping point. Tagger had just finished his critical incident stress debriefing session. He used to be a serious macho guy, although he had mellowed over the years. Still, talking about feelings wasn't his thing. This was not the first time Tagger had been close to dying in the line of duty, and it was not his first debriefing. Until now the debriefings were helpful, but not so much this time. He felt edgy, irritable. The pain from his burns made him mad. Even the bandages bothered him, reminders of his close scrape with death. Tagger needed sleep. He wanted to be alone. His cell broke out with a few bars of a familiar song. He did not have to look at the caller ID. It was Sergeant Diane Willingham, the woman he had been dating. The woman he had had a crush on since junior high. What's the deal? he thought. Why don't I want to talk to Di?

* * *

What's going on? Willingham thought. Why won't you answer your phone? He's pulling that *I'm a man, I don't need anyone* bullshit. Like hell.

* * *

Tagger ordered three quarter pounders, two supersized fries, and four apple pies from the McDonald's drive-thru. He had beer in the fridge. He pulled into his driveway, gathered his dinner, and unfolded himself from the car.

"Freeze, dirt bag!" a voice shouted from behind.

Tagger jumped, his stomach leapt to his throat. The McDonald's bag slipped through his hands. He heard it hit the ground. He felt disorientated, staring at his white bandaged hands hanging in front of him where the bag used to be. But before he could get his bearings he was attacked from the rear. Strong arms grabbed him, then spun him around.

"What do you mean not answering my calls?" said Willingham.

"I, I—"

"*I, I,* nothing," she said, looking at his bandages and his missing chunks of hair. "Don't you dare try to do this by yourself. You hear me?" "She grabbed him tightly, burying her head into the side of his neck. Tagger stood still, his bandaged hands in front of him, not wanting to touch anything, and not wanting to resist.

"Sorry, Di," I...I'm sorry."

"You better be." She pulled back and took his face in her hands and kissed him, then hugged him again, his hands still hanging in the air. They held that strange embrace for what seemed minutes.

Willingham stepped back. "You got enough in that bag for me?"

"You can have as much as you'd like."

Chapter 35

Physical First, Then the Emotional

Wednesday morning…just when you thought you were all better. Julia felt the bounce in her step as she ran down her street, her home in sight. She was feeling stronger every day. Her workout at the InsideOut Gym had been the best since her broken ribs. The time for her post-run heart rate to recover was decreasing. She could see it when she looked in the mirror—she stood taller, straighter, her stomach smaller.

* * *

Julia sat at her table in the *Deliberate Literate* drinking her coffee, eating her nutrition bar, and reading the *Commercial Appeal.*

"Looking better every day, Lieutenant," said Millie. "Heck, you're even smiling again."

"Thanks, Millie. Yeah, it's coming back. Must be your coffee."

* * *

"Morning, Lieutenant," said Teresa.

"Morning, Teresa. Anything going on?"

"Sergeant Tagger won't be coming in till this afternoon."

"He give you a reason?"

"Actually, he's not the one who called," Teresa said, pausing for effect.

"You going to stretch this out all day?"

"Wait for it, Lieutenant. Drum roll, please…The call came from Sergeant Willingham."

"Willingham? Oh."

"Ta-da!"

"Anything else?"

"I think love is in the air."

"Teresa. Please don't keep milking this."

"Dr. Blue Eyes asked about you."

"Teresa, that's not funny," Julia said.

"Yesterday, after work, I went with my brothers to see about having granddaddy transferred to a different care facility."

"At the Haven?"

"Yeah. We were there for two and a half hours. I was getting sleepy—"

"Teresa. Dr. Sanders?"

"Oh, yeah. I saw him walking down the hall. So I went over so say, *hey*. Truth be told, he didn't really bring up your name. I did. But he didn't gag or anything."

"What did you say?" Julia asked, the blush spreading on her neck.

"I just happened to mention that you were doing real well since you ran into a burning building." Julia's face contorted. "He said, 'that's good'."

Julia felt all the wind go out of her sails, again. One word about Mark and I dissolve into mush, she thought. So much for feeling in control. "I'm sure you have things to do, Miss Johnson," Julia said.

"I love it when you go all formal on me, Lieutenant."

* * *

Julia's mind was racing, keeping pace with her stomach. It took two Union Station doughnuts and a cup of police issue coffee before she regained her focus on the bombings. She licked the sugar off her fingers and dove into the internet.

She needed to know more about the health insurance business in general, and **OPRESSD** in particular.

Chapter 36

A Flashback with Instant Replay

Wednesday afternoon…suck it up. Tagger walked into Union Station.

"Hope you had a good nap," said Teresa, smiling.

"Yeah. A good nap," said Tagger, striding passed her.

Tagger found Marino in the conference room watching surveillance DVDs.

"I wish *I* could work half-days," said Marino.

"You can," said Tagger." Just get yourself blown up. You'll get a free half-day."

"Touché," said Marino.

"Find anything?"

"You sure you're up to watching this?" asked Marino, turning serious.

"Yesterday I would have said yes. Today I'm not so sure."

"Your call. We'll play it however you want."

"Is it bad?"

"Depends on who's watching," said Marino. "Me, I see one hell of an effort from an incredibly brave guy working to save a life. I can't say what you might see."

"You have anything I can watch that doesn't have the explosion?"

"Nope. I only pulled DVDs covering an area with a direct line of sight to the car."

"Okay. Show me the best one you've got."

"You want the controls?"

"You keep 'em."

"Just close your eyes if it's getting to be too much. I'll cut it off whenever you say."

Marino changed discs, cued it up to 3:25 PM, and pushed PLAY. "This is about seven minutes before the blast. It's a full-on shot from about two blocks away. You'll see Lyndale exiting the building, and passing by the man with the walker."

"Here comes your cruiser."

They watched a woman hold the door for the man in the walker, and Lyndale pull his cell. When Lyndale opened his car door, Tagger said, "I've seen this part."

Tagger watched, feeling as if he were not a part of it. He flinched, surprised by the explosion. Then he watched a tall black policeman shoot out of his car and run, first collecting a fire extinguisher, then closing on the BMW."

"You okay?" asked Marino, watching carefully.

Tagger nodded, focused on the action. He watched as the firefighters moved him out of the way, and took over. Lyndale looked dead.

One minute sooner..., Tagger thought.

Marino stopped the recorder. "Talk to me, Johnnie."

"It's weird, Tony. I feel numb, and I keep thinking it could have been me."

"I'm no shrink, but that makes sense to me."

"Can I see it again?"

"You got it. I have to say you move awfully well for an old guy. You must have been intimidating as hell on the football field."

Tagger managed a smile.

* * *

Marino loaded the last surveillance DVD. It had come

from a camera pointing away from the parking lot. He pushed PLAY.

"Stop it," said Tagger. "That man in the far parking lot. His clothes and build fit the description of the fingerless guy. Can you zoom in?"

"Not on this machine."

"And behind him looks like a small black SUV."

"Let it run. Let's see if he gets any closer."

Chapter 37

Techie Questions

Thursday morning...if it's in there, I can find it. MPD Technician Specialist Elwood Banks' fingers flew across the keyboard. The images on the computer screen grew larger, grainy.

"Looks like a Ford grill," Marino said. "Probably the *Escape.*"

"Great, El," said Tagger. "Can you make us hard copies?"

"Is the pope Catholic?" Banks said. The printer clicked on, humming out two photos—a black SUV, and a thin man in casual clothes, his hair hanging below his ears. "Let me play around with this. Maybe I can come up with something more useful."

"Okay, my turn," Julia said. She handed Banks ten pages of printouts. "These folks are using pseudonyms. I need to know who they are, and where they live."

Banks read out loud. "*Pillpopper, PRN, doctorno, trustmeimadr, Rxthewonderdog, sayahh, lastinhisclass, twiceaday, beforemeals, secondopinion.* I think I like these people already," he said, flipping to the second page.

Julia rolled her eyes.

"Sorry, Lieutenant," Banks said. "I'll check IP addresses. Maybe we'll get lucky. Why don't you give me some time?"

"The clock's ticking, El," Julia said.

"I'll email you by noon," Banks said, turning back to the PC.

* * *

"That bitch nurse Allen is next," he said.

"She's got a Doberman," said the second man. "We can't get near her."

"There are ways. This bomb's mine."

Chapter 38

Once Was Enough

Thursday afternoon…it's catching.

"That's an amazing video, Tony," Powers said. "Have to admit I'm having a little Mosul flashback of my own."

"Mosul? That where you were in Iraq?"

"Yeah. An EOD spec."

Marino made a face.

"Explosive Ordnance Disposal Specialist. That stuff can mess with your head."

"Yeah," said Marino. "I don't remember that being in my job description when I signed up."

"Sign of the times. You say Tagger watched the video?"

"Absolutely. Watched this particular one four times, then watched all the others."

"Damn. Not sure I could've done that. Once was enough."

"So, whatchathink?" Marino asked.

"I think Tagger would have made one hell of a Marine."

"No argument there. What do you think about the explosion?"

"The blast confirms what we'd gathered at the scene. Very similar to the Tuttle bomb."

"I was surprised watching it. Bigger blast than I was expecting."

"Big enough to do the job."

"I guess you're right. Big enough."

"Who you think's gonna be next?" Powers asked.

"From what the lieutenant says about the attitude and the mouth on one of the nurses, I'm betting on Donna Allen."

"You got someone on surveillance?"

"An officer's sitting outside her house. We've tried to convince her to stay inside, but she won't listen. Says it's driving her crazy."

"What do you say we pay her a visit?"

"I'm game."

* * *

Visiting hours, Thursday…it pays to be nice. Lyndale remained in a coma. An officer sat just inside ICU's double doors, beside his room. Allen sat in the waiting area. A nurse walked through the double doors.

"I'm here to see Dr. Craig Lyndale," said Allen.

"I'm sorry, ma'am," said the nurse. "No visitors allowed."

"I'm a nurse. I know procedures." Allen said.

"If you leave your name and phone number with the receptionist, someone will call you as soon—"

"Bullshit," Allen said. "I'm going in now." She brushed by the nurse, and pushed through the double doors. The officer heard the commotion and moved to the entrance. Allen ran smack into her.

"Hold it right there, lady" said the officer, left hand out in front of her, right hand on her weapon. Allen stepped into her.

"Get your hands off me," said Allen loudly, struggling to get around the officer. "I have to see him." The officer grabbed her wrist and twisted." Allen yelped. Her body turned reflexively. The officer quickly slapped one cuff on her wrist, pulled her other arm behind her back, and secured the second wrist.

"I'll have your badge, bitch," yelled Allen, driving a heel into the officer's shin. Pain shot up the officer's leg, but she only held Allen more tightly.

"Officer needs assistance!" she yelled into the two-way on her shoulder.

* * *

Allen sat in one corner of a small room, handcuffed and sobbing. Officers gathered witness statements before they'd transport her to 201 Poplar for disturbing the peace, resisting arrest, and assaulting a police officer. A nurse walked by the door.

"Please. Tell me how he's doing. Please," Allen begged.

"What's the name?" the nurse asked.

"Lyndale, Craig Lyndale. He's in ICU."

It was several minutes before the nurse returned. "There's no change," she said.

* * *

A man walked to his car in the MED parking lot, a cell phone to his ear.

"I'm telling you I saw the cops drag her off in handcuffs," he said

"What the hell'd she do?" said the other man.

"Don't' know. But I'm thinking she'll be gone a good while. That cop still sitting in front of her house?"

"Yup. It's getting dark, but I can still see him. He's been sitting there drinking coffee."

"I'm on my way."

Chapter 39

Number Three

Thursday evening...keeps the ole heart a-pumping. Marino and Powers pulled up to Allen's house. They got out of the car and walked over to the officer's patrol car.

"Everything okay, officer?" Marino asked.

"All's quiet, Sergeant. Haven't seen the woman in over four hours."

"Yeah. She's down at 201," Marino said.

"201?" said the officer. "She being questioned?"

"No, she went to the MED to see Lyndale," said Marino. "Got worked up and assaulted an officer. I'm sure she'll be able to get bail, probably not before midnight."

"We're just going to walk around the house," Powers said.

"Watch out for the Doberman," said the officer. "He's inside, but you know how they are. He might just dive through a window to get to you."

"Appreciate the heads-up," said Powers.

They started along the west side of the house, as far as the cyclone fenced backyard. Powers grabbed the top of the fence and easily hoisted himself up and over.

"I'll wait for you here," said Marino, shining his flashlight along the back of the house. Powers walked to other side and yelled back.

"I'll go this way. Meet you in the front." Powers hopped the fence again.

Marino turned and began walking to the front. As he passed the first window he heard a loud noise. Marino, jumped, dropped his flashlight, grabbed the handle of his Glock, and looked up. The Doberman repeatedly crashed into the glass, barking loudly, viciously. The window rattled, but remained intact. Marino picked up his flashlight and illuminated the snarling, barking dog. He released the Glock.

"Jesus," he said, putting his hand on his heart. He walked to the front, trying to calm down. He saw Powers on the other side.

"Sounds like you found the dog," said Powers, laughing.

"I'm getting too old for this crap," Marino said.

Powers stopped laughing. He was standing in the driveway, at the left side of the garage.

"Think this rock belongs here?" Powers asked, focusing the flashlight beam on it. Marino aimed his flashlight along the foot of the bushes on the left, then on the right.

"Nothing matches it," Marino said.

Powers lowered himself to the pavement, on both knees and one hand. A section of the bottom edge of the rock hovered above the sloping ground. He shined the light under it.

"Damn," said Powers, the hairs on his arms standing up.

"What?"

"This ain't no rock." Powers laid the flashlight on the ground, illuminating the overhanging edge. He rose to his knees, turned his baseball cap around, pulled out a pocket knife, and flipped it open. "Better stand back."

"How far?"

"You saw the DVD."

* * *

"Goddammit!" said the first man. "God *damn* it. We should blow 'em up right now. Those son-of-a-bitches. Give me your phone?"

"No. For God's sake, not the cops," said the second man. "What's wrong with you?"

"Fine. I'll use *my* phone."

Enraged, he pulled his phone, flipped it open, and began punching in the numbers.

"No," the second man whispered loudly, reaching for the phone. He grabbed it and squeezed, depressing one of the keys. The number nine repeated, interrupting the coded number.

The first man broke down in tears. "I can't do anything right," he sobbed. "I might as well be dead too."

* * *

Marino found a spot across the street. Powers waited for him, then dropped, both elbows on the pavement. Using the blade he began probing for trip wires, starting away from the rock at the lowest point of the slope, and gradually moving toward it. Then he covered the same ground, cutting away the dirt in small slices, His cuts were shallow, his movements painfully slow. He removed the dirt as if he were an archeologist, pulling slivers of earth from under the edge of the rock without moving it. Powers stopped, lowered himself to his stomach, and shined the light under the rock.

"This is hollow," Powers said quietly. "Something's under there," he shouted to Marino. "Looks like a pipe."

"Do I need to call the bomb squad?"

"I'll tell you in a few seconds." Powers cut out another quarter of an inch of dirt, lowered the side of his face to the ground, nose almost touching the rock, and strained to focus his good eye. He pulled back to his knees.

"Call 'em!" he yelled.

* * *

Police evacuated the neighboring homes, keeping

everyone outside a safety circle. The bomb squad van and trailer parked outside the protective tape. A communications center was set up—computer monitor, microphone, and telephones—all contained in the van. Fire trucks waited down the block. Television crews swarmed the area, challenging the protective boundary. Marino and Powers stood with the large crowd, watching the lead man, dressed in a protective suit, make his inspection.

"Whoever cleared this away did a nice job," the man said. "I can see the bomb. Bring up Betsy!" he shouted. "And bring the containment vessel, too."

The back of the trailer opened lazily, lowering from the top, forming a ramp. A large toy-like machine on tank treads rolled down to the street. It carried its own spot light, camera, microphone, extension arms, and x-ray, as well as sensors for chemical, biological, or nuclear agents. A female officer finessed the controls from the communications center.

The entire process was exhaustingly slow. The bomb squad was in no hurry—speed was deadly. Betsy, the remotely controlled vehicle, rolled up to the faux-rock. The technician signaled Betsy to x-ray it.

"No trip wires. Looks like a standard pipe bomb," the technician said. "Wait a minute." She altered Betsy's perspective. "We got a remote receiver."

After confirming the rock was not attached to the device, she moved Betsy into position, directing her arms to pick up the rock. The extraction went smoothly. Betsy set the rock on the driveway.

* * *

The technician brought Betsy into position. A small arm extended within inches of the bomb's remote control circuitry. The technician pressed a button releasing a high-powered jet of water, disabling the device.

"Got it!" the technician yelled.

Chapter 40

The Crime Board, Part III

*Friday morning...*Julia came in early to update the crime board with the third Memphis bomb.

KNOWN

- 3 Mphs bombs—all pipe bombs. Different from Wynne bomb
- R. Tuttle: suspended Charlie B.
- 1st: 1 dead: R Tuttle. White Station
  1 injured: S Tuttle. Pharaoh employee
- 2nd: 1 injured: C Lyndale: Pharaoh employee
- 3rd: No one injured: D Allen: Pharaoh employee

MOTIVE

- Revenge for suspending Charlie B
- Revenge against Pharaoh - Refusals
- Hate crime – Wynne, AR

POTENTIAL VICTIMS

- Pharaoh Personnel

POSSIBLE SUSPECTS

- OPRESSD
- Charlie Barrington
- Fingerless man/ black SUV
- Arkansas Militia

Everyone gathered in the conference room. A box of doughnuts sat in the middle of the table, a pot of coffee on a side table.

"We've got to stop meeting like this," said Tagger.

"The odds are against us," said Marino. "Too many *almosts*."

"I prefer to see it as getting to the scene earlier and earlier," said Julia. "The next time we'll be there before the perpetrator. By the way, great work, Special Agent."

"Please, call me Chip," Powers said. "I think I've earned membership in your club."

"Okay, Chip," she said. "Good job. Thanks for saving the Professor's butt."

"Here, here," said Marino, raising his coffee cup.

"Just doing my job," said Powers. "I was the only one with a steady hand. Tony was still shaking from the Doberman who tried to come through the window at him."

"He ain't lying," Marino said. He and Powers brought the others up to date on the bomb at Donna Allen's house.

"I talked to the officer who was on duty," said Marino. "He admitted he left his post. Said he couldn't wait for his replacement—had to pee. He was gone from about eight-fifteen to eight-twenty-five."

"That's not a big window," said Tagger. "Someone must have been watching."

"I talked to all the neighbors who'd been evacuated because of the bomb," said Marino. "Nobody saw anything."

"The watching had to have been from inside one of those houses, or just around the corner," Tagger said.

"I'm going back tonight," said Marino. "I'll extend my canvass area."

"This still feels like it's different from Wynne," said Powers. "The connection with Pharaoh Health is so strong over here. No obvious health insurance connection in Arkansas.

The good news is that now we have an unexploded device to work with. Maybe we'll get lucky."

"I'll take Elwood's pictures over to Mrs. McCall tonight," said Tagger. "And I'll drive the neighborhood to see if the fingerless man or the black SUV happen by."

"Same here," said Marino. "I'll take the pictures with me, too."

"Elwood was able to track down a pretty fair number of people who frequent the OPRESSD blog," said Julia, handing out copies. "I've done some priority ranking, starting with the ones who included any references to making the folks at Pharaoh pay. Then I selected those living within Shelby County. That brings us down to seven people."

"Good list, Lieutenant," Tagger said. "How do you want to handle it?"

"I'll start contacting them," Julia said. "Y'all have your own list of things."

"Sounds like we're getting away from Charlie," Marino said.

"I don't see any motive for him beyond Robert Tuttle," Julia said. "And it's questionable that he was the target. But I'll check with the Barringtons about Charlie's whereabouts this past Monday and last night."

"I'll run over to the school and do the same," said Marino.

"And, Professor," said Julia. "When you go back to Allen's neighborhood, take a rubber band and an empty milk jug for the officer."

Chapter 41

Line 'em Up, Knock 'em Down

*Friday morning...*Julia laid her list of names on the desk and picked up the phone. On the first run through she had scheduled three meetings.

Teresa buzzed in. "Your aunt on line two, Lieutenant," she said.

Julia punched the blinking light.

"Am I interrupting anything, dear?"

"No, it's a good time. I just finished a half-dozen calls."

"I'm calling about Sunday. Dell and Beth are back in town. I wanted to ask them to join us for dinner. Is that okay?"

"Of course. I'd like to hear about their trip."

"We might need an extra baguette and more wine."

"Got it covered. Anything else?"

"No, dear. See you Sunday."

They'd been visiting Beth's daughter, Julia thought. Didn't it have something to do with their health insurance denying payment for her grandchild's care?

Chapter 42

Going Back to the Well

*Friday morning…*The halls of White Station High School were quiet. Nobody would know there were over two thousand warm bodies in the building.

"Mrs. Patterson," Marino said. "Thanks for meeting with me."

"No problem, Sergeant. But I only have about five minutes."

"I wanted to follow up on our conversation about Charlie."

"Sure."

"I was wondering…could you tell me whether Charlie was in school this past Monday morning?"

"Monday? Let's see. Ah, yes. That was our first rehearsal for the end-of-year open house in May. Our kids have to start a little early. Almost all the parents come to the school that day."

"And Charlie?"

"I remember distinctly. He was late. Said he missed the bus. His mother, er step-mother, brought him."

"What time did he arrive?"

"Maybe eightish. You know he has to check in at the office to get wanded each day."

"And this morning?"

"I'm pretty sure I saw him going to his first period class."

"He and his buddy still getting along?"

"JR? Sure. I saw them walking out together after school yesterday."

* * *

*Friday morning...*Tagger found Franklin in a new area of the hospital.

"Morning, Sergeant," Franklin said.

"When did they make the move?"

"Yesterday, after Dr. Lyndale came out of the ICU. They set us up down here on the end of the corridor. No stairs or elevator on this end. Just down from the nurses' station. Mrs. Tuttle's in 306. Dr. Lyndale's in 308. Good vantage point. I can sit here across the hall and see both doors."

"Dr. Torruilla still seeing Mrs. Tuttle?"

Franklin nodded. "And Lyndale as well."

"He still in a coma?"

"That's what Dr. Torruilla said when she came out of his room an hour ago."

"Any people wanting to visit?"

"Mrs. Tuttle is still getting visits from her sister, the children, and her friends." She paused. "And yes, I have their names." Tagger smiled. "Two men came to see Lyndale. Dr. Torruilla gave them three minutes." Franklin pulled out two business cards. "One was the CEO of Pharaoh Health, John N. Sigforth, the other was the Board President Dr. Eric Gustafson."

Tagger wrote down their names. "Donna Allen hasn't made it in?"

"Not on my shift. She the woman targeted for bomb number three?"

"That's the one. She's a close friend of Lyndale. Most likely was at his house when the bomb was attached to his car." Franklin raised her eyebrows. "Anyone been hanging around?"

"Not that I've seen," she said.

"Here's a picture of a person of interest. He's missing some fingers. Keep an eye out."

"This the bomber?"

"I wish I knew."

Chapter 43

Chasing Down Leads

Friday...the pain of loss. Julia headed east on Park Avenue, turning south on Mt. Moriah, then left on Edenshire. She pulled into the driveway of a modest one-and-a-half story brick home, much in need of paint. The temperatures had not been high enough to change the Bermuda grass from its winter brown, and a rotting tree stump announced a yard that had seen better days. She walked up the brick sidewalk and rang the doorbell. A woman opened the door.

"I'm Lieutenant Todd, here to see Mrs. Wundt."

"I'm Matilda Wundt. I've been waiting for you. Come on in."

"The smell of wet dog was strong. Julia turned in time to catch a German Shepherd full in the chest."

"He won't bite," Wundt said.

He jumped again. This time Julie nudged him in the stomach with her knee. He backed away.

"Is there somewhere we can talk? asked Julia. "Somewhere without the dog?"

"Sure," Wundt said, grabbing the dog's collar and leading him away. She returned. "Sorry. I should have better control of him. He was Donny's dog. I just haven't given him the attention he needs."

"Mrs. Wundt, I'm investigating a homicide which may have

some connection to Pharaoh Health Management Systems."

"Homicide? Who?"

"Robert Tuttle, so far," Julia said. "I've been reading a blog belonging to OPRESSD."

"Oppressed? What in the world is that?

"The Organization of Patients Rejected for Essential Services, and Sentenced to Death."

"My word. They need a marketing person. My Donny used to be a marketing person. He would've come up with a better name than that."

"Used to be?"

"He passed last November."

"I'm sorry to hear that. An accident?"

"Heart defect. He was on the list for a transplant, but when his turn came our Pharaoh Health refused to cover their portion. They said their doctor looked at his history and determined that Donny had signs of this problem in his teens. They said it was a 'pre-existing condition,' and accused us of lying on our original health insurance forms. Our doctors disagreed. They filed an appeal, but Pharaoh wouldn't back down. We tried to sell this house to get the money, but with the downturn nobody wanted it, even at seventy percent of its value." She paused, staring. "I used to cry when I told that story, but I'm all cried out."

"Again, I'm very sorry," said Julia. "You remember the name of the insurance company's doctor?"

"Sure. I'll never forget that arrogant SOB. It was Lyndale."

"Dr. Craig Lyndale?"

"So you know him? I filed a grievance with the state licensing board. But it didn't do any good. You got something on him? Maybe something I can use?"

"Somebody tried to kill him last Monday."

"Kill him? I guess I'm not surprised. I'm sure Donny's not

the only person he denied coverage to."

"Back to the OPRESSD blog."

"What does this have to do with me?"

"You probably know more about this than I do, but computer folks can trace addresses of people who write to blogs. A person calling themselves *preexisting* has been posting some pretty angry comments on this blog, making threats. Our technician tells us the posting came from a computer in this house."

"My house? I can assure you, Lieutenant, that I have not written any such thing."

"Anyone else live with you?"

"My daughter, but…you don't think *she'd* have anything to do with this?"

"Is she here?"

"No. She's in school."

"How old is your daughter?"

"Eleven."

Julia thanked her for her time, and gave her a card.

* * *

The next home was in the Cordova area, on the east side of Memphis.

"Mr. Caruthers? I'm Lieutenant Todd."

"What's this about?"

"May I come in?"

"I guess so." He turned and walked into the living room. A baby cried. "Esther," he yelled. "See what's wrong with your sister." He dropped into an overstuffed chair. Julia sat on the end of the couch.

"You have two children?"

"Yeah."

"Does the blog OPRESSD mean anything to you?"

"What about it?"

"Is your web name *paymentdue?*"

"I was just blowing smoke. You'd be pissed off, too."

"About what, Mr. Caruthers?"

"I lost my job, and of course my health insurance. I got a half-assed job. It doesn't pay shit, and I couldn't afford the insurance. The only option Pharaoh gave me was to buy insurance with a five thousand dollar deductible. We had to cover the full cost of going to the doctor or dentist. My wife, Angela, had to skip her annual check-ups and mammograms. By the time they found the malignant lumps it was too late. She died of breast cancer in January. The doctor said he could have saved her if she'd have come in sooner."

"I'm sorry for your loss."

No response.

"Mr. Caruthers, could you tell me where you were the last two Monday mornings?"

"I work a ten-hour shift, Monday through Thursday at Wal-Mart, over here on Germantown Road. My mother watches the kids."

* * *

The third person lived in the Berclair area, north of Summer Avenue, inside the northern leg of I-40.

"Mr. Forturello? I'm Lieutenant Todd. We spoke on the phone."

"You didn't say what this is about."

"Sir, can we talk inside?"

"If we have to," Forturello said, stepping back and holding the door. He pointed to the living room. "We can talk in there."

"I'm investigating a murder of one person and the attempted murder of two others."

"Murder? What's that got to do with me?"

"Two were employees of Pharaoh Health Management

Systems."

"Pharaoh Health? Can't say as I'm sorry about that, with what they did to my Antonio."

"What happened to Antonio?"

"He got kidney problems when he was seven, on dialysis at twelve. Then he got some infection from the needles, caused him all kinds of internal problems. He was scheduled for an operation. A Pharaoh nurse told the doctor it was approved. But the day before the operation they changed their mind. Their company doctor said Pharaoh wouldn't cover the operation because it wouldn't matter. He said Antonio was going to die anyway. The hospital wouldn't perform the operation without the money...Antonio died three weeks later. We buried him last October."

"I'm sorry to hear about Antonio. Do you remember the name of the doctor from Pharaoh?"

"Lyndale."

"How about the nurse?"

"Dil-something, I think. Antonio's doctor kept trying to get Lyndale to change his mind, but he wouldn't hear of it. We called and were only allowed to speak to a secretary. Someone named Tuttle. She was nice and all, but her answer was always no."

"Do you post on a blog called OPRESSD?"

"What if I do? Ain't no law against it."

"You go by *rustyneedle*?"

"Yeah. So?"

"Can you tell me where you were the last two Monday mornings?"

"You saying I did this?"

"No, sir. I'm just ruling people out. Where were you?"

"I was right here. Sundays and Mondays are my days off."

"Anyone who can verify that?"

"Nope. My wife left me, and Antonio's dead. It's just me."

"What about last night, between eight and nine?"

"I was sitting right here, all by myself, watching a rerun of NCIS."

"Don't leave town anytime soon. We'll be in touch."

Chapter 44

Rechecking the Scenes

Friday evening…pictures in hand. Tagger knocked on Linda McCall's door.

"You catch him?" McCall asked.

"Not yet, ma'am," said Tagger.

"You certainly take your time. It's been almost two weeks you know."

"Yes, ma'am. I have a few pictures I'd like you to look at."

"Not very good pictures. What do you do with all the tax dollars I pay you?"

"Sorry, ma'am. They're a little grainy. The picture was taken from two blocks away."

"You seem to have gotten a good picture of my license plate, claiming I ran a red light."

"That's the Germantown police, ma'am. Our cameras won't be up for a while yet. Do you recognize anything?"

She walked across the room and laid the pictures under a table lamp. "This looks like the man with the missing fingers, but the picture's not good. And this certainly looks like the black car I saw."

"Thank you, ma'am. This is helpful."

"When you think you'll catch them?"

"I'm betting on *soon*, ma'am."

* * *

Friday evening…door-to-door. Marino showed his pictures to over two dozen neighbors, fanning out from Allen's house. He checked the line of sight to her garage, and decided to stop at one last house.

"I'm Sergeant Marino. I'd like to ask you a few questions about last night's incident at Donna Allen's house."

"Who?"

"Allen, ma'am. Donna Allen. She lives in the brick house with white trim around the corner. The two crepe myrtles in the front yard?"

"The one had all the hullaballoo last night?"

"That's the one. Can I get your name?"

"Madelyn. Madelyn Mott."

"You see anyone hanging around here yesterday or last night, Mrs. Mott?"

"You mean that black pickup?"

"A black pickup? Yes, ma'am. Tell me about the black pickup."

"Well, I'm always working in my yard, especially since I retired. Ask anyone. Yesterday I was digging up onion grass. I came in to eat lunch, then I got to dusting and vacuuming. When I started back outside there was this pickup parked in front of my house. I don't mind doing all that bending over, but I don't cotton to doing it in front of anyone, especially men. You never know what they're going to do."

"No, ma'am," Marino said. "What time did you first notice the pickup?"

"Let's see…Oprah was on. So it must have been around four, four-thirty."

"Tell me more about the pickup."

"Like I said, it was black."

"Old or new, big or small, any dents or bumper stickers?"

"Well, it was old. Kind of scratched up, dirty tires. Just

an old pickup, like a painter might have. I didn't see any dents, but I never saw the front or the driver's side...I don't remember any stickers."

"Did you get a look at the license plate?"

"I'm pretty sure it was a Tennessee license, but I didn't see any numbers."

"*Pretty* sure?"

"It had the same colors. At least I think it did."

"Could you tell what kind of pickup it was?"

"Oh no. I don't know anything about that kind of thing."

"You mentioned men."

"I did?"

"You said you didn't like to be bending over in front of *men.*"

Mrs. Mott blushed and looked down.

"Were there men in the truck?"

"Well, yes. And sitting in that dirty old truck, I just knew they were up to no good."

"Two or three men?"

"Two."

"Can you describe them?"

"I never could see the driver."

"But you're sure it was a man."

"Well, I just assumed...But, I'm not one to be snooping."

"Of course not, ma'am. But you're a very concerned neighbor. The type of person we recruit for our neighborhood watches."

"I suppose I am."

"Tell me about the one in the passenger seat, the one closest to your house. Was he white or black, Hispanic or Asian?"

"White."

"Young or old?"

"Maybe in his thirties or forties."

"Facial hair?"

"No."

"Was he wearing a hat?'

"A blue baseball cap and sunglasses."

"Did he look anything like the man in this photo?" Marino asked, showing a picture Tagger believed to be the fingerless man.

"I don't think so. The man I saw was kind of round in the face."

"So they stayed from maybe four o'clock?"

"He was gone when I looked out after dinner."

"He? Who was gone?"

"The man in the passenger side."

"Only the driver stayed?"

"Yeah, I saw his fingers on the steering wheel."

"What time was that?"

"I always eat at five-thirty. That's when my late husband Frank wanted to eat. He's from Michigan. Didn't go in for this southern habit of eating at eight or nine o'clock at night."

"So you saw the passenger was gone at…?"

"Six-forty. Yup. I'd say six-forty."

"Did he ever return?"

"I heard the truck start up around a quarter after eight. Saw it drive away. Can't tell you whether or not the second man was in the truck."

"You see where it went?"

"Just turned left at the corner."

"You've been a great help, ma'am."

"Can I be in the neighborhood watch?"

"You've got my vote, ma'am."

* * *

Friday evening…third times a charm. Tagger drove the neighborhood, back and forth from East Parkway to McLean, covering all the side streets. Neither the fingerless man nor the black SUV were around. He drove Madison Avenue back to Cooper, heading for the Tuttle house again. As he turned onto Court, he saw it. A small, black SUV, driving slowly in front of the Tuttle house. He approached from the vehicle's rear, turning on his flashing lights, and gave a quick double blast of his siren. The SUV pulled to the curb. Tagger typed the license plate number into his onboard computer. The driver remained in his seat, hands on the steering wheel, ten and two, like he'd been through this before. The computer came to life. The SUV was registered to Bailey Trucker Reid.

Tagger ran his name against the FBI database. The search triggered a list of arrests for drunk and disorderly, vagrancy, drug possession, and resisting arrest. His record covered several states, ending in California in 2007. Tagger called for backup. Reid was searched. No weapons or drugs on him or in his SUV.

"Hey, man. I'm cool," said Reid.

"What're you doing cruising this neighborhood?" Tagger asked.

"I'm looking for my guys."

"What guys?"

"I'm with the V.A. My job's working with vets, mostly homeless. Some of them hang out around here."

"Around here? Nothing here but homes."

"True. They often live in abandoned buildings, or they set up camp just a few blocks north in Overton Park," he said, gesturing with an upward movement of his head. "Overton Square has several vacant buildings just a few blocks west. They roam around looking for odd jobs, or handouts. They usually find their way downtown, where they can get the most food and clothing, sometimes even a shower...a bed for the night if they're really lucky."

"One of your guys happen to be missing some fingers?"

"Yeah. That's probably Trigger," said Reid. "Haven't seen him for about two weeks."

"Maybe since the bomb went off in that house over there?"

"Yeah, about that time."

"Trigger his real name?"

"No. It's Joey Carter."

"Where'd the name Trigger come from?"

"Joey was an explosives expert in Iraq, defused IEDs and other ordnance. His buddies used to rag on him for jumping into shit without thinking. You know, *quick on the trigger?* The nickname stuck. As it turned out, one of the IEDs blew up on him. Took three of his fingers, and left a whole lot of metal in his brain. From what I hear, Trigger's a tad slower than he used to be, if you get my meaning."

"You know where I can find Trigger?"

"I've been looking for him myself. We were supposed to meet, talk about him getting his act together. He never showed."

Chapter 45

Not There Yet

Saturday morning...two steps forward, one step back. Julia woke with yesterday's sadness draping over her. The stories of family members dying because of problems with health insurance didn't make sense. *I thought we had the best health care system in the world,* she thought. *How could they just let people die? I wonder what kind of health insurance Aunt Louise has.*

Julia used her morning run to regain focus. Thinking of positive things always seemed to help her. At the InsideOut Gym she chose the Turkish get-up exercise using a kettlebell, a complex exercise testing one's core strength, balance, and newly healed ribs. She did well. She felt strong, relieved. The run home felt good. She gulped down a large glass of water while her heart rate and breathing returned to normal. She began stretching, and slipped into her yoga workout.

* * *

After lunch Julia pulled her list of Pharaoh Health OPRESSD members. She found three more at home, and arranged to see them Monday. Julia turned her attention to the one unresolved aspect of her emotional recovery—Mark Sanders. She grabbed her cell and punched the speed dial number.

Mark jumped at the sound of the familiar ring tone, but

didn't answer. Her call rolled into voice mail.

"Mark. It's Julia. You didn't call back. I can't wait any longer. I know I hurt you...I'm so sorry. It was my fault, all my fault. Please. I want to start over. I miss you. I miss *us*. I need to talk to you. I need to hear your voice. You can yell at me, call me names. I deserve it. But don't ignore me...the way I did you." She added in a whisper, "Mark. Please."

* * *

Saturday morning...Jarvis. Marino pulled into Union Station.

"Morning, Sergeant," Teresa said.

"Hey, Teresa," said Marino.

"Jarvis is in the conference room. I told him you might be coming to talk to him."

"How'd he take it?"

"Couldn't tell. But I'm sure he heard me."

"Thanks for letting him know. I'm trying to understand how to talk with kids who have Asperger's."

"Take notes for me."

* * *

"Hey, Jarvis," said Marino. "Remember me?"

Jarvis nodded, but kept focused on the computer screen. Marino could hear the explosions, gun shots, and other noises coming through Jarvis' head set.

"What game is this?"

"BF forty-two," Jarvis mumbled, sounding irritated.

Did he just swear at me? thought Marino.

* * *

"I need help," said Marino.

"I'm loving it," Teresa said. "The wise professor is coming to the lowly secretary for help."

"It's Jarvis. He's clearly not interested in talking to me. I can't seem to get his attention away from that video game."

"Don't feel bad. Neither can anyone else, including his father. He's pretty stuck in his routine. He gets to play video games for another ten minutes. I take him a snack, and then he works on his math for twenty minutes. Then another snack, and back to video games. You get the picture?"

"So maybe I can go with you at snack time? In ten minutes?"

"I'll meet you there."

* * *

Teresa slipped a blueberry yogurt container to Marino for Jarvis's snack.

"Hey, Jarvis," Marino said.

"Jarvis, please answer the Sergeant," said Teresa. Jarvis looked away.

"You got water?" Jarvis asked.

"You want water?" said Marino. "I can get you a bottle."

"I have lots of water," said Jarvis. Marino looked at Teresa. "You have to have at least one gallon for each person, times three. And you have to get new water every six months."

"He's talking to you," said Teresa, smiling.

"I don't understand," Marino said.

"Christmas day, 1699" said Jarvis. "Right at Memphis. Over two thousand between December 1811 and February 1812. Yup. And four were the biggest ever in North America. Twenty-five percent chance of another when I'm forty-three."

"Forty-three?" said Marino.

"At least forty percent in Memphis," Jarvis said. "Maybe sixty percent."

Teresa stifled a laugh. Marino looked desperate.

"Church bells rang in New York City," Jarvis said.

"Jarvis, what are you talking about?" Marino asked.

"Sand blows, liquefaction, soil horizons, and ground warping," said Jarvis. "You better be ready. Three gallons of water."

Marino looked to Teresa for help.

"Earthquakes," she said, stifling a laugh. "I forgot to warn you. Jarvis is an expert on the New Madrid Seismic Zone."

Marino absentmindedly began taking the top off the yogurt.

"My yogurt," said Jarvis, snatching it from Marino.

"Church bells in New York?" mumbled Marino.

"Sorry," said Teresa, losing her battle with laughter.

"I think I've been run over by a truck," said Marino.

"Yeah," Teresa said. "Sometimes with Jarvis it's a one-way conversation, and you find yourself on the losing end."

"Is he right about all that stuff?" asked Marino.

"I'm pretty sure," said Teresa. "His parents tell me they've looked it up."

Chapter 46

Death Committees

Sunday evening…the apology do-si-do. Julia signed in at the Haven's reception desk, her left arm wrapped around two French baguettes and two bottles of wine. She strode down the hallway to the elevators. She caught movement to the left, turned to see Mark going into a meeting room. Julia got a better grip on her wine bottles and began jogging after him. She hesitated at the door, opening it slowly in case others were there. The only light came from the windows, sunlight muted by the trees. Her eyes swept the empty room until she found Mark standing against the far wall. He looked around as if seeking an escape route. Julia approached, setting the bread and wine on a chair. Mark stepped to the left. Julia mirrored his move. He took a half-step to the right. She moved with him, now only ten feet away.

"I need to be somewhere," Mark said.

Julia shortened the gap to three feet. "We need to be right here," she said.

No response.

"Remember last December, in the *Deliberate Literate?* When you just showed up that morning *trying to get to know me?* And I wasn't having any of it?"

Mark nodded once, a guarded look on his face.

"You were reaching out to me, and I was blocking you at

every turn. It was very awkward. But you kept trying. Now I know how you felt."

No response.

"That morning we agreed to start over. Later you asked me to dinner at the Tsunami. Remember?"

No response.

"Mark, I'm asking for a do-over. I'm asking for another chance."

"I can't go through that again."

"I hurt you. I'm so sorry. It's up to me to show you I'm worth another try."

Mark said nothing, but he was no longer trying to get away.

Julia sensed his softening. She pushed ahead. "This time *I'm* asking you out to dinner at Tsunami," she said. Mark's eyes flickered. "And since I'm doing the asking, I'm going to pick you up at *your* house. Wednesday evening, seven o'clock."

Mark didn't say no.

Julia backed up to the chair, collected her supplies, smiled hopefully, turned, and left.

* * *

*Again with the death committees...*Julia caught the elevator. Normally she would be worried about being late, especially when it came to Aunt Louise. But the feeling of hopefulness was intoxicating. He didn't say no, she thought. She was smiling as she pushed the doorbell.

"Here you are," said Aunt Louise. "I called the desk. They said you signed in ten minutes ago." Julia gave her a one-armed hug.

"Something came up," Julia said, holding up her packages. "I've got goodies."

"Come in, come in," said Aunt Louise. "Beth and Dell are

here."

"Hello, ladies," Julia said as she walked in. "It's good to see you." They opened their arms, smiling. Julia greeted them with hugs and cheek-kisses.

"Louise has been pacing around like an expectant father," said Dell.

"And when she wasn't pacing, she was checking her watch and eyeing the door," Beth said.

Julia rolled her eyes. Louise looked down.

"Afraid punctuality is in the Todd DNA," Julia said. "I inherited the same OC genes."

"But *you* didn't became a librarian," said Dell, winking.

"True," said Julia. "But I was raised by one." Julia stepped beside Aunt Louise and gave her a squeeze.

"Speaking of time," said Aunt Louise. "Dinner's ready."

* * *

"Tell me about your trip," Julia said.

"So sad," said Beth, shaking her head.

"Very sad," said Dell.

"My grandson Dana is just six," said Beth.

"He's so cute," said Dell. "His smile just makes you want to eat him up. And friendly…like he'd never met a stranger."

"He was born with a badly formed heart. Has asthma to boot," said Beth.

"He's already had four operations, poor little guy," Dell said. "The pictures of him lying in that big ole hospital bed, hooked up to more machines than I'd ever seen…it just tears your heart out."

"The doctors keep making adjustments in his heart as he grows," Beth said.

"Their plan is to continue until he's around twenty," said Dell, looking at Beth.

"Their health insurance company sent his doctor a letter

saying he no longer qualified for these surgeries. They said it was their medical director's opinion that his surgeries were only postponing the inevitable. Given his medical history, and his 'poor prognosis'," Beth said, using air quotes, "they're not going to cover the cost of any future 'unnecessary' surgeries."

"What?" said Aunt Louise. "That's outrageous."

"Dana's doctor was furious. He did everything he could, but his appeals were rejected," said Dell.

"My daughter's involved with other families who've had similar experiences," said Beth. "According to them, the health insurance companies are deciding who's going to live and who's going to die. They say the companies have medical staff, giving credibility to their refusals to pay. They call them death committees."

"I've heard lots of stories just like that," said Dell. "The health insurance companies are in the business of making money. The less they have to pay out, the more money they make."

"My son-in-law says most of them are publicly traded companies," said Beth. Julia looked lost. "They're part of the stock market, dear. That means there's constant pressure from the stockholders for the companies to make money, with very little concern over the morality of how they make it."

"The little family doesn't have much money," Dell said. "And since the recession, banks won't make loans. Their only alternative is to sell their house. But the market is so bad. Nobody'll buy it, even if a buyer could get a home loan. They're just devastated."

"Is there any hope for Dana?" asked Aunt Louise.

"Their church is trying to raise money," said Beth. "But people have so little, and there are so many without jobs.

In the meantime Dana will have outgrown his latest surgical correction by the year's end."

"Could they get insurance with a different company?" asked Julia.

"They wouldn't be accepted because Dana would be judged as having a pre-existing condition," Beth said. "Other companies wouldn't even consider him—too costly. He's been labeled a financial leper."

"They always say America's health care is second to none," said Dell. "They don't say how many patients are kept from receiving that health care by the wealthy insurance companies."

"So someone decided it was okay for him to die?" Aunt Louise said.

Nobody spoke.

"I have a life insurance policy that would help," said Beth, her lip quivering. Dell pressed her hand. "I know, I know. It won't pay for suicide."

Chapter 47

Looking for Leads

Monday morning...we'll need a specimen. Julia drove east on Sam Cooper Boulevard until it became I-40. Holding her breath, she crossed three lanes of traffic in order to make the first exit. She drove north on Sycamore View across the city limit into Bartlett. She passed north of Bartlett High School and slowed, looking for the house number.

"Mrs. Black, I'm Lieutenant Todd. We spoke on the phone last Saturday."

"Yes, come in."

"I'm investigating a murder and the attempted murders of two others."

"What does this have to do with me?"

"All the victims were employed at Pharaoh Health insurance."

"Good."

"Good?"

"They're getting a dose of their own medicine. Sitting up there all high and mighty-like, deciding who's going to live and who's going to die. It ain't Christian. It ain't American."

"What's your relationship with Pharaoh?"

"That's the insurance my husband Lou had. Last fall he came down with yellow jaundice—bad kidneys. One had to be taken out. The other wasn't doin' none too good. Doctors said he needed a new kidney, a transplant. He went through all the tests and everything. We got a call they found a donor. He was supposed to go under the knife on a Thursday. But that Tuesday we got word Pharaoh wouldn't pay for it. They said he was a poor risk because he was a smoker. Lou smoked since he was a kid. Tried to stop lots of times, but could never kick it. The Pharaoh *death squad* didn't think he'd survive very long even with a new kidney. Considered it a waste of their money."

"Your doctor challenge that?"

"Oh, yeah. He wrote letters, had phone calls, and even tried to get Channel 5 on 'em. But they wouldn't budge... Lou died a month later. Those bastards killed him."

"Does the name OPRESSD mean anything to you?"

"Sure. I'm always posting on their blog."

"Your web name, *peeinthecup?*"

Black nodded.

"You've written some pretty strong things."

"Nothing that ain't the truth."

"Mrs. Black, can you tell me where you were these last two Mondays?"

"I work at Macy's. Ten in the morning till seven at night."

* * *

Monday morning... my three lives. Tagger walked Bailey Reid into a conference room.

"Appreciate you coming in," said Tagger.

"No problem, Sarge," said Reid.

"Coffee? Doughnut?"

"Sure. Two drugs I'm allowed to have—caffeine and sugar."

"Tell me something about yourself."

"I'm originally from Olympia, Washington. Dropped out of college after three years. The whole 9/11 thing kept wearing on me. I became a navy corpsman, attached to the 3/4 Marines—the Thundering Third. They were the ones who pulled down Saddam's statue in Baghdad. I did two tours in Fallujah. Lots of shit in that sandbox. I was wounded three times, sent home once. Went back for the Al Qa'im deployment. Took shrapnel in the head and neck. Came home permanently."

"Man. That's a lifetime's worth."

"You got that right. But I've had at least three lives. Couldn't deal with the pain in my neck. Got hooked on painkillers. Lost my friends. Crapped on my family. Hit the streets. I was homeless for more 'n two years. I roamed around the country. I'm sure you saw my rap sheet. Ended up in southern California. Lotta homeless vets there. That's where I heard about the *Stand Down* for homeless vets in San Diego. Once a year they get thousands of volunteers and put together a weekend for about a thousand male and female homeless vets. They provide free medical, dental, counseling, food, clothing, haircuts, showers, a cot—the whole nine."

"That's huge."

"Not only that, they interview vets who are interested in getting clean and putting their lives back together. I was one of a handful who got chosen for a free ride into rehab. Spent four months in the program, brushed up on my medical skills, became a paramedic. Got one of those official certificates—one with the vaccination bumps. After I proved to myself I could do it, I decided to pay it back. Saw an ad for a street counselor for homeless vets at the VA in Memphis. I applied and they hired me. Been here since one October. Life number three."

"Mr. Reid, I'm proud to know you."

"Call me Doc. All the vets do."

Chapter 48

Variations on a Theme

Monday afternoon…making money on the breasts of women. Julia returned to I-40, east to Appling Road. She headed south, turning east on Dexter Road, and then onto one of the side streets. She found the address, an attractive two story home with a well maintained yard, lots of trees. A man stood beside a notice taped to the front door. They shook hands and entered the house. The inside was a mess. The potent smell of felt marker stung. Open moving boxes were everywhere.

"I saw the foreclosure notice," Julia said.

"Just had an estate sale. Got rid of most of our stuff. Paid through the ass for the service," said Peter McCoy.

"I'm sorry."

"Yeah, well. Everyone's sorry. But *sorry* doesn't bring Zaney back, and it doesn't pay the bills."

"Zaney?"

"My wife. Breast cancer. We had Pharaoh Health insurance through her job. They decided to stop coverage for breast cancer treatment. Apparently lots of women get it, and it was costing them too damn much money. So they fixed their predicament. They just let 'em die. Problem solved. Tons more money in their pockets."

"I'm sorry to hear about your wife," Julia said. "But I don't understand. The health insurance company is allowed to just stop covering medical treatment for breast cancer?"

"They make up their own goddamned rules, and the politicians let 'em do it. From what I hear, it's not just Pharaoh. They're *all* in bed with Washington..."

Julia empathized with McCoy's wife. Her mind drifted. She felt vulnerable, angry. It's bad enough Zaney got breast cancer, she thought. Then, just as she's struggling with it, her insurance company takes away her only chance to beat it. Julia became aware of her neck warming as it turned red. She heard the last words of McCoy's sentence.

"...lost her job. No way we could hold the line on just my salary. The medical bills piled up. I missed one house payment, then another. No way to catch up. Zaney died in February. Just the kids and me. Soon, no house. The kids'll lose all their friends and have to change schools."

Julia said nothing.

"So what are you doing here anyway?"

"I'm investigating one murder and two attempted murders," said Julia.

"Who was killed?"

"Robert Tuttle."

"Never heard of him."

"Maybe you've heard of his wife, Shelly, or her boss, Dr. Craig Lyndale, or his nurse, Donna Allen."

"Lyndale? The poor excuse for a human being who works for Pharaoh? The jerk who calls himself a doctor?"

"That's him."

"Yeah, I heard someone tried to blow him up."

"Same with Shelly Tuttle and Donna Allen."

"Too bad they didn't finish the job."

"You sound pretty angry."

"Damn right. Zaney would be here now if it weren't

for Pharaoh."

"You acquainted with OPRESSD?"

"Seems like you already know."

"You post on their blog?"

"I bet you know that, too."

"You use the web name *antiboob*?"

"It's for Zaney. Pharaoh Health decided to shit on all women because they've got breasts."

"Just a few more questions," Julia said quietly. "I need to know where you were the last two Mondays."

"You accusing me of planting bombs?"

"No, sir. I'm trying to rule you out."

"I still work over at International Paper. They've been great. I used up all my sick days and vacation taking care of Zaney, the funeral, and now moving. I've been back to work for a month."

* * *

Monday afternoon…I didn't sign up to be a shrink. Tagger walked around the corner. Franklin jumped to her feet.

"Sergeant," she greeted. "Good to see your bandages are gone."

"Just got in my way," said Tagger. "Where are we?"

"Dr. Torruilla said she'll be releasing Mrs. Tuttle soon, maybe Wednesday."

"How's she holding up?"

"The stronger she gets physically, the more emotional she becomes. She's distraught about losing her husband, she can't believe she was the target, and she's scared she's still a target. Having Lyndale next door is a constant reminder of how serious the bomber is. I wish I were a psychologist or a clinical social worker."

"Welcome to the force, Officer."

"Of course, she's worried about her kids—and her job,

her house, her car, where they'll live, whether it would be safe to have a funeral for her husband. There doesn't seem to be an end to her worries."

"Okay, Franklin. Breathe. You've obviously done a good job of listening, of *serving*. I'll give you that. But now comes the part about *protecting*. We're going to need a plan to cover her outside the hospital. Nothing's as easy as sitting across from a single door."

"I'd like to be part of that plan, Sergeant."

"Good. You've earned it. Now, what about Lyndale?"

"Nothing new. Still in a coma."

* * *

Monday afternoon...too much of a decent thing. Julia approached the Mississippi River, just north of St. Jude Children's Research Hospital. A new, single-family neighborhood rose from the rubble of a dismantled housing project and trashy streets. Several of the new homes had sold before the recession hit. Julia found the house of Murphy and Tosha Yates.

"I'm Murphy Yates."

"Lieutenant Todd. Thanks for seeing me." They entered. Yates led Julia to the living room. "Your wife here?"

"She works first shift at St. Jude's. She's a biochemist. I work third shift at the FedEx hub, down by the airport."

"Mr. Yates, I'm investigating a murder—"

"A murder? Who was murdered?"

"Robert Tuttle, car bomb?"

"Oh, the car bombs."

"Are you familiar with an organization called OPRESSD?"

"Yes. The dues to that club are way too steep."

"Dues?"

"Yeah. Somebody has to die. Somebody you love."

"Do you post on their blog?"

"Tosha and I both do. Is there a problem?

"Is your web name *urinsurancewont?*"

"Yes…"

"You've put up several threatening posts."

"So?"

"So, three Pharaoh Health employees have been targeted by car bombs."

"And you think *we* did it?"

"What's your complaint with Pharaoh?"

"'Complaint'? Is that what you call it when they kill your son? A complaint?"

"I apologize," said Julia, holding her hands in front of her, palms out. "Let me try that again. Tell me about your history with Pharaoh Health."

"You have any children, Lieutenant?"

"No, sir."

"Well, if you ever do, you'll know what it's like when one of your kids is in pain, especially when you can't do anything to help. You'll know what it feels like when he struggles just to breathe."

Julia waited.

"Our first child, Dorsey, was born with sickle cell disease. He tried so hard to be normal, go to school, run around with the other kids. But he couldn't do it. He was always at the doctor's, and then the hospitalizations started. Two of our other children developed asthma. Again, lots of doctor visits, some to the ER," said Yates, becoming emotional. He paused.

"Dorsey had a series of crises," he said. Do you know what sickle cell crises are, Lieutenant?"

"No, sir."

"It's horrible. Dorsey'd have excruciating pain in his bones. In his *bones* for God's sake. Then he'd start coughing up blood. Of course his immune system was weakened by the disease, and he was always catching something. His kidneys started giving him trouble. And on top of all that, he had a stroke."

"A stroke?" said Julia.

"That's what we said. Strokes are for old folks." Yates stared, his eyes watery.

Julia waited.

"The hospital in Tulsa wanted to give Dorsey some new treatments," he said. "The doctors were optimistic. The date was set. Then the hospital was told by Pharaoh that they wouldn't cover the cost of the treatment. Not only that, we received a letter from them saying we had submitted too many medical charges *as a family* on our insurance policy, so they were terminating coverage on all of us. We tried to switch to the insurance carrier at my wife's job. But they refused to cover Dorsey because of his pre-existing condition. We started the process of changing jobs and moving to Memphis to be close to St. Jude and their sickle cell treatment program. But we didn't move fast enough. Dorsey had an attack at school last September. Paramedics worked on him all the way to the hospital. By the time Tosha and I arrived, he was gone."

"I'm so sorry."

No response.

"Mr. Yates, I have to ask. Can you account for your whereabouts for each of the last two Mondays, from seven AM to four PM?"

"I was right here, getting our other three kids ready for school, and right here when they came home."

Chapter 49

Bringing Everybody Up To Speed

Tuesday morning...new information. Julia walked into the conference room carrying freshly copied papers. Tagger, Marino, and Powers had already settled in.

"Morning, fellas," she said. They nodded

"Whatcha got, Lieutenant?" asked Marino.

"I've waded through six months' worth of the OPRESSD blog," she said. "I've followed up with national news stories on the web. The news stories and research claim tens of thousands of Americans have been victimized by our nation's system of health insurance—people are dying because health insurance companies have refused to fund medical treatments. The personal stories I've listened to this past week all seem to confirm it. I have to say it's really getting to me. The greed. The public relations BS spewing from the health insurance companies. The tragedies of patients and their families. All blatantly supported by paid-off politicians at every level of government. It makes Bernie Madoff look like a kid stealing candy. At least the government took action against Madoff. But no one's intervening with the health insurance companies. The level of corruption is amazing. I'm not sure who to trust."

"Do we need to sweep the room for bugs, Lieutenant?" asked Marino.

"Let's say no, for now," said Julia. "But I'm keeping my options open."

"I'm lost," said Powers.

"You're just not up to speed on the Lieutenant's spidy senses," said Tagger.

"We've learned to trust the Lieutenant's instincts," said Marino. "If she says something smells fishy, I'm buying tartar sauce."

Julia rolled her eyes. "Let me tell you what I've learned, then you can decide," she said.

"Can you start slow, Lieutenant?" said Powers, shaking his head. "I'm not as sharp as these guys."

"I'll start with a story, a real horror story," said Julia. "It's been covered by the AP, New York Times, the major networks, and the 2008 presidential candidates. It involves a seventeen year-old girl from California named Nataline. Nataline was diagnosed with leukemia just before her fourteenth birthday. Initial treatments were successful, but the leukemia came back. She got a bone marrow transplant from her older brother. The follow-up chemotherapy and radiation damaged her liver. Doctors said she needed a transplant. A donor was found, but CIGNA, the family's health insurance company, denied coverage, calling the surgery 'experimental.' Appeals from the treating physicians were denied. A huge media campaign was launched on Nataline's behalf, backed by the California Nurses Association. On December 20, 2007, a crowd demonstrated in front of CIGNA's offices in Glendale, California. CIGNA relented, said they would cover the costs of the transplant. But it was too late. Nataline died that night."

"Jesus, Mary, and Joseph," said Marino.

"Bastards," Tagger said.

"What a horrible story," said Powers. "But still, I can see

CIGNA's point. They can't approve *every* experimental surgery. It would just be money lost that could be used to help others. And besides it would end up raising the insurance rates for everyone else."

"I'd probably agree if this were just an occasional event," said Julia. But from what I've been reading, it seems there are hundreds, maybe thousands of stories like it across the country each year. Nobody's denying health insurance companies the opportunity to make money. The question is: Should they be making that money on the lives of so many people? Or like OPRESSD says, *refused essential services and sentenced to death.*"

"So, even when the insurance company is justified in denying coverage, given all this history, the family members of the patient will never believe the company acted honorably," said Marino.

"Which ends up being a solid motive for murder," said Tagger.

"And that brings me to this chart," Julia said, handing out copies. "The first seven names on this list were found by Elwood, all from Shelby County. Their postings to the blog are the angriest, often threatening toward specific Pharaoh Health employees."

"You're thinking one of these people has been planting the car bombs?" asked Powers.

"I think we've pretty much ruled out the guy from Arkansas," said Julia. "And nobody's found a connection to any militia, at least on this side of the river. Then there's Charlie. We can't find a tie to anyone but *Robert* Tuttle. I admit. Trigger's still a question mark."

"You pull all this information from the blog?" Marino asked.

Julia nodded. "I've interviewed the first six. Haven't found number seven yet," she said.

"Does this mean that someone died from each of these families because Pharaoh Health refused to cover a medical procedure?" asked Tagger.

"We may never know if these patients died *because* of Pharaoh's refusal," said Julia. "But yes, Pharaoh denied coverage, *and* yes, someone died from each family."

SUSPECTS

OPRESSD	EVENT	BLOG NAME & cancellation rationale	ALIBI
1-Matilda Wundt	Husband died waiting heart transplant	"preexisting" Smoker since adol Claim falsified appl	11-yr old daughter?
2-Torrence Caruthers	Wife died no preventive mammograms	"paymentdue" excessive deductable	Alibi: work
3-Sammie Forturello	Son died awaiting kidney transplant	"rustyneedle" infect—considered poor risk	No alibi
4-Eileen Black	Husband died awaiting kidney transplant	"peeinthecup" smoker—considered poor risk	Alibi for two days: work not 1st day
5-Peter McCoy	Wife died from Breast Cancer	"antiboob" policy to avoid paying for BC	Alibi: work
6-Tosha & Murphy Yates	Son died sickle cell	"urinsurancewont" too many med procedures	Tosha – alibi work Murphy -no alibi
7-unknown		"rescission" Too many medical procedures	Can't find
OTHER			
1-Charlie Barrington	Threatens to blow up people		No alibi
2-Joey Carter "Trigger"	Stranger in neighborhood		Person of interest Can't find

"So the ones without alibis are possibles?" Marino asked.

"I'd say so," said Julia. "And I need to find the person with the web name *rescission*. He or she was the angriest of the bunch. It turns out health insurance companies throughout the country have been using a policy they call 'rescission'."

"In English," said Powers.

"Companies have cancelled policies retroactively when they judged that the family had submitted too many insurance claims," said Julia.

"Retroactively? You mean the family ends up owing for previous bills?" asked Marino.

"Usually for the most recent medical bill," Julia said. "Say I had an operation, one that I and the hospital believed was covered by my health insurance. Then when I'm recuperating, I get a letter from the hospital telling me I owe for the entire cost because the health insurance company cancelled my policy as of a date prior to my surgery."

"I'd be more than angry if that happened to me," said Marino.

"Point, set, match," Julia said.

Chapter 50

No More Mistakes

Tuesday...she's next. One man sat on the couch sipping one hundred percent agave Tequila. The other man paced, holding a half-empty bottle of Bud.

"Will you sit down? You're driving me nuts."

"How can you just sit there? We screwed up—three times."

"It's been the cops—lucky SOBs. Just showing up at the last second."

"If we'd have done it better. They'd all be dead. We screwed up."

"Not totally. The bombs have worked beautifully. Lyndale is still in a coma. That has to count for something. And Tuttle lost her husband. She'll remember that forever."

"Not as long as I'll remember her. So *nicey-nicey*, all the while lying to my face. She knew damn well Lyndale was denying coverage. She's as guilty as the rest. I'm not willing to let her off."

"She's being watched. Let's put her on hold."

"What about that bitch Allen?"

"We'll get her. We just have to be patient."

"And those bastards in the head office?"

"Their time is coming, soon. We'll have to see what security precautions they'll be taking."

Chapter 51

Bringing Everybody Up To Speed - 2

"How about Charlie and Trigger?" asked Julia.

"I don't know what to say about Charlie," said Marino. "I checked. He was late to school on that second Monday. We can't say when the bomb was planted on Lyndale's car. But the other two bombs were planted at homes. I wonder about the change in location. Maybe something went wrong, and the killer couldn't set off the bomb at Lyndale's home."

"Good point," said Tagger.

"Neither Mr. Barrington nor Mrs. Barrington were at home Monday until seven, and Thursday evening until about ten," Julia said. "Charlie was supposedly home alone both times."

"Still no alibi?" said Powers. Julia cocked her head and raised her eyebrows in agreement.

"You called him Trigger. Right, Tag?" Julia asked.

"Right," said Tagger. "Doc Reid is the guy with the black SUV we'd been looking for. I found him cruising the Tuttle neighborhood. Turns out he's a VA counselor for homeless vets. Trigger's one of his clients. He was a no-show, and Reid was looking for him. He told me Trigger was kissin' kin to you, Chip—an explosive ordinance disposal specialist in Iraq."

"You know his whereabouts in Iraq? When?" asked Powers. "Maybe I can run down some information on him."

"Reid never said, but maybe he knows," said Tagger. "I'll check. He did say that Trigger lost his fingers to an IED, and had some nasty head wounds, bad enough to affect his thinking process. Said he was 'slow'."

"Stay with those two guys," said Julia, passing out another chart. "Let's look at the targets and possible targets. Tag, fill us in on Tuttle and Lyndale."

TARGETS

Shelly/Robert Tuttle	Shelly Recep PH Hospital / Robert dead	surveillance
Craig Lyndale	Medical director PH coma	surveillance
Donna Allen	Nurse PH bombing attempt	Was under surveillance
Frances Dilworth	Nurse PH	
John Sigforth	CEO PH	
Eric Gustafson	Board President PH	
Troy Conway	Public Relations PH	

"Lyndale's still in a coma," said Tagger. "Doctor's not sure he'll ever come out of it. Tuttle's a different story. Talked to her yesterday. She'll be getting released tomorrow. We couldn't plan any surveillance without knowing where she'd be living. Her local family and friends are too afraid to take her in. Her only option appears to be her mother who lives in Wisconsin. That might work. We can escort her and her kids to the airport, even fly with them if you think it's necessary, Lieutenant."

"Let's think on that," Julia said. "We'll talk later. Professor, Chip. Fill us in on Nurse Allen."

"The bomb was the same pipe bomb as the others," said

Powers. "It had a ring magnet, but no duct tape."

"Duct tape?" asked Tagger.

"Yeah. We found pieces of duct tape at both the Tuttle house and at the Pharaoh Policy Review office. I'm guessing it provided more security than just the magnet."

"Belt and suspenders, huh?" Marino said.

"One more thing," said Powers, pausing. "It also had wiring for a phone switch."

"That means he could have dialed in while y'all were messing around with it?" asked Tagger.

"Yup," said Powers. "I guess that brings up an important point."

"Which is?" Marino asked.

"Why didn't he blow our shit away when he had the chance?" Powers asked.

"You thinking he or she is pretty selective about who to blow up?" Julia asked.

"Hell, I don't know," said Powers. "But it'd be nice to think he *or she* ain't going to take us out."

"Nice thought," Tagger said. "But I wouldn't hang my hat on it. Remember, whoever it was almost took my head off."

Everyone was quiet.

"Getting back to Allen," Marino said. "We still haven't made any progress on finding the old black pickup. The neighbor, Mrs. Mott, told me that truck was parked in front of her house Thursday, at least from four-thirty to eight-fifteen."

"She have anything we can use—plates, descriptions," Julia asked.

"Not much," Marino said. "The passenger was the only one she could see. He wore a baseball cap and sunglasses. She guessed he was white, medium build, thirties or forties, clean shaven."

"She say if he had all his fingers?" Tagger asked.

"She didn't say," said Marino. "She told me the passenger left sometime between five-thirty and six-forty."

"On foot?" asked Powers. "Taking a leak? Buying food? What's the closest grab 'n run?"

"There are a handful of places within a half-mile," Marino said. "I had some guys check with employees of neighborhood stores last evening, during that timeframe. Nothing."

"Maybe he had a car parked nearby," Julia said.

"Good point," said Marino. "I'll have them expand the door to door, further out from Allen's."

"Is Allen home now?" asked Tagger.

"She made bail," said Marino. "She drove home, gave the surveillance officer the finger, went inside, returned with two suitcases, got in her car, and gave the officer another digital salute as she drove away."

"Any idea where she went?" Julia asked.

"Her attorney told me she was staying with friends," said Marino. "But he wouldn't reveal her whereabouts. He assured me she'd be in court for her hearing. What do you want to do about the surveillance on her house, Lieutenant?"

"I supposed we'd be better off pulling the surveillance, then, when she's ready to return, have our dogs sweep the house," Julia said. "Let the attorney know to alert us so Miss Allen doesn't just show up."

"Will do," said Marino.

"What about these other names, Lieutenant?" asked Powers.

"Dilworth is rarely mentioned on the OPRESSD blog, but she's a decision-maker at the Policy Review office. I included the three men because their names were frequently mentioned. According to the postings, the first two tend to be unresponsive to subscribers, and their names are on all the official stationary. So naturally they generate a lot of hostility."

"And the last one?" asked Tagger.

"From what I can gather, Conway has an interesting job," said Julia. "It's his responsibility to display Pharaoh Health in the best possible public light. That includes the development of marketing campaigns, slogans, media announcements, and the like. But more importantly for our purposes, Conway ghost-writes all responses for the upper echelon. If any subscriber does get an email or a letter response from Sigforth or Gustafson, it has been written by Conway. All responses to media inquiries are also answered by him or his department. He's the one responsible for saying *no* in such a way as to keep the company's skirts clean. The blog posters call him the 'spin doctor,' or the 'spinmeister'."

"A guy who talks out of both sides of his mouth at once? I don't like him already," said Tagger.

"I bet he's one slimy dude," said Powers. "And he gets paid for being himself."

"He gets paid big bucks," Julia said. "All three of these guys make an ungodly amount of money, at least compared to the MPD. And that's just their reported salaries. Their bonuses are gargantuan, and then there are the stock options."

"That brings us back to motive," said Marino. "Isn't that what we heard about Lyndale—his bonuses increased when he denied coverage to subscribers?"

"That's right," said Julia. "Now you understand why I began this morning with my concern that the great American health insurance system may not be all it's been cracked up to be."

"I got a bad feeling Lyndale's just a little fish in this ocean," Tagger said.

Chapter 52

Filling in the Chart

Tuesday afternoon...for want of a lawnmower. Julia had been on the phone. Both Sigforth and Gustafson were out of town until Thursday afternoon. She tried to leave a voice mail message at the number Elwood had given her for "rescission," but the mailbox was full. She arranged a meeting with Bertrand Tankersly, the head of security for Pharaoh Health Management Systems, and planned to swing by *rescission*'s home on the way. She drove east on Union Avenue until it became Walnut Grove. She turned north, passing St. Dominic School for Boys. She found her turnoff, and began checking street numbers. She pulled up in front of a sizable house sitting behind a neglected front yard, weeds blocking the view. So much for curb appeal, she thought. I'm going to guess nobody's home. She walked up the driveway.

"It's about time," called a voice. Julia turned to see a woman walking quickly toward her from the house next door.

"Ma'am?"

"I've been calling city hall for months. Someone needs to do something about this yard."

"Looks a tad overgrown, doesn't it?"

"You some kind of comedian?"

"No, ma'am. I'm Lieutenant Todd. You know who owns

this property, Mrs...?"

"Halderman. Mrs. Theodore Halderman. I suppose First Tennessee Bank owns it," she said gesturing to the foreclosure notice on the front door.

"Who used to live here?

"The Wallaces."

"You know where they are now?"

"Dead. Well, three of them, anyway. Their son is still alive, but I don't know where he is."

"What happened?"

"You need to know all this to get the grass cut?"

"No, ma'am. Sorry, I don't have anything to do with having this yard cleaned up."

"Makes me so mad. *It's not my job*," she mimicked. "I guess my only option will be one of the TV stations. Maybe they can get something done."

"Before you make that call, could you tell me what happened to the Wallaces?"

"Amy died of cancer. So pretty. So young. Their daughter Pandora died because she couldn't get an operation she needed. And Scott Senior. Well, he just shot himself, he did."

"Suicide?"

"That's what they said."

"You have doubts?"

"Like I told the police back then, I saw a man come out of the house and drive away, around the time they say he died."

"Did you give them a description?"

"Of course I did. What do you think I am?"

"You happen to know the name of the officer you talked to?"

"It was two months ago. I don't remember his name."

"You know how old the son is?"

"I don't keep up with his birthdays."

"How about taking a guess? Ten, Fifteen, Twenty—"

"High school. I think he's in high school."

"Thank you, Mrs. Halderman. You've been very helpful."

"You're not going to take care of the grass?"

"No, ma'am. I've got my own to keep cut."

* * *

"Lieutenant Todd. I'm Fuzzy Tankersly." They shook hands. "Like I said on the phone, I'd've been more than happy to come to Union Station to meet with you."

"I appreciate that, Fuzzy. But I had to be out anyway. Besides, I wanted a first-hand look at how the other half lives."

"I can give you the ten-cent tour after we talk, if you'd like," Tankersly said, leading her into his office.

"I might just take you up on that."

"We really appreciate what you and Sergeant Tagger did, saving Shelly Tuttle and Dr. Lyndale."

"I'll pass that along to him. Last I heard, Lyndale was still in a coma. You hear anything different?"

"No. I'm afraid the longer he stays in the coma, the worse his chances."

"Fuzzy, have you ever heard of an organization calling themselves the OPRESSD?"

"Sure. They're one of a handful of groups that blog or have websites across the country. The health insurance company security personnel keep up with them through a monthly newsletter. More often when something seems to be brewing. Disgruntled Pharaoh subscribers tend to post on OPRESSD. I have a woman who follows their blog for us."

"Have things changed, the last six months or so?"

"Not that we've seen. New blog posters always tend to be a little more energized."

"Do you keep track of them by their real names?"

"Absolutely. We want to know who's saying what. We've got a dynamite computer consultant. Lives and breathes binary code. If you ever need help, his name is Barrington."

"Lindsey Barrington?"

"So you know him."

"We've met."

"You think the bomber's one of our disgruntled subscribers?"

"Makes sense. Pharaoh Health is the common denominator."

"Like I said. We haven't seen anything different."

"You have any ideas who it might be?"

Tankersly shook his head. "But all the victims, or intended victims, work in our Policy Review office downtown."

"I'm thinking the bomber might be coming here next."

"What?" said Tankersly.

"I'm only giving you what I've read in the blog postings. There were specific references to Lyndale and Allen, as well as Sigforth, Gustafson, and Conway."

"Shelly Tuttle never gets any threats. In fact she's usually one of the few to receive positive comments from the subscribers."

"Yeah," Julia said. "She's the outlier. Haven't figured that one out."

"So what do you need from us?"

"Do you have a protection plan for these three folks?"

"Sigforth has always had a bodyguard— his chauffeur. And when Gustafson's in town for board meetings, we assign a bodyguard to him as well."

"Twenty-four-seven?"

"There any other way?"

"And Conway?"

"We've never assigned anyone to him. You think we

should?"

"It can't hurt. There's been a bomb each of the last three weeks. If the pattern continues, number four is about due."

* * *

Tagger was driving the neighborhood. His cell rang.

"Tagger."

"Sarge, this is Doc."

"You find Trigger?"

"That's why I'm calling. I can't find him anywhere. I've touched base with all the guys he hangs with—nothing. Nobody's seen him for over a week."

"What's your guess?"

"Either he left town, or something bad happened to him."

* * *

"Marino."

"Tony, this is Johnnie. I just talked to Doc Reid. Trigger seems to have disappeared. None of his buddies have seen him in over a week."

"That's interesting."

"I was thinking, you still have those surveillance DVDs?"

"Sure."

"Any chance you could track Trigger from where we spotted him?"

"I'll give it a shot."

* * *

Tuesday afternoon…found her. The two men drove slowly down the winding street of an old country neighborhood—no sidewalks, deep front yards, heavily treed, white clapboard-sided homes.

"You sure she's staying down here in Mississippi?" asked the man in the passenger seat.

"Relax. She called to let HR know where to send her leave papers," the driver said.

"I can't find any house numbers. These people don't put up their numbers."

"On the mailboxes. See, G-10753. And this one, G-10863. Should be just ahead on the right."

"I'll be damned. Bet her car's in the garage."

"We'll come back tonight."

Chapter 53

How To Fix a Bruised Mojo

Tuesday evening...it's a do-it-yourself project. Julia sat on the carpet of her living room, in the lotus position. She was calm, respiration lowered. It was her habit to take advantage of this centered state to help her problem-solve. The lack of emotion allowed her to consider existing problems objectively. She could then select a particular problem, and choose actions leading to a desired ending. She breathed ever so quietly. She took time to affirm the progress she had made. I saved Aunt Louise's life, Julia thought. I've recovered from an assault, and three broken ribs. I recovered from my close encounter with death in the burning building. I saved Shelly Tuttle's life. I've regained my self-confidence, my courage to act. I'm back to normal in every way but one—my relationship with Mark Sanders. As Tonya would say, if you want to improve a relationship, you need to focus on the only person you have the power to change—yourself. Julia was anticipating tomorrow night's date with Mark. It was much more than a date. It could be her last chance to reclaim the relationship they had before she scuttled it.

Julia came away from her exercise with a commitment to exuding confidence, respectfulness, tolerance, and happiness. Tonight it's *me*, she thought. Tomorrow it will be *us*.

Sleep came easily.

Chapter 54

One Never Knows

Wednesday morning…big boys do cry. "Sergeant, you have a visitor," Teresa said over the phone. "He says he knows you from a *different life*. He's waiting in the lobby."

Marino walked to the entrance. An African-American man stood with his back to him, facing the glass doors, a hand in his pocket, jiggling a set of keys.

"I'll be darned," said Marino, smiling. "Good morning, *Major* Johnson." The two men shook hands.

"Good to see you, Tony," Johnson said.

"It's been too long, Raif." Marino said. "I missed your promotion ceremony, but I've been keeping up with your rise through the ranks. And Teresa's always talking about you."

"I hear my sister's been giving y'all grief," said Johnson.

"I'm sure you didn't hear that from her," said Marino. They laughed.

"Say, Tony, I'm here about Jarvis," said Johnson. "I almost fell over when he mentioned your name."

"Me? Hope I didn't do anything wrong," said Marino.

"Wrong? Hell no," said Johnson. "You're only like the third or fourth person he's ever talked about, including his teachers."

"That's good to hear. Of course I don't want to say this too loud," Marino said, looking over his shoulder. "But I never would've been able to strike up a conversation with Jarvis if it hadn't been for Teresa."

"I know," said Johnson. "She's been great."

"Is Jarvis going to keep coming to the Station?"

"Long as we don't wear out our welcome. Saturday's are the best time for us to visit my granddad."

"Yeah, I heard about your grandfather," said Marino. "I'm sorry. It's got to be a bear."

"I never would have believed it, Tony. He was always so active, so quick intellectually. Hell, he was taking Spanish classes eight months ago. Then he just dried up, like his *being* got up and left. Alzheimer's is a horrible disease, for everyone."

Marino waited.

Johnson cleared his throat. "It's really hard. First Jarvis is born with Asperger's, and now Granddad. That's why it means so much to me to hear that you've been spending time with Jarvis. Thanks, Tony."

"Glad to do it. But I've got a lot to learn about Asperger's."

"You and me both."

Chapter 55

Still Behind

Wednesday morning... Julia focused on her computer screen. She found Scott Wallace, Sr. in the foreclosure listings. She pulled up the *Commercial Appeal* website, and searched for Wallace. There were three articles. The first was captioned, "Man Found Dead in Home." The headline was more informative than the article. The second article appeared the following day, "Apparent Suicide." Julia skimmed it.

> *...gunshot wound to the temple...suicide note..."I'm sorry. I just can't take it anymore"...wife and daughter deceased...leaves son, Scott...student at White Station High School..."*

The third article was his obituary. No new information. Julia picked up the receiver and punched one number.

"Marino," he answered.

"Professor, got a minute?"

"You know I do."

"I need the address and phone number of a student at White Station. His name is Scott Wallace. Since you've established all those good contacts, I thought it'd be easier for you to get that information."

"Turns out I'm heading over there this afternoon. Hope to learn more about Asperger's, maybe get to talk to Charlie's assigned student buddy."

* * *

Julia tracked down the incident report on Scott Wallace's suicide. Officer notes substantiated a suicide. The Coroner's conclusion was also suicide. She found the notes regarding the man Mrs. Halderman said she saw.

> *Nbor, Mrs. Torrance Halderman saw a man lvg the house around the time of the shooting. Said he was walking fast. Did not remember exact time. Gave vague description: white, forties, nicely dressed – suit, tie. Drove fancy car.*

* * *

Wednesday morning...gotcha. The two men sat in the pickup, just past the curve. The house wasn't visible, but the driveway was.

"How long we gonna wait?" the man in the passenger seat asked.

"Not long," said the driver.

"What'd she say when you called?"

"Said she'd be there in thirty minutes."

"So she should be—"

"Here she comes. Remember. We don't want anyone else hurt. Wait till she gets in the street."

"Yeah, yeah." He started punching numbers...6, 3, 9...4. BOOM!

Chapter 56

The Magnolia State

Wednesday afternoon…bomb number three, again. Julia, Tagger, Marino, and Powers had all driven across the state line into Desoto County, Mississippi. They passed an ambulance headed in the opposite direction. Smoke wafted from the burned out car. Firefighters, along with Sheriff's Deputies of the Crime Scene Unit, remained on the scene.

"We get enough of your big city crap down here," said Deputy Sheriff Wendell Thurston. "Now Memphis is sending us car bombers?"

"Believe me, Deputy, we're as put out as you are," said Julia.

"Marlene Pilsner, the homeowner, ID'd the victim as Donna Allen of Memphis," said Thurston. "But I suppose you already knew that. She said Allen was hiding from the car bomber."

"We didn't know where she was," Julia said. "Her attorney wouldn't give that up. We were hoping she'd stay hidden."

"And how'd that work for you?" said Thurston. "We used to have a nice little community. But all your Memphis shit keeps oozing across Stateline Road."

"Welcome to America," said Marino. "Now how about we focus on the bombing?"

Thurston eyed him and Tagger, started to say something, but thought better of it. He turned to watch the firefighters and sheriff's deputies expand the crime scene, tape it off, and leave the investigation to ATF agents.

"This is different again," said Julia. "The bomb goes off in the street in mid-morning. It doesn't fit the pattern. And how'd the bomber find her? How'd the bomber know Allen would be driving her car? The bomber must've been sitting around here for hours, maybe days. So how can we help?"

"You can tell me what the hell we're dealing with here," said Thurston. Julia caught Marino's eye and threw a glance at Pilsner sitting on her porch steps. She turned to Thurston. "Be glad to tell you what we know, Deputy."

* * *

"Mrs. Pilsner, I'm Sergeant Marino with the Memphis Police Department. Was Donna Allen a friend of yours?"

"Donna is…*was* my cousin's daughter."

"I'm sorry for your loss."

"I was waving good-bye when she blew up. Knocked me down."

"Were you hurt?"

"I don't think so."

"Did the paramedics check on you?"

"No. They were busy with Donna. But I'm okay."

"Was she staying with you?"

"Yes. Poor dear. She called me. Scared to death. Told her she could stay with me."

"Did anyone know she was here?" asked Marino.

"Well, she had a lawyer. He knew."

"Anyone else?"

"I don't think so."

"Did she use her car while she was here?"

"Oh, no. She said it wasn't safe," said Pilsner. "Kept it in the garage."

"Why did she drive it today?"

"She got a call from the hospital. They said her boss had come out of his coma and wanted to see her."

"What time was that?"

"Just before it blew up."

"So that would be…?"

"About nine-forty, I guess."

* * *

The Memphis team huddled outside of the crime scene tape. AFT agents were gathering evidence, taking pictures, and measuring the blast radius. Marino walked up.

"Anything?" asked Julia.

"Pilsner is Allen's cousin—well, second cousin. She was staying here. She said Allen got a phone call just before the explosion. The caller claimed to be from the hospital saying that Lyndale was out of his coma and wanting to see her."

"No wonder she left," said Tagger.

"How'd the bomber get this address?" Julia asked. "And her cell?"

"Pilsner said only the attorney had the address," Marino said.

"I don't suppose Allen's phone survived the blast," said Tagger.

"We need to check on that," said Julia. "If it did, maybe I can convince Deputy Thurston to let Elwood have a look at it."

"Anything on your end?" Marino asked Powers.

"Looks familiar," said Powers. "We've retrieved pieces of a pipe bomb, some with duct tape. There's also a piece of wiring that looks like the configuration used for a distant trigger or cell phone."

"The bomber sat right here," Julia said, looking around.

"In broad daylight, again," said Tagger. "Somebody had to have seen something."

"The Sheriff's Deputies are talking to the neighbors."

A car eased down the street, the only occupant a woman, seated in the passenger seat.

Tagger did a double take. "What the..."

"The mail carrier," said Marino. "They drive with their left foot stretched over the hump, and reach the mailboxes through the passenger window."

"And you thought carpel tunnel was a problem," said Powers. "I can't imagine what job-related injuries she has."

Julia looked up. Mrs. Pilsner was waving something in the air. The others turned.

"Professor, I think she's waving to you," Julia said.

Marino left the group, spoke with Pilsner, and returned. "May not need Allen's phone after all," Marino said holding up an envelope. "Here's a letter addressed to Donna Allen, at *this* address."

"Who's it from?" asked Tagger.

"Pharaoh Health," said Marino. "Human Resources, the Poplar Avenue address."

Chapter 57

Taking No Chances

Wednesday...growing into her responsibilities. They shouldered new backpacks, filled with basic clothing, a favorite toy, a stuffed animal. Shelly Tuttle walked between her two children, one small hand in each of hers. Jacquelyn Forest walked behind, side-by-side with Franklin. Memphis International Airport was in the middle of the mid-day push. They took the jog to the left, passed the restaurants, and found their departure gate. The plane sat at the end of the jet way. Franklin had been watching for anyone following them. She scanned the waiting area. Nobody looked like the picture Tagger had given her. She eyed all the carry-on bags, hoping the x-ray machines had done their job. If the bomber was going to be on this plane, she thought, he wouldn't have been able to purchase a ticket ahead of time. She walked behind the desk and spoke with one of the two gate agents.

"I need to know which people on the passenger list made last minute purchases," Franklin said.

"That's above my pay grade," said the ticket agent, ignoring her. "You need to be talking to my supervisor."

"Fine," said Franklin, stepping in front of him and reading his nametag. "Agent *Wiley*." Wiley looked surprised. Franklin glared.

"I'll get her," Wiley said.

* * *

Franklin stood next to the agent as he collected boarding passes. Each swipe of the boarding pass brought up the name of the passenger. Franklin's copy of the passenger roster had five names highlighted in yellow—last-minute ticket purchases. None of the names matched the ones on the suspects' chart Tagger had given her. She held a bad photocopy of the picture of the fingerless man beside the roster. She knew that a last minute purchase of this ticket to Chicago was an extra three hundred dollars, not something people would normally do. She questioned each of the highlighted passengers about why they had just bought their ticket. When she was satisfied with their answer, she jotted a physical description on her roster, and let them board. Tuttle, her two children, and her sister would be met at O'Hare by airport security. They would escort them to her mother's waiting car for the drive to Janesville, Wisconsin.

* * *

Julia found the business card and punched in the numbers.

"Security, Tankersly."

"Fuzzy, this is Lieutenant Todd."

"Yes, Lieutenant," Tankersly said. "I'm watching the news right now. The bastard got Miss Allen."

"We were at the scene when the mail carrier delivered a letter—addressed *to* Donna Allen *at* the Desoto County address."

"Who sent it?"

"Y'all did."

"I don't understand."

"The letter came from your Human Resources office. Somebody in your organization is feeding information to the bomber."

"I'll get back to you, Lieutenant."

Chapter 58

Is It Really Like Riding A Bicycle?

6:58 Wednesday evening…one foot in front of the other. Julia pulled into Mark's driveway. She took a deep breath, checked herself in the mirror, put on a big smile, and opened her door. Stay positive, be respectful, and have fun, she repeated to herself. The walk to the front door was surreal. It felt as if she had to push her way through the air. But push on she did. The thicker the air, the more she smiled. She rang the doorbell—attractive, confident, welcoming, happy.

Mark opened the door.

Julia saw his far-away look, his hesitancy—he didn't want to do this. Her courage faltered. But she recalled her mantra and smiled, "Hey, Mark."

"Hey," he said.

"Not too early, am I?"

"No."

"Okay. Shall we?"

Mark nodded, then turned to lock the door.

Julia had hoped for some physical contact. If not a kiss, she thought, maybe a hug. If not a hug, maybe a hand squeeze, or the briefest of finger touches. But Mark was sliding past her as if surrounded by a magnetic force field. She dared not challenge—not yet.

Chapter 59

Always Teaching, Always Learning

Thursday morning...never too old to learn. Marino stood as Nelly Patterson walked into the school office.

"Thanks for meeting with me, Mrs. Patterson," said Marino.

"Please call me Nelly. And it's no problem, Sergeant," she said.

"I met a friend's son about two weeks ago. He has Asperger's. I've tried to talk to him, but I didn't do so well. I thought you could give me some pointers."

"I'm impressed, Sergeant. Somehow I didn't think you would be—"

"The type," he interrupted.

"Well, when you put it that way, yes."

"What is it you thought I was missing?"

"To tell you the truth—patience."

"Yeah. You're right about that. I'm known for my Italian short fuse."

"But I can see now that you're probably also known for your Italian big heart."

Marino looked down, slightly blushing.

"Come with me, Sergeant. I think I have something you might find helpful." She walked him to the teacher's lounge.

"Here is one of the manuals we use to prepare our student buddies. It's written in understandable language, and addresses key basics."

"This is exactly what I need. Well, this and the opportunity to keep asking you questions."

"Sergeant, I think you'll find that one of the characteristics of all special education teachers is that we love it when anyone expresses an interest in knowing more about *our* kids. Whatever the disability."

"Maybe I could ask you about something now."

"I'm all yours."

"I asked Jarvis...that's his name, he's twelve. I asked Jarvis to tell me what he'd been doing that day."

"Oh, my," she said smiling. "What did he say?"

"Well he told me he woke up, got out of bed—"

Patterson began laughing. "And when you interrupted him to say that you wanted to know what things he did that were fun, he began by telling you that he woke up, got out of bed, and so on."

"How'd you know?"

"Our kids have a very difficult time summarizing, whether summarizing a story they've just read or summarizing their day. It's not a memory problem. Many recall every minute detail. But they simply lack the skill to summarize, at least without a lot of teaching and support."

"And last Saturday, Jarvis's aunt encouraged him to talk to me," said Marino. "He just went gangbusters about earthquakes."

"Was it pretty much a one-way conversation?" asked Patterson, smiling.

"It was *all* one-way."

"I'd say you've had a great initiation. Most of our kids gravitate to one or two topics, and just vacuum up all the information on them—baseball stats, the Memphis Grizzlies, the Latin name for flowers, you name it. It really is amazing."

"Advice about situations like these—I'll find it in this manual?"

"Yes. Please study it, and then we can talk. I have to get to my second period class before the bell rings. You always want to be ready when the students come in."

Chapter 60

Devastating

Thursday afternoon...yet another heartbreaking story. Julia drove to the home of Miller and Dottie Sinclair, north of Memorial Park Cemetery in east Memphis.

"Mrs. Sinclair, I'm Lieutenant Todd. I called about Scott Wallace."

"Yes, Lieutenant. Please come in." They walked into the den. "Is there something wrong? Is Scotty in trouble?"

"Nothing like that. I came across his father's name, and wanted to talk to him. Then I found out he had died, leaving only his son. I wondered if you could tell me about Mr. Wallace."

"Scott was my brother," Sinclair said. "Forgive me. I still can't talk about it without crying." She dabbed her eyes with a tissue. "He married my best friend in school—Amy. They had two lovely children, Scotty and Pandora. I'm ashamed to admit I was jealous for a long time."

"Jealous?"

"We could never have children. After a while I just adopted Pan and Scotty in my heart."

"What did Scott and Amy do for a living?"

"Scott was an architect, quite successful. Amy was an interior designer. Worked for some of the big home builders in Germantown and Collierville. But then she got sick—pancreatic cancer. One of the deadliest kinds, you know. Such a blow to the family. The malignancy had spread too much for surgery. She was weak, in a lot of pain. She stayed at home under hospice care. Scott cut back his work hours to spend more time with her. In only six-to-eight months, Amy was gone."

"I'm sorry."

"Thanks...We were all finally beginning to cope when Pan had a freak accident on campus. Dislocated her shoulder and broke several ribs."

"Broken ribs, too?"

"She was rollerblading, hit a crack in the sidewalk, and went headfirst down a flight of concrete steps. Anyway it turned out she needed emergency surgery because one of her ribs pierced her lung."

"She recover?"

"At first. But there was infection. Other surgeries were required. It was then that Scott learned his health insurance company had cancelled his policy. Said he had had too many medical claims. Not only that, they refused to cover the emergency surgery Pan had already had."

"That's horrible."

"Scott was already working fifty-hour weeks trying to cover the normal costs of a home and raising kids. There was no way he could cover the cost of that surgery, let alone future surgeries. He couldn't get a loan. My husband Miller was on disability. We could only help a little. The bigger issue was that no one would treat Pan without insurance. Scott was in a panic, broke, and exhausted. Pan died while the medical establishment sat on their collective thumbs."

"My God."

"God indeed. I had always been a Christian. I have never prayed so hard in my life. But not only did Jesus not answer my prayers, he let Scott's home go into bankruptcy. Last November Scott shot himself. He left a note saying he was sorry—he just couldn't take it any longer." She dabbed her eyes. "I haven't read the bible since."

"What about Scotty?"

"Scotty was a zombie. He just sat and stared. I can only imagine what he must have felt. Everyone in his family gone. On top of which, I'm sure Scott had no energy left for his son those last years. Amy and then Pan took all his attention. Regardless, Scotty refused to leave their home, even when the authorities kicked him out and changed the locks. He just found a way to sneak back in."

"But he lives with you now?"

"That's right. He's eighteen, so he can do what he wants to. We finally convinced him to stay with us, at least through his senior year. He's been here for a few months. I marvel, I really do. I don't know how he goes on. He's a wonderful kid. Even volunteers to help others."

"Mrs. Sinclair, did you ever hear of an organization calling itself OPRESSD?"

"Yes. Scott was very high on that group. Lots of people in a similar situation, having lost a family member."

"What did he tell you about that group?"

"He said it was a crying shame it even had to exist. He had a notebook with names in it. I think there were also names of employees at Pharaoh Health. He was never without it. He was always calling or writing someone."

"Do you have that notebook?"

"I believe Scotty has it."

Chapter 61

Trigger

Thursday afternoon…where oh where has my person of interest gone? Tagger found Marino watching surveillance DVDs.

"Anything?"

"Maybe. I was able to follow Trigger as he went to the Greyhound Bus terminal. Then I lost him. I got a DVD from Greyhound. That's what I'm looking at now. Pull up a chair."

"Here he comes," said Tagger. "This face-on shot is much better than the one we have. We need to get a picture from this."

"I'm writing down the location number," Marino said, changing discs. "Okay, here's a shot from an inside camera."

"This the same door he was walking to?"

"Sit tight, he's coming."

"There. An even better picture."

"He going into the men's room?"

"Looks like it. Let's stay with this camera till he comes out."

Fifteen minutes passed.

"What the hell's he doing in there?" asked Marino. "If he's getting high, he could be in there most of the day."

"Think he's changed clothes?" asked Tagger.

"You're the expert on picking a person out by their gait. You tell me. Has he already come out?"

"Go back to where he's coming in, so I can learn his walk."

Chapter 62

Intuitively Obvious

The close of shift Thursday... like a bloodhound. Julia was going through the two stacks of file folders on her desk—one of old cases ready to be filed, and one of new cases waiting to be assigned. Teresa buzzed in.

"Lieutenant, your Aunt Louise on two."

Julia picked up. "Aunt Louise. How are you doing this fine day?"

"Aha."

"Aha, what?"

"I just saw Mark downstairs, coming from one of his family sessions, and he looked different."

"Aunt Louise. Do I have to handcuff you and drag you into the interrogation room? What are you going on about?"

"The two of you. Something's happened. Hasn't it?"

"Aunt Louise."

"You're both different."

"What are you—FBI?"

"It doesn't take a professional. What is it you say...It's intuitively obvious to the most casual observer? Well, it is."

"What is?" Julia asked.

"He looks like the cat that ate the canary, and you sound all warm and fuzzy."

"And you put two and two together and got eight?"

"I'm right, aren't I?"

"Geez, Louise," said Julia.

"You two got back together, didn't you?"

"Don't get all whipped into a lather, just yet."

"Fill me in. Let me know how excited to be," said Aunt Louise.

"Okay, okay. I asked him out."

"*You* asked him? Well, considering you were the one—"

"Do you want to hear this or not?" Julia interrupted.

"Sorry, dear. Go ahead."

"I asked him out last Sunday."

"That's why you were late to dinner."

"Your memory will be the death of me, and maybe of you, too," Julia said.

"So what'd he say?"

"Not a word."

"Whoa. It was worse than I thought," Aunt Louise said.

"What was worse?"

"He was hurt a lot more than I thought."

"Oh, that. Yeah. I guess he was…"

"Well go on, go on," Aunt Louise said.

"You've interrupted me so often, I don't remember what I was saying."

"You asked Mark out, and he didn't say a word."

"Oh, yeah. So I just plunged ahead anyway. I apologized, told him we were going out to dinner, and I'd be at his house at seven Wednesday to pick him up."

"And what did you do when he didn't say anything?"

"I turned around and walked out of the room."

"Phew."

"*Phew?* That's all you got?" Julia said.

"I'm processing it. I think you did it right. Clearly, he had no intention of initiating anything with you. But at the same time, he was open to you initiating something."

"I guess."

"And, sooo?"

"The short version—"

"What's with the short version?" said Aunt Louise. "You're lucky to have *any* version."

"Okay. *Uncle.* What's the short version?"

"I remained confident, respectful, and smiling the entire evening," Julia said, recalling her mantra. "Mark was very reserved. Not hostile. Well, maybe a little angry. But more like he wasn't convinced it was safe."

"For the entire dinner?"

"Pretty much. When I got him home, I reached for his hand. I can't say he squeezed it, but he didn't pull away. I told him I was going to call him over the weekend. He kinda nodded okay."

"So, how are you feeling about it all, dear?" asked Aunt Louise.

"Better than I was yesterday. I'm going to keep trying... till he stops me."

"From what I've seen over here, your date made a positive impact on Mark. He's a good man, Julia. You're a good woman. You deserve each other. You deserve to be happy. Together."

Chapter 63

The Promise

Friday morning...but that's not the way I planned it. Julia laced up her running shoes and left for her morning run and workout. She found exercise addictive. She enjoyed feeling her muscles respond and bounce back. She felt excited when she saw the InsideOut Gym. She smiled at the thought of taking on the heavy bag, and the free weights. Her *runner's high* lasted through her workout, run home, and even into the shower. She felt strong and confident—feelings she had doubted she would ever have again. She toweled off, shook her hair into place, dressed, and drove to the *Deliberate Literate.*

* * *

"Morning, Millie," Julia said.

"Hey, Lieutenant. Your coffee and a treat, a Luna nutrition bar—chocolate-dipped coconut."

Julia pulled her wallet.

"Not *this* morning, Lieutenant," Millie said, throwing a glance over Julia's shoulder.

Julia had a déjà vu, a distant chill. She turned to see Mark sitting at her regular table.

More than surprised, Julia felt disoriented. She had prepared so carefully, anticipating every possibility. This wasn't part of her plan. What am I going to say? she thought as she walked to the table feeling out of control.

"Okay if I buy you coffee?" asked Mark.

"Yes. Of course," Julia said, overwhelmed by the fact that this was already more words from Mark than she had heard in a month.

She sat across from him. "Thanks," she added after a pause.

"It's not exactly in the same sequence since you already took me to dinner at Tsunami's, but I thought maybe I could reprise our first *unofficial* date," Mark said, opening his hands, palms up.

"I was surprised to see you sitting here then, too."

"Julia, it's my turn to apologize."

"You don't—"

"Yes I do. I've been acting like a despairing teenager who'd been rejected by his fantasy girlfriend. I was only thinking of myself. I crawled into my old shell of self-pity, getting a strange pleasure from reliving the pain, yet vowing never to allow myself to be hurt again. I know better." Mark slowly sipped his coffee. "I know better."

Julia intercepted the tears running down her cheeks with the back of her fingers.

"I know you've been running into burning buildings and the like," said Mark. "But what you did for me, for us, this week was the bravest. It reminds me why I fell in love with you. Thank you."

Julia grabbed his hands. He squeezed back.

Chapter 64

Curiouser and Curiouser

Friday mid-morning...cloud nine. Julia pulled into Union Station, parked and headed inside.

"Running late, are we, Lieutenant?" said Teresa.

"Good morning to you, too," Julia said.

"Your cheeks are a little rosier than usual. Anything happen you'd care to talk about?"

"I'm sure you've already been in touch with your sources."

"I can't imagine what you're alluding to, Lieutenant. But I'm sure Dr. Blue Eyes has red cheeks, too."

Julia rolled her eyes and walked to her office, smiling.

* * *

*Bits and pieces...*The tone in the team meeting had shifted—personal emotion replaced by a focused sense of urgency.

"Remember the web name *rescission* from the suspects' chart?" asked Julia. The men nodded. "Turns out I couldn't find the man because he was dead, an apparent suicide. His name is Scott Wallace. It's another one of those health insurance horror stories involving the death of his wife *and* daughter, followed by the foreclosure on his house, and his suicide. He left an eighteen-year old son, Scotty. He's a senior at White Station."

"You thinking Scotty's picking up on his father's anger at

Pharaoh?" Powers asked.

"We're on the same page, Chip," Julia said. "Scotty's living with his aunt and uncle. His aunt said the father kept a detailed notebook of his correspondence, emails and telephone calls, including names of Pharaoh Health employees." Julia paused. "She said Scotty has the notebook."

"What's the date of the last posting from *rescission?*" asked Tagger.

"Last week," said Julia. "Professor, why don't you have a little chat with Scotty today?"

"Will do, Lieutenant," said Marino.

"Tony and I've been looking at DVDs," said Tagger. "We started with our sighting of Trigger on the thirteenth, the day of the Lyndale bombing. Tony was able to piece together DVDs from different cameras. Tracked him to the Greyhound station."

"We followed him as he entered the station and into the men's room," said Marino. "Never saw him come out. That's when Johnnie started checking out his walk."

"Do I want to know about this?" asked Powers.

Julia rolled her eyes.

"Johnnie used to evaluate the strides of runners for his college track coach," said Marino. "He nailed the walk of our serial-killing nurse a few months back."

"I feel much better now," said Powers.

"As I was about to say, Johnnie found him," Marino said. "He'd changed clothes and boarded a bus."

"Where to?" asked Powers.

"Los Angeles," Tagger said.

"What do you make of it?" asked Julia.

"We're thinking someone bankrolled him," Tagger said. "We know he didn't have any money, or a change of clothes. The whole thing looks orchestrated by someone to hustle him out of town."

"Makes you wonder whether Trigger performed a service for somebody," said Powers. "Like maybe bomb construction?"

"I put in a call to a buddy in the LAPD," Marino said. "Gave him the specifics, and asked him to see what he could find."

"I heard from our friendly Desoto County Deputy Sheriff," said Julia. "Neighbors did see an old black pickup parked just around the bend from the house. Thinks it was a Dodge."

"Get a plate?" asked Marino.

"They did," said Julia. "A Mississippi tag belonging to a 2003 Toyota Camry."

"Any descriptions?" Powers asked.

"The most they got was two white men, baseball caps and sunglasses," Julia said.

"Damn," Marino said. "Nothing more?"

Julia shook her head.

"Moving along," said Tagger. "We put Shelly Tuttle, her two kids, and her sister on a plane to O'Hare. Airport authorities met them and escorted them to her mother's car for the trip to her home in Wisconsin."

"One more item," Julia said. "I talked to Tankersly, the head of security at Pharaoh Health, brought him up to speed on that letter from corporate sent to Allen. He's looking into it."

"Anything on Lyndale?" asked Powers.

"Despite what Allen was told, he's never come out of his coma," Tagger said. "We still have surveillance on his room."

"Speaking of surveillance, we have cars rotating through the neighborhoods of Forturello and Yates, keeping an eye out for a black Dodge pickup," said Julia.

"What're we going to do about those three bigwigs at Pharaoh?" Powers asked.

"Tankersly said Sigforth has his own bodyguard, twenty-four-seven. Gustafson comes into town just for meetings. He's assigned a bodyguard while he's here. Conway is the only one not covered. Tankersly said he'd get with Conway about setting something up."

"So where's that leave us, Lieutenant?" asked Powers.

"We keep on digging," Julia said. "These guys aren't letting any grass grow under their feet. If they keep on schedule, the fourth bomb goes off next week." She let that sink in. "Tag, get the names of guys Trigger hung around with. See if anyone knows who he's been talking to. Professor, follow-up with Scotty. Also gather up more security DVDs and see if you can retrace Trigger's steps. Maybe we can find out who he was talking to before the blast. I want to meet the Pharaoh big three. They're supposed to be in town today. And, Chip?"

"We'll keep checking on hardware stores," Powers said. "But if Trigger did build the explosive devices, these guys could be working off a stash of bombs. They'd have no need for more supplies."

"A *stash* of bombs," said Tagger. "Sweet Jesus."

Chapter 65

Watch Your Back

Friday morning...politics. Julia's brain was in fifth gear—questions flying in from all directions. How do we get a handle on this? she thought. We have a motive. Everything points to a family member who's lost someone due to Pharaoh denying coverage. But then there's Charlie. No reason for him to be after anyone but Robert Tuttle. Then there's Shelly Tuttle who's supposed to be the subscriber's favorite. Why would she have been the target? Do we have two bombers with separate agendas? Is Charlie one of the men in the black Dodge pickup? He can't be the brains behind this, can he? Teresa buzzed in.

"Major Williams on line one, Lieutenant."

She punched one. "Lieutenant Todd, sir."

"I need to do some chewing, Lieutenant. I've had lots of calls today. One from our neighborly Deputy Sheriff from across the border. Then there's the handful of politicians all mentioning their close relationship with Pharaoh Health Management Services, and last but not least, our Director. The CEO of Pharaoh Health didn't lower himself to call little old me. He called the mayor and members of the city council."

"Where would you like me to start, sir?"

"Seems the Deputy Sheriff felt disrespected by you and

your team. But after having listened to him carry on for ten minutes, I think we can consider his complaints addressed. Let's move to the CEO."

"Sigforth?"

"Yeah, Sigforth."

"We think he's one of the next three most likely targets—him, the board chairman Gustafson, and Conway, their publicity guru. Sigforth's been out of town, but it's my understanding all three are in Memphis now. We also believe someone from their shop is leaking information to the bombers. That's how they found Donna Allen hiding in Mississippi. We think there are at least two, because two men have been seen parked in the neighborhood where the bombs were planted."

"You still think this is being done by family members who are mad at Pharaoh for pulling their coverage."

"We do, sir."

"Be careful with Sigforth. He's a powerful man with loads of political contacts, including those who oversee the MPD."

"I'm hoping to meet with him and the two others this afternoon, at their corporate offices out east."

"I'll be surprised if he lowers himself to give you an audience. In any case, Good luck, Lieutenant. And watch your back."

"Thank you, sir. I will, sir."

Chapter 66

Scotty

Friday afternoon...showing his gentler side. Mrs. Seymour escorted Scotty Wallace to the school office. Scotty froze when he saw Marino.

"I'm Sergeant Marino. Come on in. I need a word." Seymour gently touched his back. Scotty turned to look at her, then back to Marino. They walked into Seymour's office.

"He's one of my students, Sergeant," she said. "I'd like to be present."

"He's eighteen, and this doesn't have anything to do with school," said Marino. "Besides, if this ever did go further, you might be subpoenaed. You don't need that hassle."

She sighed.

Marino closed the door. "Scotty, I need to ask you about the blog postings under the name, *rescission.*"

Scotty's eyes grew large. "What about it?" he said softly.

"That was your father's web name, right?"

"Yeah."

"You're still using it, right?"

"Yeah."

"You've been saying some pretty heavy things. Some people could interpret your comments as threats."

"They killed my sister. I have to do what my father would be doing if he...." Scotty looked down.

"I understand what you're trying to do, son. And I'm sorry you've lost your family."

Scotty continued looking down.

"You've named a lot of people. Have you carried out any of those threats?"

"No."

"Do you intend to?"

"No."

"Will you stop posting those comments?"

No response.

"I'm sure your mother would want you to stop."

Scotty sobbed.

Chapter 67

The Gauntlet

Friday afternoon...protocol. Julia met Tankersly in his office.
"They'll be ready for us in seven minutes," Tankersly said.
"*Seven* minutes?" Julia said, raising her eyebrows.
"Yes," said Tankersly, double checking his watch. "And we
need to be on our way. I don't want to be late."
They took the elevator to the sixth floor. Julia was taken
aback by the change in décor. This was not the same time
zone as the security offices—plush carpeting, artwork, stylish
furniture, ten-foot high wooden double doors at the end of
the hall.
A man walked out of a side office, carrying a leather-bound
planner against his chest. "Fuzzy," he said, as if speaking his
name were beneath him.
"Mr. Cranston," said Tankersly.
"I take it this is the lieutenant," Cranston said to Tanker-
sly, choosing not to look at her.
Julia stepped in between them. "I'm Lieutenant Todd.
And you are?"
Cranston leaned back, his feet frozen. "Raoul Cranston."
"Okay, Mr. Cranston. What's your job?" she asked.
"I'm Mr. Sigforth's personal assistant."
At that moment the two large double doors burst open.
"Cranston!" a man bellowed. "I'm waiting."

"Yes, sir, Mr. Sigforth. I was just clarifying her credentials," he said herding his two guests with his free hand."

"I know her credentials. Lieutenant Julia Todd, one of the MPD's fine *female* officers, advancing through the ranks on the fast track," Sigforth said as if announcing her. He extended his hand. Julia took it. He attempted to intimidate her with his powerful grip, but Julia matched him. She watched as a little air went out of his self-importance.

"Mr. Sigforth," she said. "Thank you for meeting with me." He released his grip and turned back to his office. Julia took in the room. A heavy Mediterranean desk dominated the wall overlooking Poplar Avenue. Three leather chairs sat before it. Behind them, a long, highly-polished maple table with seats for about twenty. Two men were standing at the near end.

"This is Doctor Eric Gustafson and Troy Conway," said Sigforth. They nodded. "Please, have a seat."

Julia waited to make sure she didn't sit in the wrong seat. Sigforth took the seat at the head of the table, Gustafson and Conway to his right and left. Julia chose to sit beside Conway. Tankersly and Cranston both stood.

"Tankersly here assures us you have information worthy of interrupting our busy day," Sigforth said. "I hope he's correct, Lieutenant, and that you are about to inform us you have caught the person responsible for killing one of our employees and seriously injuring two others."

"Mr. Tankersly is correct," said Julia, becoming aware her neck was getting warm. "This is important. And, no, we haven't found the person or persons responsible. My purpose for coming today is to tell you all signs point to you three gentlemen being the next targets of the bomber."

"The three of us?" said Gustafson. "Why in the world? I don't believe it. John?"

"This is a joke, right, Lieutenant?" said Conway, smiling.

"Tell them to get in line," said Sigforth. "That's why I have Furman."

"Who's Furman?" Julia asked.

"My bodyguard," said Sigforth, raising his voice. "Bull Furman. Used to be a professional football player. Been with me for six years."

"What makes you think we're targets, young lady," said Gustafson.

Julia paused before answering. "Do y'all have any idea how many people you've pissed off?"

"This meeting is over," Sigforth said, standing.

"Not just yet, sir," Julia said, keeping her seat. The two stared at one another. "I've read hundreds of blog postings from people who feel they've lost loved ones because Pharaoh Health declined to cover the cost of an important medical procedure."

"We're one of the top health insurance carriers in the country," said Sigforth, still standing. "We have millions of satisfied subscribers."

"I'm not challenging that point, sir," said Julia. "But what I am saying is that it only takes one or two angry subscribers to start putting bombs under the cars of people they blame for the death of a loved one—"

"They have no case," Sigforth interrupted.

"What difference does it make when you're dead?" Julia asked, feeling the heat rise from her neck to her face. The men sucked the air out of the room. Sigforth sat down, not breaking eye contact.

"Tankersly," Gustafson said. "What do you know about this?"

Tankersly lowered his head. "I've seen the comments, Mr. Gustafson, sir," he said. "And I've seen all three of you mentioned by name." He turned to his right. "And your name as well, Mr. Cranston." Cranston's eyes opened wide, his jaw dropped. "The Lieutenant and I have discussed the need for safety plans."

"What kind of safety plans?" demanded Sigforth.

"Something of a twenty-four-seven nature, sir," said Tankersly. "Probably not much different than you already have with Furman."

"Twenty-four-seven? Do you really expect us to have live-in bodyguards?" Gustafson asked.

Tankersly looked at Julia.

"What we can tell you," Julia said, "is that there have been three successful bombs. We know two of them were placed under the victim's cars while they were at home. We suspect the third one was as well, but it was not set off until Dr. Lyndale attempted to drive away from your downtown office."

"Jesus, John," Gustafson said. "How'd we get into something like this?"

"Shut up, Eric," snapped Sigforth. "Troy, can't you work your magic and generate a kind of publicity smoke screen convincing subscribers what good people we are?"

"Not a bad idea, sir," said Conway. "Perhaps a direct posting on that blog?"

"In the meantime—" Julia said.

"In the meantime," interrupted Sigforth, "it's business as usual."

"If I may, sir?" said Tankersly. "We've already taken some measures. We're patrolling the parking area, and we've assigned additional men to help Furman and Mr. Gustafson's usual bodyguard for times when you're home. They know to sweep your cars and garages each morning."

"There, Lieutenant," said Sigforth, smiling. "That sounds like a plan, does it not?"

"A good plan," said Julia. "We'll just need to include something for Mr. Conway."

"And me," said Cranston, suddenly aware he had spoken out of turn.

"And one more thing, sir," said Julia. "Donna Allen died because someone leaked information from this building. She was hiding at her cousin's house in Desoto County. *We* didn't even know where she was. Only her attorney and your human resources office had that information."

"That true?" Sigforth said, looking at Tankersly.

"Yes, sir," Tankersly said. "We haven't found the source of the leak, yet."

"Thank you for an informative meeting, Lieutenant," Sigforth said, standing. Julia stood. Neither offered to shake hands.

* * *

Conway caught up to Julia and Tankersly as they reached the elevator.

"Lieutenant," Conway said. "I hope you understood how grateful we all are that you met with us. It's been a particularly bad week in the stock market for Pharaoh Health, and Mr. Sigforth has been very worried. He's really a great guy. He's under a lot of stress from his shareholders to increase the company's profit margin. I hope you'll forgive anything that may have seemed, well, discourteous."

"Why, Mr. Conway," Julia said. "I think I need to have someone just like you on my team. Yessiree, I need a person who shovels BS with such eloquence."

The elevator bell dinged and the doors opened. Julia and Tankersly gestured good-bye to a smiling Conway.

"He always so upbeat?" asked Julia.

"Never seen him any other way," said Tankersly.

* * *

Julia sat in her car, taking slow, deep breaths. She closed her eyes, visualizing a cool, bubbly stream. Voices interrupted her. She didn't see anything at first. Then the back of a head popped up on the far side of a green Lexus.

"Well, then, use your compact mirror," a man said roughly. His head dropped from view.

Julia decided to investigate. She left her car and walked until she saw a woman in a dress, on her knees, reaching her hand under the car. The man she had seen was hovering over her and giving directions. The woman struggled to stand, brushed her knees, and straightened her dress.

"I'm telling you, Mr. Cranston," she said. "There's nothing under there."

"Did you use your mirror?" he asked.

"Yes, sir. Now can I go back to the office? I'm sure the phone's been ringing like crazy."

"Go, go," Cranston said, waving her away.

"Lose something, Mr. Cranston?" Julia asked.

Cranston turned, startled. "You think this is funny? You tell me I'm going to have a bomb under my car. Then you just leave?"

"Well, I think you're lower on the list."

"Lower than someone like Tuttle or Allen? I don't think so."

"You're right. It's not funny. Why don't you get with Tankersly and make sure you're going to be protected as part of his safety plan?"

"I'll do just that. Good day, Lieutenant."

Chapter 68

Making the Homeless Rounds

Friday evening...the underside of the city. Tagger and Doc made the rounds at mealtime in the downtown area, hitting the usual free-meal spots—St. Mary's Catholic Church, Holy Names Catholic Church, First Presbyterian Church, St. Patrick's Catholic Church, Union Mission, and others. They talked to no fewer than eight of Trigger's buddies before they caught a break.

"Friday's our day to hit St. Mary's for evening chow," said Donny Brown. "I waited for Trigger in front of that burned down church."

"First United Methodist?" asked Doc.

"I guess. The one on Poplar by the mall," said Brown, gesturing. "Anyways, when he didn't show, I started looking for him. That's when I seen him talking to a dude in a Lexus down the block. I figure he's working on a sweet gig in G-Town or in the Ville."

"He get in the car?" Doc asked.

"Like a pro," Brown said.

"What'd this dude look like?" asked Tagger.

"White, I think," said Brown.

"Help me out, Danny," Tagger said. "If I were trying to pick him out, what would help me the most?"

"The Lexus, man," Brown said. "I don't remember the

color, but the shiny Lexus thing on the front was clear."

"Was the Lexus dark or light?" asked Tagger.

"Bright," said Brown. "It was bright. You know, flashy."

"What else?" Tagger asked. "Was he the same height as Trigger, same weight, age?"

"Couldn't tell," Brown said. "Never got out of the car."

"Ever see Trigger with this guy before?" asked Doc.

"Nah," said Brown. "Jes' that one time. Never saw Trigger after that. You find him, you tell him Danny's waiting on him."

"I'll do that," Doc said. "Thanks."

Chapter 69

Weekend-Schmeekend

Saturday morning...the sky is bluer when you're relaxed. Julia decided to change up her exercise routine with an hour's worth of Yoga. She felt relaxed as she pulled into Union Station to do some paperwork. Two stacks of files called to her from her desk. She settled in. Her phone buzzed.

"A Mr. Tankersly on line one, Lieutenant," said Teresa. "Says you told him to call this morning."

"Todd," she answered.

"Sorry to be bothering you on a Saturday, Lieutenant," Tankersly said.

"No problem," said Julia. "Remember? It was my idea."

"Yeah. Well, here's what we've put together. We've assigned extra bodyguards for Mr. Sigforth and Dr. Gustafson. Cranston was almost in tears begging for a bodyguard, and Conway refused one. Said it would interfere with his love life. Regardless, we have experienced men assigned to all four, guys who will check their cars before they leave home, and again before they leave the office."

"When will all this be in place?"

"The first sweeps were conducted this morning. We mounted two more cameras in the parking lot. And they're being monitored twenty-four-seven."

"Any success tracking down the leak?"

"Nobody's owning up to it. Allen's Mississippi address was entered into a secretary's computer. I suppose somebody could have been watching her."

"Or somebody hacked in."

"We have all the top firewall protection. It's hard for me to believe anyone could get in."

"Didn't you say Lindsey Barrington was one of your consultants?

"Yeah. Good man. A little strange, but knows his stuff."

"What time do you get cranked up Monday morning?"

"The offices officially open at eight, but some people come in earlier, some later. The big four usually are at their desks by seven-thirty."

"I'll be there myself, maybe bring a few folks."

"You're always welcome. I really appreciate your help."

"Good to be working with you, Fuzzy."

"And, Lieutenant, I apologize for the way the big four treated you. There's no call."

"Appreciate it. See you Monday."

* * *

"Morning, Sergeant," said Teresa. "Our boy's here today."

"Hey, Teresa. I was hoping to see him," Marino said, handing her a manual. "I've been going through this. Got it from one of the White Station teachers. I'm trying to learn what to do, and what not to do. Can I tag along with you again today?"

"It'd be my pleasure. Heck, you can give him his snacks."

"Actually, I brought him a gift. I've been doing some research on video games. I hope he likes it."

"You know he likes the shoot-'em-up kind," Teresa said.

"The White Station teacher who works with students with Asperger's said that *Battlefield 1942*, the one Jarvis has, is what's called a *linear* game. They have a pre-written story and the player chooses to be a particular type of soldier. She's found that her Asperger kids have difficulty with it because it focuses on teamwork. As we've seen, it's mostly about shooting."

"I've seen Jarvis get angry when he's playing the game. But I just thought he was reacting like anyone else does when they lose."

"This one," said Marino, holding up a brightly colored disc cover, "just came out this year for PCs. The teacher says it's what's called a *sandbox-style game*. She says there's no formatted right way of playing it, gives the players lots of freedom to do whatever they want. Her students love it. And of course there's lots of explosions. Thought it'd be worth a try."

"Sergeant Marino, I never knew you were such a softy."

* * *

Saturday afternoon. Marino picked up his phone and punched in a number.

"It's Saturday, Tony," answered Tagger.

"Johnnie, you need to see this. I'm at the station."

"Be right there."

* * *

Tagger, Marino, and Julia watched surveillance DVDs.

"I stayed with the same camera," Marino said, "and when I backtracked, this is what I found."

"The black pickup," said Julia.

"I'll be damned," said Tagger. "It was sitting in the foreground all the time, and we never saw it."

"I've gone through a handful of DVDs," said Marino. "I pulled the two that give us the best views. In this one, Trigger approaches the pickup and talks to the driver."

"There's the link between Trigger and the bombers," said Julia.

Marino switched DVDs. "This angle gives a shot of the plate," he said. "It's the same stolen Mississippi tag."

"Can we see their faces?" Tagger asked.

"Not on any of the DVDs I've looked at," said Marino.

"Any dents or markings on the truck?" asked Julia.

"None I've seen," Marino said.

"Good work, Professor," Julia said. Marino managed a grin.

"How'd it go at the Pharaoh Health meeting?" Tagger asked.

"Except for me losing it with the blowhard CEO, I guess it went okay," Julia said.

"They handling the safety plan?" asked Marino.

"Yeah. Tankersly, the head of security, has coverage for all four guys," said Julia. "The top two have fulltime bodyguards, and all will have their cars swept for bombs before they leave home or the office."

"Who's number four?" asked Tagger.

"Sigforth's personal assistant, Julia said. "Guy named Cranston. He's every bit as sympathetic to the plights of subscribers as Lyndale."

"Real jerk, huh?" said Marino. "His name show up on the blog?"

"Only a few times," said Julia. "But like he said when he begged for protection, he considers himself more important than Tuttle or Allen."

"So how do we fit in?" Tagger asked.

"I want to know how they're doing their bomb sweeps at the office building," Julia said. "Y'all meet me there Monday morning, say around seven. I'll call Chip and put the bomb squad on alert."

* * *

The phone rang. "Marino."

"Sergeant," said Teresa. "Check in on Jarvis. He's loving the *Saints Row* game you gave him."

Chapter 70

Catching Up

Sunday evening... ain't love grand?

"This dinner is perfect," said Julia, nursing her second glass of wine. "Simple but elegant."

"What in the world, child?" Aunt Louise said. "You've hardly eaten a thing. And that language—*simple but elegant?* Have you been reading *Gone With the Wind* again?"

"No, ma'am."

"If it ain't *Gone With the Wind*, it must be Mark."

No answer.

"Okay. Out with it. The last I heard you took him out to dinner, but he still wasn't talking to you. Something's happened."

"I told him I'd call him on the weekend," said Julia, becoming animated. "The next thing I knew he was sitting at my table at the coffee shop, just like that first day."

"What was he doing there?"

"Just buying my coffee again."

"So you're back together? Is it official? Is it a secret, or is anyone allowed to know?"

"It's not a secret. Even Teresa knows."

"She didn't say anything to me."

"I'm sure she's just waiting for the right time."

"So what happened after the coffee shop?"

"Let's just say he asked me to the movies on Saturday."

"What'd you see?"

"I don't remember."

* * *

3:00 AM Monday... The two men moved quietly, forced the lock on the garage side door, and slipped inside. One lay on his back and scooted under the car. The second man eased a pipe bomb from a gym bag and placed it in his outstretched hand. He felt the magnet pull the pipe to the undercarriage with a light click. He ripped off pieces of duct tape, and secured the bomb.

"They'll be at the office in four, five hours."

"It's your turn."

"I've been waiting for this one."

Chapter 71

Alive But Less Wealthy

Monday morning...staying one step ahead. Tagger sat in the Pharaoh Health Security office watching the surveillance monitors. He skimmed through the past twelve hours looking for anything suspicious. Tankersly and his men stationed themselves throughout the parking lot. Everyone knew to be on the lookout for an old, black, Dodge pickup. Marino joined Julia and Powers. Only a dozen or so staff had arrived, two of them Cranston and Conway.

Powers was carrying an electronic device, a little smaller than an old fashioned cell phone.

"What's that thing?" asked Julia.

"Something that saved my butt a few times in Iraq," said Powers. "It jams electronic signals to a bomb."

"So the bomber can't set it off?"

"Theoretically."

"Theoretically?"

"Well, if it's banging the right frequency we're probably good."

"Probably?"

"Depending on the circuitry, the jammer may just delay the explosion."

"I feel *so* much better now."

"I'd say we're eighty-five percent to the good."

"Will it take out our cell phones as well?"

"Yeah. There's always a downside."

All eyes turned as a large Mercedes pulled in—Sigforth, easing in slowly.

"Eyes out, damn it," yelled Tankersly in his mouth piece. His men turned, scanning their assigned portion of the parking lot and neighborhood.

* * *

A man watched Sigforth's car, his cell phone open.

"Almost there," he whispered, punching all but the last number of the code—...6, 3, 9...

* * *

Marino watched the limo, then his gaze fell on the parking sign that read "CEO." His eyes widened and he began running.

"Stop that car," Marino roared. Julia and Powers closed in.

"What'd you see?" yelled Julia. Marino pointed to a light blue Honda Accord, already parked beside the designated CEO's spot.

"Check that car," Marino yelled. Powers ran to it and dove to the blacktop, landing first on his hands and lowering his body and legs in one fluid motion.

"Damn," Powers said. He pulled his jammer and hit the switch. "Call the bomb squad!" he yelled.

* * *

Goddamn meddling cops," the man said, considering the last number of the code. He mashed the final key. Nothing happened. He swore, pressing the number 4 repeatedly.

* * *

They watched from across the parking lot as Betsy did her magic, breaking the electronic relay with her water jet, and placing the pipe bomb in the spherical containment vessel. Patrol cars scoured the area looking for the black pickup.

"I don't get it," Chip said. "How'd you know there was a bomb under the Honda?"

"It's kind of crazy," Marino said. "I've been learning how to relate to a kid who has Asperger's Syndrome. Saturday I bought him a new video game called *Saints Row*. I watched his character set satchel charges and blow them up. One time he had to take out a car but it was heavily guarded. So he attaches a charge to a second car and has it drive by. Then, when the cars are side by side, he blows the satchel charge, taking out the targeted car. I guess I was watching a mirror image as the targeted Mercedes was driving to a parking spot beside the Honda. It was a lucky guess."

"Better—" Powers began.

"Yeah, yeah," said Marino. "Better lucky than good,"

"Good, lucky, or Harry Potter's wand," said Julia. "We're all grateful you saved our bacon. We were clearly within the blast radius."

"Yeah, that goes for me too," said Powers. "The best bomb is the one you can walk away from. Thanks, man."

* * *

"I'm not sure Sigforth understands y'all saved his ass," said Tankersly. "He's still carrying on about having been on the phone with his stockbroker working on some European deal. He claims he lost a half-million dollars because his phone went dead."

"Better the phone than him," Julia said.

"Now may not be the best time to try to convince him of that," said Tankersly.

"And the others?"

"Gustafson just came in. I think the reality of the danger hit him. He never got more than a few inches from his bodyguard all the way in. And you can imagine Cranston. He locked himself in the women's restroom. My guys found him squatting in a corner, hugging his knees."

"That leaves Conway."

"He was unusually upset when I saw him," Tankersly said. "First time I've seen him at a loss for words."

"So how're you going to modify your safety plan?" asked Julia.

Chapter 72

Grains of Sand Sifting Through Our Fingers

Monday afternoon...into thin air. The Pharaoh Health Security office conference room was full. The remains of three platters of sandwiches, chips, and snack bars sat on the table. Individual staff reported to Tankersly. Julia, Tagger, Marino, and Powers were participant observers.

"That's it," said Tankersly. "Nobody saw anything. No black pickup, nobody hanging around, nobody observed watching the parking lot. The surveillance DVD shows Sigforth's secretary arriving in her Honda at five after seven, and parking in her spot next to Sigforth's. Nobody touched it."

"The bomb had to have been planted at the secretary's house, maybe last night or early this morning," said Julia, nodding to Marino to follow up.

"No change in the bomb itself," said Powers, "like they've been made by the same person. Can anyone spell *Trigger?*"

"The bombers have moved up their timetable," said Tagger. "This one's right on the heels of the Mississippi bombing."

"The security has been heightened around here, and will only get tighter," said Julia. "Maybe we should be expecting a change in the MO."

"You thinking they'd use other means than bombs?" said Marino.

"Can't rule it out," said Julia.

"You think they'll start targeting us?" said Tagger.

"We don't know they weren't trying today," Julia said. "Chip had his jammer going. Maybe a couple of us would have been taken out, even if only as collateral damage."

"We need a break," Marino said. "Somebody's seen something. Someone knows."

"Anything from your friend in Los Angeles?" asked Powers. Marino shook his head.

"We have four names without alibis for the initial bombings," said Julia. "We need to turn up the heat."

* * *

Monday afternoon...trying to catch a break. Katrina Stallings unlocked the front door. She and Marino walked inside her home. He had followed her blue Honda Accord from the Pharaoh Health parking lot.

"I don't understand," she said, jingling her keys. "Why would anyone want to kill *me*? I've never hurt anyone."

"They weren't trying to kill you, Miss Stallings. They used your car to get at your boss."

"I can't believe I drove all the way to work with that thing stuck under my car," she said, tears starting. "I could've been blown to smithereens." She blew her nose, and dabbed her eyes.

"I want to make sure that won't happen again," Marino said. "I need you to help me. First, let's make sure your home is safe. I'll go through every room with you." She nodded. "Tell me all about your locks."

* * *

"Alright," Marino said. "Everything looks good, and your deadbolts are strong. No signs of forced entry anywhere in the house. You're secure in here. Now let's check the garage."

They walked out of the kitchen door through a short

breezeway and opened the door to the garage. He flicked on the overhead light.

"Tell me when you put your car in the garage," he said.

"You mean yesterday?"

"Let's start with yesterday."

* * *

A team of officers were knocking on doors looking for a lead. One of the officers reported to Marino.

"Sergeant," said the officer. "I found a guy who was getting ready for work. Says he works crazy-ass hours. He didn't get in until almost three o'clock this morning. Said he saw an old black pickup with a Mississippi tag parked in the street. He'd never seen it around here before. He didn't see anyone, and assumed they were from out of town, staying with one of his neighbors."

"He notice when it left?" asked Marino.

"He said he went to the store at about eleven this morning. He didn't remember seeing the pickup then."

* * *

Monday afternoon…a long shot. Officer Franklin reported to Tagger's office.

"I've got a job for you," Tagger said. "I think you'd be the best person because you've done such a good job of noticing people and learning their names."

"Yes, Sergeant," said Franklin.

"We've been trying to get a lead on these bombers. I'm thinking you might have seen at least one of them."

"Me?"

"In the visitor's lounge, or maybe even walking past their rooms. It's a long shot, but I'm guessing at least one of the bombers made a trip to the MED to check on Tuttle and Lyndale."

"Tell me what to do?"

"I want you to pull the MED's surveillance DVDs, starting with the day Tuttle was taken to the ER, right up through today."

"When do I start?"

"I can't believe you're still here."

Chapter 73

Wrapping Up Loose Ends

Monday afternoon...one by one. Julia left Pharaoh Health and drove the short distance to the International Paper offices. It only took ten minutes to verify that Peter McCoy had in fact been at work for the past month—eight to five, Monday through Friday. That's one less, she thought. Julia drove north to Walnut Grove, east to Germantown Road. She pulled into the *WalMart* store parking lot. Another ten minutes, and she had verified Caruthers' alibi. She retraced her path to Macy's on Poplar Avenue, confirming Black's alibi, at least for all but the first bomb. That's three, she thought. That leaves Wundt, Forturello and Yates.

Julia called Teresa to obtain the phone numbers for Forturello, Yates, and Wundt. When she called, only Mrs. Wundt answered.

"Yes, Lieutenant. Clarisse is home from school."

"I want to talk to her about her posting on the OPRESSD blog. I can be at your house in fifteen minutes."

* * *

"How do you do, Lieutenant Todd," said Clarisse. "Is that a real gun?"

"Yes, it is," said Julia.

"Can I hold it?"

"No, ma'am."

"Why not? Is it because I'm a kid?"

"The real reason is because there is a strict Memphis Police Department policy that says nobody is allowed to handle my weapon."

"Well, how about you pull it out of the holster, and I'll just look at it."

"Actually, Clarisse, there's a policy against that, too."

"I hate being treated like a little kid. I'm almost twelve. I'll be going into middle school next year," Clarisse said, lifting her chin.

"You're a very impressive almost twelve year-old. You're even tall for your age." Clarisse stood taller.

"Clarisse," Julia said. "I'm trying to find a bad guy, one that's been hurting people. I need your help."

"Okay."

"I understand you're very good on the computer."

"Yup. But Mom isn't."

"Tell me about a blog for a group called OPRESSD."

Clarisse looked down. "Mom told me the police were mad at me for what I wrote."

"I wouldn't say the police are mad," said Julia. "Do I look mad?"

Clarisse shook her head.

Julia touched her shoulder. "Like I said, I need your help. First I want to make sure I know who *preexisting* is."

Clarisse looked down again.

"Is that you? Do you post on the blog using the name *preexisting*?"

Clarisse nodded.

"Tell me how you found out about that blog."

"From Mommy."

"Me?" said Mrs. Wundt. "I don't even know what a blog is."

"You gave me the card," said Clarisse.

"What card?" Mrs. Wundt asked.

"You remember. When we were going through Daddy's stuff? You gave me things to put in my memory box."

"I remember that. But I don't remember anything about a card."

"You said a man gave it to you at Daddy's funeral."

"Funeral?" said Mrs. Wundt, trying to remember. "My gracious. It was just a business card."

"Tell me about the man, Mrs. Wundt," said Julia

"I'd never seen him before," said Mrs. Wundt. "He introduced himself, but I can't remember his name. He told me his daughter died because of Pharaoh Health refusing to cover her operation."

"Do you still have the card, Clarisse?" asked Julia.

"Sure, it's in my memory box."

"May I see it?"

Clarisse nodded and ran off.

"Really, Lieutenant. I can't imagine what this has to do with anything," said Mrs. Wundt.

Clarisse came trotting into the room. She held the card out in front of Julia.

"You can look, but you can't touch it," Clarisse said.

"Clarisse Susan Wundt," scolded Mrs. Wundt. "Where are your manners?"

Julia struggled to stifle a laugh. "That's all right, Mrs. Wundt," Julia said. "I understand. It's policy, isn't it, Clarisse?"

"Policy or no policy, young lady," said Mrs. Wundt. "You give that card to the lieutenant right this instant."

"Yes, ma'am," said Clarisse, handing Julia the card.

"Thank you," said Julia, taking the card. "It's a business card for the OPRESSD organization, giving their blog site." She turned the card over. "Scott Wallace had printed his name and phone number on the back."

Julia looked at Clarisse. "So you went to this blog site and read what other people had been writing?"

Clarisse nodded.

"And you started posting your own messages?"

She nodded again.

"I know you are a very smart girl," said Julia. "But there were some big words in your messages. And pre-existing is really a big word. Did you write those messages all by yourself?"

No response.

"Clarisse," Mrs. Wundt said, "answer the lieutenant."

"Not all of them," said Clarisse.

"Who helped you?" Julia asked.

"Mr. Wallace," said Clarisse.

"The man on this card?" asked Julia. Clarisse nodded. "How did he help you?

"I called him," said Clarisse. "Then we emailed."

"You called a stranger? A man?" asked Mrs. Wundt. "And you were *emailing* him?"

Julia spread her fingers slightly to signal Wundt, while watching Clarisse. "What things did you email about, Clarisse?" Julia asked gently.

"The blog," said Clarisse.

Julia dropped to one knee, maintaining eye contact. "Can you show me?" asked Julia. Clarisse nodded and turned. Julia and Mrs. Wundt followed.

Chapter 74

What Have You
Done For Me Lately?

Monday, late afternoon…the glass is sixty percent empty. Teresa buzzed in.

"Lieutenant, Major Williams on line two."

Julia picked up. "Afternoon, Major—"

"Your friend John Sigforth is pulling the chain of all his political contacts, all the people he donated funds to. Says the MPD's incompetent."

"But it was the MPD that saved his sorry—"

"I know that, Lieutenant, believe me. And I'm very proud of what you and your team have done. Two out of five bombs dismantled. But *one* bomb's too many. One more bomb is intolerable."

"Yes, sir. I understand, sir."

"Lock this up tight, and soon."

* * *

Julia's cell began playing a tune.

"Hey, Mark."

"Hey yourself. You have some time for a tired psychologist?"

"You know I do. Whatcha got in mind?"

"For starters, I was thinking of a margarita at Molly's La Casita."

"That sounds perfect. For starters."

Chapter 75

The Politics of Cooperation

Tuesday morning...solutions generate problems. Julia and her team returned for the second day of bomb security at Pharaoh Health Management Systems. Tankersly had secured several long-handled mirrors designed to view the undersides of cars. All cars were forced to use one entrance. Each car was inspected with the mirrors, while their trunks were opened and checked. The line was snaking out Poplar Avenue, backing up traffic for a half-mile in each direction.

When Sigforth's Mercedes pulled in, he was fit to be tied. He forced his bulk out of the back seat and looked for anyone to blame. "Get that damn mirror out from under my car," he barked. "You there, get the hell out of my trunk."

Tankersly hurried over. "Mr. Sigforth. Please, sir. We have to do this."

"No, you don't have to do this," Sigforth snapped. "My car was checked before I left my house. I promise you nobody planted a bomb on my moving car."

"No sir," said Tankersly, waving his security guards off.

"I want a sit-down with you and that lieutenant," said Sigforth. "*This* morning."

"Yes, sir," Tankersly said.

* * *

Tuesday morning...mine's bigger than yours. Julia and

Tankersly were ushered inside. As before, Sigforth, Gustafson, Conway, and Cranston were there.

Sigforth stood. "For the life of me I can't understand what you're doing," said Sigforth. "You've caused the worst traffic jam I've seen since moving here. How are we supposed to get any work done? And you're no closer to catching this murderer than you were yesterday."

"Sir—" began Tankersly.

"I'm not speaking to you," said Sigforth, focusing on Julia. "Well? How long is this going to take?"

Julia stepped toward him. "Am I correct in my assumption that if anyone died in your parking lot, you'd be the first person to complain to high heaven about it?" she asked.

"Why you arrogant b—"

"I wouldn't use that B-word if I were you, Mr. Sigforth," said Julia, taking another step toward him." It's really un-*be*-coming."

Neither Julia nor Sigforth blinked. Tension hung in the air. Sigforth appeared to be about to say something.

"Sir," said Conway. "May I suggest that it is in the company's best interest for us to *continue* to work cooperatively with the police. Pharaoh Health has been a good community-minded neighbor. We've maintained the most cordial of relationships. And I must say, Mr. Tankersly has gone above and beyond the call in cooperating with the MPD—an exemplary display of Pharaoh Health's commitment to the community."

Silence.

"Of course he's right, John," said Gustafson. "Our company has indeed enjoyed an exemplary working relationship with our men—and women—in blue."

"This might be the perfect time for Mr. Tankersly and Lieutenant Todd to evaluate the effectiveness of their latest safety strategy," said Conway. "And come back to you this afternoon with any revisions?"

"John?" Gustafson said, more pleading than asking.

"I suppose we need to...what was your word, Conway? *Continue?* Yes. We need to continue our exceptional working relationship with the MPD." Conway gave small waving motions of his hand out of Sigforth's view.

Tankersly saw it first. "Yes sir," He said. "We'll be back this afternoon with our revisions." His eyes pleaded with Julia.

She followed. "See y'all this afternoon," Julia said.

* * *

They walked to the elevator without speaking. Tankersly worried about his job. Julia hot. The elevator doors closed. Neither moved to press a button.

"Please, Lieutenant," Tankersly whispered. "Don't do that again."

"I already know the only mistake we made in the implementation of this safety plan—we saved that blowhard's worthless hide." Julia said through a clenched jaw.

Tankersly closed his eyes, took a deep breath, found the button to the basement, and pushed.

Chapter 76

Consequences, Always Consequences

Tuesday afternoon…me and my big mouth. Teresa buzzed in. "Major Williams on line one, Lieutenant."

Julia picked up the receiver, put her finger on the flashing button, closed her eyes, and pushed. "Yes, Major Williams," she said.

"You trying to start World War III?"

"No, sir. I—"

"I warned you. I specifically remember telling you to be careful with Sigforth."

"I know, sir. I—"

"Sigforth has his financial boot so far up every politician's ass they have to say 'Ah' for him to get a shoeshine."

"I understand, sir. I—"

"Lieutenant, you have any idea how much shit is raining down on me? Everyone wants your ass, and I'm just a whisker from giving it to them."

"Sir, is the Director standing next to you?"

"You better believe it, Lieutenant. Now get your shit in order or there'll be hell to pay. And I want that bomber *yesterday.*"

Julia held the receiver in front of her, mesmerized by the flat dial tone.

"You have a good day too, sir," she mumbled.

* * *

Tagger and Marino showed up at Julia's door.

"Got a second, Lieutenant? Tagger asked, leaning through the door jamb.

"Sure, fellas," she said. "Come on in."

"Lieutenant," said Marino, "you sound as if you just got bad news."

"My fault," she said. "I lost it. Got into a pissing contest with Sigforth, and naturally his *is* bigger than mine. That was Major Williams on the phone. Seems that Mr. Sigforth is mighty unhappy with yours truly, and he's been telling everyone he ever bought and paid for."

"You like some time alone, Lieutenant?" asked Tagger.

"Nah," she said. "But if I can't control my mouth I may have *lots* of time alone."

"Sounds like we need a plan B, Lieutenant," said Marino.

"Maybe so," said Julia. "Why are y'all here?"

"We just wanted to bring you up to speed," said Tagger.

"Go for it," she said. "I hope it's good news."

"I followed Sigforth's secretary home," Marino said. "She was pretty shook up. I checked her locks, windows, and closets for her. I couldn't find anything. I'm guessing the bombers got in the garage through the side door."

"Did you calm her down?" she asked.

"I think so. I gave her the name of a good locksmith and told her to put deadbolts on the garage side door, and the side doors to the breezeway," said Marino. "That seemed to help. She was calling him when I left."

"You need to thank Jarvis for helping you save the day," said Julia.

"I'm not going to see him until Saturday," said Marino. "But I do think his father and mother would love to hear it."

"Franklin is going through the MED's surveillance DVDs playing *which one of these is not like the others*," said Tagger. Julia looked lost. "She's looking for anybody who looks suspicious, who doesn't seem to fit the visiting room profile."

"That's a stretch," said Julia.

"I know," said Tagger. "But we're down to stretching."

"As long as we're playing show and tell," Julia said. "I checked on the alibis for a handful of the blog posters. I think we're down to Forturello and Yates. But on a hunch, I mean a *stretch*, I drove out to talk to that eleven year-old who was posting threatening messages. She's bright all right, but she also had help. Turns out Scott Wallace was ghost-writing her posts."

"That's the guy who killed himself, right?" asked Marino.

"That's right," said Julia. "Except Clarisse has been posting right along."

"She find another ghost-writer?" asked Tagger.

"She did indeed—Scotty Wallace," Julia said.

"The Scotty Wallace I questioned?" Marino asked.

"The same," said Julia. "Seems Scotty told her he had all the names from his father's notebook, and he was going to 'finish his Daddy's work'."

"What does that mean?" Tagger asked.

"Clarisse didn't know," said Julia.

"I guess I missed something when I talked to him," said Marino. "He seemed like a genuinely nice kid."

"A genuinely nice kid who lost his entire family and his home inside of twelve months," said Julia.

"I'll check on him at school in the morning," Marino said.

Julia nodded. "In the meantime, I agreed to meet with Sigforth and his band of worshipers this afternoon," she said. "It might be a good idea for y'all to come along, and keep me out of trouble."

Chapter 77

The Spinmeister

Tuesday afternoon...the doctor is in. Gustafson stepped inside Conway's office, and closed the door.

"Nice work this morning, Troy," Gustafson said. "Things were getting kind of dicey in there."

"Like I keep telling everybody," Conway said. "We save our attacks for our enemies. And we tell our *friends* what they want to hear."

"Like focusing on the word *cooperation?*"

"Everyone loves a company that's cooperative and civic minded."

"How're you handling these bombings?"

"We want the media and the public to see the bombers as the villains, not Pharaoh Health. I've been sending out news releases highlighting the careers and families of our people who've experienced these unwarranted attacks. We want them to appear as human and cuddly as possible. Then I load up on statistics like the number of our subscribers and the dollar amount spent to cover medical care. Then I throw out a sampling of high-profile cases—little kids whose lives have been changed for the good by the medical care we've covered. And I end up with how Pharaoh Health provides all these services at a reasonable rate, one of the lowest in the industry.

"Brilliant. What about the subscribers on that blog?"

"It's critical never to make any comment about OPRESSD. I never even use that name in any of our interviews or press releases. I don't respond to specific questions about the subscribers who've died. I only give a general statement of the company's sorrow at the loss of any life. And then I site our company's confidentiality policy that prohibits me from discussing our subscribers and former subscribers."

"Do you have the talking points you always send us for handling the media?" asked Gustafson.

"You'll have a complete playbook by this afternoon," said Conway. "Just keep to the two- or three-word phrases we've developed, and you'll be fine."

"You mean like 'government takeover' and 'socialized medicine', or 'consumer-driven healthcare'?"

"Exactly. Don't stray from the messages. When everyone keeps giving the same short messages, the public will hear it from all quarters—newspaper, TV, radio, and politicians. The short messages are easy to remember, and after a while they'll sound familiar. It won't be long before the public will begin to think they're true. Hell, they'll even believe they're core 'American values,' ones they'd be sure to promote."

"How're we going to deal with John?" Gustafson asked.

"He especially needs to follow the same playbook. It might be good if you sit down with him once it comes out, maybe limit his contact with the media. His temper and attitude will destroy our image with the public. If that happens, it will take years to get it back."

"You have an ace in the hole?"

"We can always play *hide the pea*, and get the public energized about some off-target issue—the incompetence of the police, or the *American value* of 'consumer-driven health care' through which the public has shaped the health insurance industry's fight to contain escalating medical costs."

"Damn. You're good. I can't wait to see the playbook."

Chapter 78

A Hammer Is Rarely the Best Tool

*Tuesday afternoon...*After watching three hours of DVDs, Shawna Franklin had worked out a system. She focused on the Tuttle family and friends she remembered seeing— their patterns of coming and going, their interactions, their demeanor. Using this as a template, she identified other individuals and small groups she judged to be legitimate visitors. She made note of everyone else. So far, two men stood out.

* * *

Tuesday afternoon...from the bottom up. Julia stood beside a security guard in the Pharaoh Health parking lot as she wheeled the four-foot mirror pole under a white Ford Escort.

"The trick is to get used to seeing things inside-out and upside-down," said the guard. "I think of this like my dentist's mirror on steroids. I never realized how crazy it must be to look at teeth through a mirror."

"Let me try," said Julia, reaching for the pole. "What do you call this thing?"

"An *under vehicle search mirror*. Not too creative. They must've named it at the end of a very long day. Usually they at least have a catchy acronym, but *UVSM* doesn't work for this baby."

"I see what you mean about the mirror," said Julia. "And it helps if you're familiar with the typical underside of a car."

"You got that right," said the guard. "My father and mother are both auto mechanics. I've seen lots of undercarriages."

"Let me try a few more," Julia said.

"Go for it, Lieutenant."

* * *

late Tuesday afternoon...leveling the playing field. Tankersly led them down the hall—Julia, Tagger, Marino, and Powers. Cranston stepped out of his office, as if on cue, and escorted them into Sigforth's office. Two new men stood by the wall.

"Well, looks as though we had the same idea," said Sigforth. "I'll introduce mine if you'll introduce yours."

Tagger could almost hear Julia's eyes rolling. He took a half-step sideways until his arm touched hers. She took a breath. "These are members of my team," said Julia. "In fact, this is the team that found the bomb meant for you." Sigforth winced. Julia called their names.

"Special Agent Powers, is it?" Sigforth asked.

"Yes, sir."

"Do you always wear your cap indoors?" Sigforth asked, his lips tightening.

"I wear it to bed, sir," said Powers, smiling.

Sigforth broke his stare from Powers. "These gentlemen are our bodyguards," he said. "Mr. Furman works for me, and Mr. Echols is assigned to Dr. Gustafson when he's in town."

"Did you say Johnnie Tagger?" asked Furman, speaking out of turn. Tagger perked up. "From the University of Michigan? Tight end?"

"Are you the Furman from Perdue?" asked Tagger, his eyes getting larger. "Linebacker?"

"I'll be," said Furman. "I still can't raise my arm all the way because of the hit you laid on me my junior year." Tagger walked over. They shook hands.

"I hate to interrupt this reunion," said Sigforth. "But I

think we have more important things to talk about."

Tagger slapped Furman on his good shoulder and returned to the MPD side of the room.

"Bring us up to speed on your progress," Sigforth said.

"We've checked every car in the parking lot while people are working," said Tankersly. "We're monitoring the turnover in cars. All will be checked before leaving. There'll be no holdup on exiting the lot."

"I don't give a damn about people getting out of the parking lot," Sigforth said. "I want them in the office tomorrow, *on time.*"

"We've streamlined the search process, sir," said Tankersly. "We've added three extra guards screening cars into the parking lot. You gentlemen will be picked up on Poplar and escorted past the line of cars. Since you will have been screened at your homes, you will be able to drive directly to your parking spots."

"And this will move our people into the lot more quickly?" Sigforth asked.

"MPD will be directing traffic on both sides of Poplar," said Julia.

"We'll see if it works," said Sigforth. "Now, Lieutenant, where are you with finding this bomber?"

"We continue to track down every lead," Julia said.

"But you still don't know squat," Sigforth said. "Right? Hell, if I ran this company as effectively as you do your job, we'd be bankrupt."

"And if we did our job like you run your company, they'd still be scraping pieces of your sorry ass off the black top," said Julia.

Sigforth's eyes flashed. Tagger stepped closer until his arm touched Julia's arm again. She took another deep breath. Marino's eyes bore into Sigforth, and Powers broke out in a huge grin. Gustafson shot a pleading look at Conway.

"And we at Pharaoh Health Management Systems will be forever grateful for the bravery and quick actions of the MPD," said Conway.

Powers waved his hand.

"And the ATF, of course," said Conway. "Obvious progress has been made. Speaking for everyone, I feel much safer."

Sigforth stared at Conway, then back at Julia. He said nothing.

"We look forward to an update this time tomorrow," said Gustafson.

Tankersly led them out. Tagger and Furman made eye contact.

* * *

"Thanks, Tag," said Julia. "You didn't stop me from digging my grave, but you kept me from jumping in."

Tag gave her a single nod upward.

"I can see why you lose it with that clown," said Marino. "I'd a taken him out."

"All that disrespectful ranting and raving. I thought I was back in the service," said Powers. "Nice move, Lieutenant. I can't wait to tell Masterson."

Chapter 79

Look What I Found

Wednesday morning...learning something new in school every day. It was the usual controlled chaos of two thousand people, mostly students, all seemingly heading someplace else. Grimacing from the din, Marino spotted Nelly Patterson.

"Mrs. Patterson," he called, walking toward her.

"Well, Sergeant Marino. We'll have to stop meeting like this," Patterson whispered.

"I wanted to tell you the manual is fantastic, and Jarvis loved *Saints Row*. Thank you so much."

"I'm glad everything is working out so nicely. I see you finally got to meet Charlie's student buddy."

"Student buddy?"

"Yes. I saw you walking him down the hall last Friday."

"You mean Scotty?"

"Of course. Scott Wallace, Junior. Everyone calls him JR."

"Have you seen him this morning? Or Charlie?"

"Not yet, but there's still a few minutes before the tardy bell."

"Can you take me to his room?"

"Let me make some arrangements, and I'll be right with you."

* * *

Marino walked outside and grabbed his cell.

"Todd."

"Lieutenant, looks like we've got something."

"Talk to me, Professor."

"Turns out Charlie Barrington's student buddy is Scotty Wallace. And they've been late every Monday morning for the last month.

"Transport them to 201 for questioning."

* * *

Wednesday mid-day…right under our noses. Julia gave the assistant DA a heads-up about the boys being brought in for questioning. Then, on a hunch, she drove to the Wallaces' former house. She checked the garage. The main door and the side door were locked, the windows painted over.

"Back again?"

Julia turned to see the neighbor. "Just curious, Mrs. Halderman."

"I wondered how long it'd take you guys."

"How long for what?"

"Before you'd be checking on those boys."

"Boys?"

"I've seen those two boys going in and out of the garage for months now. They drive that old black truck around, then park it back in the garage."

"A black pickup?"

"Yup."

"You sure?"

"Hey. If you ain't going to listen to me, then why ask?"

"Sorry. The two boys. You recognize them?"

"Duhh. I've been living next to Scotty since he was in short pants."

"You said *boys.*"

"I don't know the name of the other one. But he seems a little off to me."

"Off?"

"Yeah. He gets loud. A funny loud. What do they call that? *You* know."

Julia shrugged.

"Monotony."

"Monotone?"

"Yeah. That's it. He talks in a kind of monotone. And he's not all that coordinated either. Has a funny run."

"Have you seen this other boy before?"

"No, just since they've been breaking into the house."

"You ever report them?"

"Why would I do that? I liked the Wallaces. They always kept their yard up. At least till everything started going to hell in a hand basket."

* * *

Julia returned with Tagger and a search warrant. They snapped on rubber gloves and Tagger broke through the garage side door. Julia found the light switch and flipped it. No lights. They pulled their flashlights. An early-model pickup sat on the far side of the garage. They walked toward it.

"Whoa. I never expected this," Tagger said.

"I was hoping it wasn't true," said Julia.

Tagger found the handle and raised the garage door. The afternoon sun streamed in. The garage was littered with trash, mostly fast food wrappers and cups.

"No dents or marks," said Julia, walking to the back of the truck. "This is a Tennessee plate."

* * *

Wednesday afternoon...just me and my buddy. The two boys were seated in an interrogation room at 201 Poplar. Marino was attempting to engage them.

"You play video games, Charlie?" Marino asked.

"My Dad said not to talk to you," said Charlie. "So I'm not talking to you."

"Yeah, he does," said Scotty.

"He any good?" asked Marino.

"He's very good."

"What games does he play?"

"He only really likes *Saints Row*."

"What about you, Scotty? You play *Saints Row*?" Marino asked.

"Sometimes."

"Lots of explosions in that game," said Marino.

Lucy Collins pushed through the door.

"What's going on here, Sergeant?" Collins said. "You can't be talking to my clients without benefit of attorney."

"I was just making small talk, counselor," said Marino.

"What are the charges?" Collins demanded.

"No charges yet," said Marino. "They're persons of interest. Did you say clients with an *s*?"

"That's right. I've been retained by Mr. Barrington to represent both boys."

"Generous of him," Marino said. "Where is Mr. Barrington? We need to ask him a few questions too."

"What?" said Collins. "This is harassment. I think we're done here."

"Cool your jets, counselor. We're waiting on the Lieutenant. Seems she found a vehicle that's been seen at three of the bombings—parked in the old Wallace garage. I know she'll have a few questions." Collins looked at Scotty, who held his head down, staring at his hands.

"Sergeant, I need a few minutes with my clients, alone," said Collins. "And cut off that microphone."

"Certainly," said Marino, scooting his chair back.

* * *

Julia and Tagger arrived, and found Marino outside the interrogation room talking to Diggs.

"What's up?" asked Julia.

"That attorney, Collins, is in the house," said Marino. "Says Barrington retained her to represent both boys. Got her usual uppity self until I told her you found a certain vehicle in the Wallace garage. She asked for some time with her clients."

They looked through the one-way mirror. Collins was listening to Scotty. Her mouth opened in surprise.

"Oops," Julia said. "Looks like Ms. Collins heard something she didn't expect."

"Looks like he just spilled the beans," said Diggs.

Chapter 80

The Interrogation

Wednesday late afternoon…chasing the truth. Julia and Marino sat across from Collins and the two boys, Scotty and Charlie. "We have nothing to hide, Lieutenant." said Collins. "In fact we welcome the opportunity to be helpful. I'm going to let the boys answer your questions, up to a point."

"Why the change of heart, counselor?" Julia asked.

"Because this time I know their story," Collins said.

"And Mr. Barrington?" asked Marino.

"I've advised him to stay away," said Collins. "I think we can handle this just fine."

"Scotty," said Julia. "I'm Lieutenant Todd. I believe you've met Sergeant Marino."

Scotty nodded, shoulders rounded forward, hands on the table, fingers interlaced, head slightly down, looking just below his eyebrows.

"We know about your family—your mother, your sister, and then your father. We're very sorry."

Scotty began to cry silently, wiping his eyes on the upper portion of his sleeve.

"Tell me about the pickup in your family's garage."

"It was Dad's. He loved that truck."

"Why's it in the garage? Isn't the house in foreclosure?"

"My Uncle Miller used to work on the truck with my Dad.

They'd spend hours together. I suppose he loved the truck almost as much as my Dad. Anyway, Uncle Miller said the bank was taking everything. The truck and the old Mazda were paid for. He told me to park the car in his garage, and when the bank finished changing the locks, park the pickup at the house. So I did."

"Nobody found it?"

"I spray-painted the windows. My uncle said the economy is so bad no one will be looking to buy the house, so it'd be safe, at least for a while."

"You have a Tennessee plate on it."

"The inspection sticker is still up to date. No problem."

"What about the Mississippi plate?"

"What Mississippi plate?"

"Haven't you ever used a Mississippi plate?"

"No, ma'am."

"Your neighbor Mrs. Halderman said you boys have been breaking into the garage and driving the truck out." Charlie began to fidget, wringing his hands. Scotty reached over and put his hand on top of Charlie's. It calmed him.

"Yes, ma'am. I was trying to help Charlie. He loves *Sonic* soft drinks, all crazy combinations. But he'd never done the ordering himself. So we'd go to the *Sonic*. I'd back into an end slot and angle the truck so Charlie would be next to the speaker, and he'd order our drinks. He's getting pretty good at it."

"Which *Sonic*?"

"The ones on Summer Avenue. You know, there's three— one at Sycamore View, one at Stage Road, and one just past Appling."

"That's all you did with the truck?" Charlie started to fidget again. Scotty touched his hands.

"We know we weren't supposed to do it. We figured we'd

298

get caught one of these times."

"Weren't supposed to do what?"

"We'd pull into an empty parking lot, and I'd try to teach Charlie how to drive. It's a stick, and he has a hard time."

"What parking lot? What time?

"We'd go after we got our *Sonics,* around nine-thirty. I guess mostly it was the Perimeter Mall at Summer and White Station."

Julia sat back. She and Marino exchanged looks. "I understand you and Charlie have been tardy every Monday," she said.

"Not me. I think Charlie might have missed the bus once, a while back."

"But the school records show you being absent from homeroom every Monday," said Marino.

"Someone's screwed up," Scotty said. "Mrs. Patterson has been pulling us out for the end-of-year performance. That's our practice time. We're not supposed to be marked absent."

"Tell us about your father's notebook."

Scotty looked surprised. "How'd you know about Dad's notebook?"

"A moment please, Lieutenant," said Collins. "I need to talk to my client. Please."

"Okay," said Julia. "We'll take a stretch break. We'll pick up in fifteen minutes. If the boys need to use the restroom, one of our officers will escort them."

* * *

"What's going on in there?" Diggs asked. "The kid's answers come too easy. He's either the best liar I've ever heard, or—"

"Or he's telling the truth," said Marino.

"I've been watching him and Charlie," said Tagger. "Scotty's taking care of him, even here. He looks like a hell of

299

a kid."

"That's what their teacher Mrs. Patterson says" Marino said. "She thinks he walks on water. And another thing. Patterson *is* working with the special kids in the mornings to put on a show for the parents at the end of the year."

"Professor, check out their story at the *Sonics* and at least the Perimeter Mall," said Julia. "And see if anyone remembers a Mississippi plate, especially since he backs in."

"Already had it on my list," Marino said.

"What's with Collins?" asked Diggs.

"She got their story first, and felt good about it. But clearly she didn't know anything about the notebook," Julia said. "We'll see how cooperative she is when we get back in there."

Chapter 81

The Interrogation II

*The notebook...*Collins tapped on the one-way glass, and motioned for Julia and Marino to come back in.

"Okay, Lieutenant," Collins said. "We're ready." She nodded to Scotty.

"My Dad was awfully upset about the way the health insurance company refused to pay for my sister's operation. Pan died because we couldn't afford to pay for the one she'd had *and* the one she needed. Dad spent hours in his office, on the computer and the phone. He kept a notebook with the names of every person he talked to or emailed. He left it in the desk drawer with a note to me to keep on giving it to Pharaoh Health."

"That's how you found Clarisse?" asked Julia.

Scotty looked surprised. "Yeah. She's a smart little girl. I shouldn't have..."

Collins looked surprised again.

"Have what? Julia asked. "You shouldn't have what, Scotty?"

"She didn't need to be involved with all those posting adults. She's just a kid. She needed to get on with her life."

"You know someone has been planting bombs under the cars of Pharaoh Health employees, don't you?" Charlie started rocking.

"Yeah," said Scotty.

"We think one of the people who've been posting on the OPRESSD blog is the bomber. You've read the postings, you even know some of the people. Who do you think is the most angry?"

"We're all angry."

"The *most* angry," said Julia.

"I think that would be Mr. Yates and Mr. Forturello."

"Why them?"

"They used to come over to the house to talk to Dad."

"You've seen them?" Julia asked.

"Sure, especially Mr. Forturello. One of the reasons he and my Dad hit it off was they both had old Dodge pickups."

"His black too?"

"Yeah, two years older." Julia looked at Marino. He left the room.

"Was your Dad friends with Yates and Forturello?" Julia asked.

"Maybe in the beginning. I didn't see Mr. Yates very much."

"Something change?"

"I don't know. But I remember Dad and Mr. Forturello arguing."

"Arguing?"

"Yeah. They were yelling. Well, Mr. Forturello was yelling the most. He stomped out of our house and slammed the door."

"What were they yelling about?

"I was in my room listening to music. I couldn't hear the words, only that they were yelling."

"When was this?"

"Not long before Dad…"

"So…that would have been last October or November?"

"Yeah, I guess."

"Anybody else come to visit your father?"

"You mean about the blog?"

"Yes."

"I can't say for sure. Most people I only saw once. I didn't always know why they were at our house."

"Can you describe any of them?"

"It was a long time ago."

"I'd like to see your father's notebook."

"Sure."

"Take it to school with you tomorrow, will you?" Julia said. "Leave it in the school office. Sergeant Marino will pick it up."

Scotty nodded.

"Are we done here?" asked Collins.

"Yes, for now. And counselor?" Julia said.

"Yeah."

"Thanks. This has been very helpful."

"I've never been thanked by anyone who interrogated my client. I think I like it."

* * *

Tagger's cell buzzed.

"Sergeant Tagger, this is Franklin."

"What's up, Franklin?"

"I've found three men who just don't seem to fit in. Maybe one of them is the guy you're looking for."

"Be there in twenty."

* * *

Wednesday, late afternoon. Tagger watched while Franklin arranged her DVDs and set up the Union Station equipment. She flipped on the projector.

"I've looked at ten days of DVDs," said Franklin. "There seems to be a kind of pattern for most people. They enter the waiting room unsure of where they're going, often emotional—crying, looking worried, hugging, pacing, talking loudly, or saying nothing. Then they settle in, become part of the entire group. They chat with others in the waiting room. They help new people, tell them the basic goings on. You know—where they can find coffee, the bathroom, and when to expect the nurse to come through. And they all look up when the phone rings with news of one of the patients. Anyway I found three men who didn't seem to fit in at all."

* * *

Tagger knocked on the doorjamb of Julia's office.

"Lieutenant, I think you'll want to take a look at this."

He left, Julia followed.

"Lieutenant, this is Officer Shawna Franklin. She's been providing protection for Shelly Tuttle and her kids. I asked her to look at the MED's DVDs to see if she could see anyone who might just be hanging around for Tuttle or Lyndale."

"Officer Franklin," said Julia extending her hand. "Show me what you've got."

Franklin pressed PLAY. They watched a man fidget in his seat, looking at everyone in the waiting room.

"We can get a good print of his face," said Julia.

Franklin changed discs. A man sat in the corner, eyes down, a brown valise next to his chair.

"Good," said Julia. "He's looking up here. We can get his mug too."

Franklin changed discs again. Pushed PLAY.

"Here's the third—"

"That's Forturello!" Julia interrupted, slapping the table. "You got him. Good work, Franklin. Tag, make sure we get a good print of his face, and send it to everybody."

* * *

Teresa buzzed in.

"Sergeant Marino on two, Lieutenant.

"Whatcha got, Professor?"

"Forturello's gone," said Marino. "Just pulled up stakes and disappeared. The neighbors didn't see anything, and his employer said he never showed up for work yesterday."

"We've got his picture," Julia said. "Somebody has to have seen his truck."

Chapter 82

The Trigger Connection

Wednesday evening…fine tuning. Trigger's cell played *Hound Dog.* He fished it out of his pocket.

"Yeah."

"Is that how you talk to your employer?'

"No…er…no, sir."

"I trust your accommodations have been satisfactory."

"The place is great, the clothes are great. I could use more money."

"More money? Tsk, tsk. That's why I set up the account so that you could only withdraw a certain amount."

"Yeah, but I need more. It's the cost of living."

"It's the cost of *your* living."

"I have needs, you know."

"I'm sure you do. Tell you what. I'll raise the limit on your withdrawal as soon as you do me another service."

"You told me I was all done, I didn't need to be involved. That's why I blew town."

"I know, my dear Mr. Carter."

"Trigger. Call me Trigger."

"Okay, Trigger. Give me some help, and I'll expand your ATM limit."

"Whatcha need?"

"We're having a little problem with something I'm sure

you're quite familiar with."

"Which is?"

"Jammers. The ATF agent is using a jammer to block our signal. Pretty effectively, I must say."

"Shouldn't be a problem. All I gotta do is tell you, and you up my money?"

"That's correct, Trigger."

"Okay. You need a different frequency for your signal."

"And how do I get a different frequency?"

"You go see my friend Paul. He'll set you up."

"And where do I find Paul?"

"At the *WalMart* in West Memphis, Arkansas. He usually hangs around the gun case."

"What do I ask for?"

"I'll give him a call, as soon as I see my ATM limit has been increased—sizably increased."

"Deal. Now, how do I find him, and what's it going to cost me?"

Chapter 83

Getting Help Where You Can Find It

Thursday morning…breaking through. Teresa buzzed in.

"Lieutenant, there's a Mr. Barrington and an attorney out here to see you."

Julia walked to the entrance and shook hands with Lucy Collins. Barrington did not extend his hand. She took them to her office.

"Thanks for coming in," Julia said.

"This is harassment," said Barrington. "Charlie has every right to a free and appropriate education."

Julia looked at Collins.

"Sorry, Lieutenant," Collins said. "I only agreed to get him to come."

"Mr. Barrington—" said Julia.

"I have my attorney," Barrington interrupted. "I don't have to answer any of your questions."

"Mr. Barrington," said Julia firmly. "Look at me."

Barrington looked over Julia's shoulder.

"Look at me, please."

Barrington glanced at her eyes, then away again.

"I'm trying to help Charlie," said Julia. "He and his buddy Scotty helped us yesterday."

Barrington looked surprised.

"And I think you can help us even more."

No response.

"I understand from Mr. Tankersly that you do consulting for his security office at Pharaoh Health."

"That's confidential. I can't discuss confidential contracts," Barrington said.

"It was Mr. Tankersly who suggested I talk to you," said Julia.

Barrington glanced up.

"Here's the situation. One of Pharaoh's employees, Donna Allen, was killed by a car bomb last week." Barrington flinched. "This situation is different because Ms. Allen had been hiding. No one was supposed to know she was staying with her aunt in Mississippi. No one except the human resources office. A secretary put Allen's Mississippi address in her computer. Someone found that information. That's how the killers knew where to find her."

"And how does this involve my client?" asked Collins.

"I don't think it does, counselor," said Julia. "But I think Mr. Barrington can help us find out who hacked into the secretary's computer."

Chapter 84

The Notebook

Thursday afternoon, April 30, 2009...coincidence? Julia, Tagger, Marino, and Powers sat around the conference table.

"Scotty and Charlie's story checks out," said Marino. "The *Sonic* folks, in particular, remember, because Scotty always backed the truck in. They seemed to enjoy imitating Charlie's voice. Oh, and several remember a Tennessee plate on the truck."

"And the parking lot driver training?" Julia asked.

"I watched the Perimeter Mall's DVD," said Marino. "Lots of jumps and stalls. Looked like someone learning to drive a stick."

"Did Scotty take his father's notebook to school this morning?" Julia asked.

"He did," said Marino. "I've gone through it twice. What's that mental health term for people who write about every single detail?"

"Obsessive-compulsive," said Julia.

"Yeah, that's it," said Marino. "And that's Wallace."

"Anything we can use?" Tagger asked.

"Overall, it pretty much verifies what everyone's found so far," Marino said. "It has all the names the Lieutenant gave us as suspects and targets. And there are entries for his phone calls and meetings with Forturello and Yates, just like

Scotty said. And there are politicians he's talked to and corresponded with."

"Sounds as if there's a *but* coming," said Julia.

"Yeah. All the entries are clearly named except one, who's only identified as *pms*,"

"Don't y'all look at me," Julia said. "I never met the man."

"We didn't say a word, Lieutenant," said Powers. "I didn't even bring up your trashing of Sigforth."

Marino cleared his throat loudly. "Wallace had two telephone conversations with *pms*, one in October and one in November," he said. "*Pms* is listed in his appointment log for the day he's supposed to have shot himself."

"Do the times match?" asked Tagger. "The time of the appointment and the time of the gunshot?"

"The appointment falls within the timeframe of the coroner's estimated TOD," said Marino.

"What're you thinking, Professor?" Julia asked.

"Sounds like one of them *coincidences* to me," Marino said.

"Me, too," said Julia.

"So maybe Wallace's death wasn't a suicide?" asked Powers. "Who the hell's pms?"

Tagger passed out pictures of the three men Franklin had identified. The top picture was clearly labeled as Forturello.

"We pulled these prints from the MED's security DVDs," Tagger said. "As you can see, the top one is Forturello. He's the guy with the black Dodge pickup. The other two are just persons of interest. We haven't ID'd them yet."

"So Forturello was at the MED checking up on his victims?" asked Powers. "That's pretty gutsy."

"Or pretty dumb," Marino said.

"Forturello showed up two times," said Tagger. "The last time was the night we arrested Donna Allen."

"The same night he planted the bomb at her garage,"

Powers said.

"That's how they knew she wouldn't be coming straight home," Tagger said. "He saw Allen being arrested."

"I'm going to meet with Sigforth and his merry men this afternoon," Julia said. "Anything you want me to tell him."

"We aren't going with you?" asked Tagger. "I was already thinking of things to say."

Julia shook her head.

"How about letting us go in your place?" Marino asked.

"That's a good idea," Powers said. "None of us would ever lose our cool with that wiseass."

"Thanks, fellas," Julia said. "But I think I need to shoulder my load. I promise to use my *indoor voice.*"

"How much you going to share with him?" Tagger asked.

"Very little," said Julia. "There's a leak at Pharaoh. I don't want to show our hand. Not yet anyway."

"My money's on that strange Cranston," said Powers. "I think I saw his picture when I looked up *snitch* in the dictionary."

"Any progress on finding the leak, Lieutenant?" asked Marino.

"I'm working on it," said Julia.

Chapter 85

Progress

Thursday afternoon...the long-handled whatchamacallit.

"How'd it go this morning, Fuzzy?" Julia asked.

"Much better," said Tankersly.

"Walk me through it," said Julia.

"The congestion on Poplar was minimal. I'm thinking the longest any car had to wait to enter the parking lot was five to eight minutes. And that was for the last cars. Most folks arrived early, like we asked."

"Any flack from Sigforth?"

"Not a whimper. I'd say we're in good shape, and only going to get better."

"Of course we can't do this forever. Even Pharaoh Health can't afford that."

"Any breaks in the case?"

"Not much. It's a slow slog."

"Hey, Lieutenant," yelled a security guard. "Want another run with my handy-dandy under-vehicle search mirror?"

"Actually, that sounds like a good idea," said Julia, turning from Tankersly. "See you at five, Fuzzy."

* * *

The elevator doors closed and Tankersly pushed the button for the basement.

"Why was Sigforth in such a good mood?" asked Julia.

"Beats the hell outta me," said Tankersly. "But I'm not complaining."

"Conway didn't even have to spout any of his classy bull."

"Yeah. Good meeting."

Chapter 86

The Mississippi Lake House

Thursday evening...a hideaway. The Lexus headed south on Highway 72, out of Collierville, into Mississippi. The road had been improved to expressway standards for a short distance, but then returned to the familiar country road. Twenty minutes later it turned right on a narrow, dark, ill-paved country road. The driver kept his speed up, sitting on the centerline as he watched for deer. He drove until he came to a small sign, and turned into the Snow Lake community. He crossed over the spillway, climbed the hill, and pulled behind a black pickup.

"About time," said Forturello. "I'm going stir crazy."

"Calm down, my friend," he said. "There are provisions in the car."

Forturello made two trips to the car, collecting cardboard boxes from the trunk.

"*Costco*, huh?" said Forturello.

"Sure. I love munching my way through the samples. Get something to snack on and tell me how we stand."

* * *

"I drove my car to the West Memphis WalMart and found Paul. Not the most pleasant person I've ever met."

"And?"

"I got new receivers and a new pair of phones, all set to

315

a frequency rarely used by jammers. I made the changes on the pipe bombs. We're good to go."

"I'm afraid we're running out of time, Sammie. Security's getting tighter. Not much room to maneuver."

"Yeah. I've been thinking about that. There's not much room to maneuver *if* you're planning to get away." Forturello let that thought hang. "I don't think we're going to get away with this, and I don't want to go to prison."

"I understand. I've been thinking the same thing."

"I'd say we have two more in us, three at the outside. I really want that pig Lyndale dead so he won't hurt anybody else."

"And I want Sigforth for sure, and at least one other person from the head office."

"Lyndale'd be dead if it weren't for that big black cop. Hell, Tuttle'd be dead too. Damn broad."

"Can't blame them for doing their job, Sammie."

"I can. They interfered. Lyndale and Tuttle should be dead, just like my Antonio."

"I hear Tuttle left town, and Lyndale's still in a coma."

"Maybe I'll just blow up his damn house. Maybe one of those cops."

"I promised Scott I'd take care of Sigforth."

"Yeah, but Scott's dead."

"A promise is a promise. Besides it's personal. That self-centered, greedy, inhumane bastard should not be allowed to breathe our air."

"Well, we have four bombs. I figure two each. If I can get away—great. But I'm willing to die trying."

"Well said. Pop open the Moet Chandon I brought, and we'll drink to that."

Chapter 87

Burning Up the Wires

Friday morning, May 1, 2009...she's gonna do what? Julia drove away from the Pharaoh Health headquarters. The morning had gone smoothly, she thought. Yes, very smoothly. Tankersly will be increasing the guards on the top four administrators for the weekend, beginning after work, extending through Monday morning. Sigforth had been tirade-free. I bet Conway had something to do with that. Julia's cell sounded off.

"Hey, stranger," she said.

"I'm not that strange," said Mark.

"I'm glad you called. I've been thinking about you."

"That sounds promising. Say, I have a dilemma in social etiquette."

"Well, I'm your girl. I know all there is to know about social etiquette. I remember getting a B+ on that paper in sixth grade. I'm pretty sure you start with the outside fork."

"A woman just invited me to dinner."

"I can fix that dilemma in a heartbeat."

"Ordinarily I would agree. But this time it's more complicated."

"More complicated because she's rich, really good looking?" Julia said.

"More complicated because she's your aunt."

"What? Aunt Louise invited you to dinner?"

"Yup. Today at the Brooklyn Bridge Italian Restaurant. Her treat."

"What's up with that?"

"That's why I'm calling you," Mark said.

"Well, what'd you tell her?"

"I said *yes*, naturally."

"Oh. Well, I guess I'd have advised you to do the same," said Julia.

"Anything I should know? Anything the two of you've been cooking up? Anything I can get prepared for?"

"You kidding? I knew nothing about this. This is all Aunt Louise. I'd say to just be yourself. She loves you. Asks about you all the time."

"So you think it's safe?"

"Definitely. And, Mark?"

"Yes."

"Order *Bridgette's Eggplant.*"

* * *

"Hello," Aunt Louise answered.

"Good morning, Aunt Louise," said Julia.

"Oh. Good morning, dear."

"A little bird just told me you are going to dinner at the Bridge."

"That little bird chirp to the name of Mark?"

"That's the one."

"And you're calling to find out why I asked him?"

"That'd be right again," Julia said.

"My, child, don't I have the right to ask a young man to dinner?"

"Normally I'd say yes, and congratulate you. But I'm curious as to the purpose of this particular invitation."

"You've been thinking like a cop for too long."

"It keeps me on my toes."

"I just thought that now you two are a couple again—"

"Aunt Louise..." Julia interrupted.

"Now that you're a couple again, I wanted to get to know Mark better."

"How much better do you need to know him?"

"You're sounding suspicious."

"It's just that I've worked so hard to get him back..."

"Trust me, dear. Nothing's going to change that."

* * *

Thursday afternoon...a break. Marino knocked on the door jamb. Julia looked up. Tagger appeared beside him.

"They found Trigger," said Marino. "Just got a call from my buddy. Trigger's been locked up since last night for possession. Seems he had quite a roll of bills on him. LAPD thinks he was selling. I'm not so sure."

"Be great if *we* could talk to him," said Julia, cocking her head and raising her eyebrows.

"I've seen that look before," said Marino. "I'll pack a bag."

"Why does *he* always get to fly around the country on the department's dime?" Tagger asked.

"Because, big guy, you don't fit in the new economy class seats," said Julia.

* * *

Thursday afternoon...maybe another break. Teresa buzzed in. "Lieutenant, attorney Collins on line two."

"This is Todd. What can I do for you, counselor?"

"It's what *I* can do for *you*."

Chapter 88

The Plea Bargain

Friday afternoon, May 1, 2009...a guilty conscience can be a good thing. The conference room was full, the atmosphere serious, the tone formal. Assistant District Attorney Diggs sat at the head of the table, Julia to his right. At the foot of the table was Lucy Collins. To her right were the Barringtons, father and stepmother flanking Charlie. To her left, down from Julia, sat Scotty Wallace.

"Ms. Collins," said Diggs, gesturing to her, "you called this meeting."

"I want to thank everyone for being here," said Collins. "As you know, Charlie Barrington and Scotty Wallace were picked up for questioning last week. I think the lieutenant would attest to my client's openness in answering her questions. Indeed, it was due to Mr. Wallace's forthcoming that the police were able to make progress on this car bombing case."

Julia nodded.

"So I understand, Ms. Collins," said Diggs.

"Mr. Wallace called me yesterday as his attorney," said Collins. "He said he wanted to tell the police about a specific event I had advised him against sharing in last week's questioning. Being the attorney of record for both Mr. Wallace and Charlie, I found myself in a difficult ethical position.

I approached Lieutenant Todd with a few straw horse scenarios. I met with my clients, and Mr. and Mrs. Barrington. We're here because of your response to one of those straw horse scenarios." Collins took a deep breath.

"Don't stop now, counselor," said Diggs. "I'm all ears."

"Okay, let's proceed by the numbers. First, Mr. Wallace," Collins said, nodding.

"It was my idea to confess," said Scotty. "I want to make it clear that Charlie would never have done this without my influence. I take full responsibility." He paused, watching Charlie rock.

"Go on," said Collins.

"Y'all know about my family—all dead," said Scotty. "I guess I've been so lost...so sad. Charlie's been my only real friend. Then on top of everything else, the bank took our house away. That was all I had left. I got angry. When the car bomb exploded in Wynne, Arkansas I got the idea to blow up my old house, the pickup, everything. Charlie's always been talking about blowing people up and stuff. I asked him if he could make a bomb. He said he could."

Charlie was rocking so hard he was bumping into the table. Neither his father nor his stepmother seemed to notice. They looked down at the table. Scotty slid his chair back and walked over to Charlie. He pushed in between Mr. Barrington and Charlie, leaned over and put his hand on Charlie's until he calmed down. He straightened up and stepped behind Charlie.

"Charlie built a bomb," Scotty said. Mr. Barrington looked up. His wife shuddered. "I placed it under my pickup, and tried to detonate it. But it wouldn't work. Charlie had been so nervous, and he hadn't been taking his medication...he just didn't wire it right. Then three days later the car bomb kills Mr. Tuttle, and all hell broke loose for Charlie. We knew we had nothing to do with *that* bomb. I told Charlie every-thing would be okay if he just kept his mouth shut about what we'd tried to do."

He touched Charlie's hand.

"Charlie would never have done this if I hadn't begged him," Scotty said. "I take full responsibility. It was my idea. It was my fault. I never even thought of anyone getting hurt. But now I can see it was a stupid idea."

"As I understand it, there's another important element in this request for a plea bargain," said Diggs.

"The Lieutenant requested the services of Mr. Barrington in helping to solve the car bombing murders," said Collins. "It involves making use of his unique talents to find the person who's apparently hacked into a computer in the human resources office of Pharaoh Health."

"May I speak to this?" asked Julia.

"Please do," said Diggs.

"Time is of the essence," Julia said. "The bomber or bomb-ers are striking at least weekly. Donna Allen is dead because someone obtained the Mississippi address where she had been hiding. That address came from a human resources computer. We're convinced the next target of the bomber will be another Pharaoh Health employee. It's imperative we find the person who's stealing information."

"Mr. Barrington?" said Diggs. "Are you capable of finding this information?"

No response.

"Mr. Barrington," said Collins. "Please answer."

"I am capable," Barrington said.

"And if I agree to a plea arrangement of no jail time for your son and Mr. Wallace, will you assist the Memphis Police Department in their investigation?" asked Diggs.

"Yes," said Barrington.

* * *

Friday evening... not the one on the bear skin rug. After her Yoga workout, Julia nuked a frozen dinner, one supposedly free of chemical additives. This tastes like cardboard, she thought. Thankfully there's plenty of Michelob. Her cell sounded.

"So how'd it go?" Julia asked.

"Good. You were right, the eggplant was great," said Mark.

"You know what I mean. What'd my aunt have to say?"

"She showed up with three photo albums. We looked at pictures of you and your brother for the entire dinner. Pictures of you mostly."

"Pictures? What's that about?"

"She's very proud of you. I think she should be in sales."

Chapter 89

It Was An Overcast and Rainy Morn

Saturday morning...speed and power. It had been a relatively dry April, but this past week had been overcast and drizzly, with occasional claps of thunder. I wonder if this will be enough rain for those *May flowers*, thought Julia, as she adjusted her runner's cap to keep the rain out of her eyes. She wore a windbreaker. Real runners run in all kinds of weather, Julia reminded herself.

The InsideOut Gym sign came into view as she rounded her last turn. She passed her membership card under the scanner, grabbed a towel and squeaked with every step to her locker. Julia peppered the heavy bag with combination punches and kicks. She pulled off her gloves, dried the sweat on her forehead, and dropped to the mat for push-ups and sit-ups. Then she hit the free weights. Julia was feeling good. For extra measure she mounted the stair-climber, adjusting it to the third highest setting.

* * *

Forturello sat in his car, the engine running, the defroster keeping his windows clear. He chewed his fingernails, watching the numbers change ever so slowly on his dashboard clock.

"Where the hell is she?" he murmured. He eyed the cell

phone on the passenger seat.

* * *

Julia's neighbor Mrs. Woozley was worried. Her new puppy had run off. She stood at the front door as the drizzle picked up, her cell in her hand. She was calling neighbors, asking them to keep an eye out for her puppy. There was no answer at Julia's home.

* * *

Julia felt pumped. Grabbing a bottle of water, she sat until her normal heart rate returned. She walked to her locker, opened the combination lock, and stared at her soaked cap and windbreaker. Wincing, she eased into the wet jacket. A chilly, damp blast of wind got her attention as she opened the gym door, gluing the jacket to her skin. But she overcame the gross-out factor, as she acclimated quickly on the run home. Within twenty minutes she was on her street.

* * *

Forturello saw a hat-covered head bobbing in the distance. "That her?" he said. He reached for his phone, his eyes still focused on the runner. He dared to click on his wipers for a single pass. "Yes. The bitch is back." He opened the cell.

* * *

Coming up to her house Julia saw a small puppy shivering, halfway under her car. She stopped at the bottom of the driveway and squatted, looking up the small incline, coaxing the puppy to come to her. The soaked puppy looked at her with pitiful eyes, no intention of leaving the shelter of the car. Julia duck-walked six feet up the drive with her hands out, talking to the puppy. At last it walked to Julia, and stood on its back legs to lick her face. Julia turned her face away to protect her eyes. That's when she saw it—a pipe bomb!

* * *

"That's it," Forturello whispered. "Walk right up to the car. Get nice and close. Daddy's got a surprise for you." His finger was on the six. "Shit! She's seen it." He looked down at the cell and punched in the code: ...6, 3, 9, 4.

BOOM!

* * *

Julia grabbed the puppy and took off like a sprinter out of the starting blocks. A six-foot wooden fence separated the neighbor's yard from hers. Two strides brought her within a foot of the barrier. She pushed the puppy over the fence as she jumped, grabbed the top, and pulled—swinging her legs to the side and diving over the fence in one continuous motion. She saw the flash and heard the explosion just as she cleared, then dropped to the ground next to the puppy. Mrs. Woozley watched in terror as her puppy came flying over the fence, followed by Julia and a terrible explosion.

"Call 911," yelled Julia. "Fire *and* police."

Woozley hesitated, trying to understand.

"Do it now!"

Julia started to turn when she realized she was holding the whimpering puppy. She kissed it on the top of its head and sat it on the ground as she ducked and ran to the edge of what was left of the fence, sweeping the street, left then right. She saw taillights of a car as it fishtailed around a corner. Julia sprinted back to Woozley.

"I need your phone," Julia barked. She punched in the Union Station direct line, described as much of the car and its direction as she could, and ordered a thorough search.

"Awww, Parsley," said Woozley.

Julia looked down to see the puppy licking her ankle.

"You saved Parsley."

"Actually, Mrs. Woozley," said Julia, picking up the puppy. "Parsley saved me."

Chapter 90

Too Close

Saturday morning...don't tug on superwoman's cape. The Memphis Firefighters and the rain-soaked houses helped to keep fire damage to a minimum. The top half of Woozley's fence was gone. Julia's car was totaled. Umbrella-covered onlookers stood outside the barriers. Powers had his team working the scene. The fishtailing car was nowhere to be found.

"Julia. My God, Julia," said Mark, reaching for her.

"I'm okay," Julia said, soaked and goose-bumpy. "Really. A little puppy saved my life."

"You're shivering. You need to get out of these wet things," Mark said. "You're going to catch pneumonia."

"After I've talked to my guys," Julia said.

Tagger had been questioning onlookers as well as the home owners down the street where Julia had seen the car. He walked up. "Lieutenant," he said. "I have three people who agree they saw a light gray car parked at the curb this morning, possibly a Chevy Impala. They all saw a lone male driver inside."

He been there long?" asked Julia.

"From their stories, I'm guessing he'd been waiting there for thirty or forty minutes," said Tagger.

"You show them Forturello's picture?" Julia asked.

"Nobody saw him clearly," said Tagger, gesturing with his thumb. "Lieutenant, is it true you dove over that fence?"

"Yeah, I guess I did," said Julia, looking back. "Me and a dog. But it was much higher then."

"We're chipping in to get a cape," Tagger said. "One with a *big red S.*"

"Now look, Tag," said Julia. "You need to assume we're all on Forturello's hit list, including Powers. Take precautions. Check your cars and the surrounding area regularly."

"We got the message," said Tagger.

"Apparently, having a dog helps," said Mark.

Chapter 91

Frustrated

Saturday morning...hapless. Forturello sped down Airways Boulevard, pulling into the fairgrounds and parking behind one of the old buildings scheduled for demolition.

"How'd I miss her?" he asked himself out loud, banging on the steering wheel. "I'm such a dip shit. I can't do anything right...a damn cat. She's a damn cat with too many lives left. I only have one bomb."

Forturello checked his watch. Still talking to himself, he got out of the car and went to the trunk, retrieving a gym bag and a folding chair. He opened the driver-side rear door, setting the gym bag on the blacktop. He unfolded the chair and laid it on the seat, backside down, securing it with the seatbelt. The four legs extended to the door. He jiggled the chair to test the tightness of the seatbelt.

Forturello pulled his last pipe bomb and a roll of duct tape from the gym bag. He secured the bomb to one of the top chair legs, placing it at window height. He tested the steadiness of his creation, dropped the tape back in the bag, stowing it on the floor. He closed the door carefully, clicking it shut by leaning against it.

Forturello checked his watch again as he slid into the driver's seat and started the car. Gustafson's limo should be leaving the Peabody Hotel right about now, he thought. I'll be waiting.

Chapter 92

Checking In

breaking news from the bluff city... His cell rang. Marino read the caller ID.

"You know what time it is in California?"

"It's time to get your sorry butt out of bed," Tagger said.

"Tony, the bomber's hit again. This time he went after the lieutenant."

"Jesus. She's not dead, is she?"

"No, but she should be. You know she's always exercising. Well, she finished her morning run and started up her driveway. Some small dog's whizzing on the tire of her car. She sees it, thinks it's cute, and calls it to her. When she squats down to pet the dog she happens to see a pipe bomb under her car."

"Don't tell me. She threw herself on the dog to protect it."

"Almost. She high-jumps the neighbor's six-foot fence... get this...carrying the damn dog. Falls on the other side just as the bomb explodes."

"You're pulling my chain."

"As God's my witness. You can't dream this shit up."

"You catch those SOBs?"

"No. But this time it was only one male, and he wasn't in a pickup."

"Oh-oh. The MO's changing. At least one of them's

going rogue."

"Or desperate. Maybe suicidal."

"You need to watch yourself, Johnnie."

"Yeah. Say, when you going to question Trigger?"

"In about three hours. I'll call. Y'all be careful."

* * *

Julia's cell rang. Before she could say anything, Teresa said, "Lieutenant, you okay?"

"I twisted my arm a little, but I'm fine," Julia said.

"Thank God."

"Your nephew with you today?"

"Yeah. He's in the conference room playing the game Marino gave him."

"I'm afraid I sent Marino to California. You might want to tell Jarvis it's my fault Marino's not here."

"Got it. Say, Lieutenant? Mr. Tankersly called saying he heard on the news about the bomb this morning. He wanted to know which of his employees were targeted. I told him it was you. He was shocked. I told him that as far as I knew, you were all right. He asked me to have you call him."

"Will do. And Teresa?"

"Ma'am?"

"Thanks."

* * *

"Tankersly," he answered.

"Fuzzy, this is Todd."

"I'm so happy to hear your voice, Lieutenant," said Tankersly. "Glad you're okay."

"Me, too. Ms. Johnson said you wanted to talk to me."

"Remember we were trying to figure out why Sigforth was so uncharacteristically nice yesterday?"

"I remember."

"Turns out Sigforth's heading down to Tunica for a

weekend of gambling and partying. He's taking Conway. Gustafson is flying back to New York this morning. And Cranston left town to stay with his mother in Baltimore."

"Sigforth and Conway dating now?"

"They make this Mississippi run every so often. They usually stay at Harrah's Casino Resort. There are plenty of *dates* down there to choose from."

"I assume you're handling security."

"Cranston's car was cleared before he left. We'll clear Gustafson's limo before he leaves the Peabody Hotel. A guard will be waiting for him at the airport, and will stay with him till he boards. We'll cover Sigforth and Conway twenty-four-seven, and their car won't move until we've searched it."

"Good luck."

"Keep your head down, Lieutenant."

Chapter 93

It's For You, Antonio

Saturday morning...no failure this time. The gray Impala crept from behind the building toward Airways Boulevard. Forturello focused on the southbound traffic coming from his right, on the far side of the wide boulevard. He saw the limo stopped at the Central Avenue traffic light. Perfect, he thought, he's in the left hand lane. I can drive through the boulevard opening and pull up beside him in the middle lane. The bomb will be right next to his head. He opened his cell phone, holding it in his left hand, and inched the Impala onto Airways.

Horns blared and braking tires squealed, snapping his attention to the traffic coming from his left. He slammed on his brake and, cussing, dropped the gear into reverse. Drivers yelled and threw him the finger as they drove past.

Officer Hartsfield drove east on Central, moving slowly as he scanned the side streets. He'd been on the lookout for a gray Chevy Impala since the bombing. He entered the Airways intersection, crossing in front of the waiting Limo, when he heard the commotion. He caught a glimpse of a large gray car backing into the fairgrounds driveway. He hit his brakes, turned on his flashers and siren, waited for traffic to clear, and made a crazy right turn—driving headlong into on-coming cars on the northbound side of the boulevard.

More squealing tires. The police car swerved in and out of traffic, as it closed on the Impala.

Forturello reacted immediately to the siren. The intensity drained from his face, replaced by a look of hopelessness. His tense muscles released. His rigid posture slumped, and he sank in his seat.

"No, God. Please," he said, hitting and shaking the steering wheel.

He sat up straight, determination returning in his eyes. He punched in numbers as the police car closed in ...6, 3, 9....

"The happiest day of my life was when you were born, Antonio," Forturello said. Then he punched in the last digit of his son's birthdate: 4.

BOOM!

Hartsfield stomped on his brake. Pieces of the gray car rained on the cruiser, and flames engulfed the Impala. Stunned, it took several seconds before he could move. He radioed for assistance.

Chapter 94

Suicide Mission

*No exit strategy...*Tagger and Julia arrived at the second bombing scene of the day. Powers was on their heels. Fire-fighters extinguished the last of the blaze. A covered body lie on a stretcher.

"Officer Hartsfield is it?" asked Julia, "I understand you observed the explosion?"

"Yes, ma'am," said Hartsfield, staring. "The car blew up right in front of me."

"You okay?"

"Yes, ma'am. Just a bit shook up. I've never seen anything like it."

"What did you observe?"

"I was driving east on Central," he said, pointing back over his shoulder. "I'd been searching for the gray Impala. Cars were honking. I looked to see what was going on. That's when I saw the Impala. I cut through the traffic. Next thing I know, there was an explosion and the sky lit up, fifty feet in front of me. My windshield is smashed, my ears are still ringing. I can't believe it."

"See that sergeant over there? The big guy?" asked Julia, pointing. "The same exact thing happened to him a few weeks ago. Make sure you talk to him before you leave."

"Yes, ma'am."

* * *

"It's Sammie Forturello," Julia said. "His wallet confirms it."

"That guy tried to kill you this morning," said Tagger.

"Maybe even the same guy who almost took you out," Julia said. "

"Looks like the bomb was rigged to sit up level with the window of the back seat," said Powers. "Nothing to slow down the blast but glass. I'm wondering who his target was."

"Tankersly told me Gustafson was flying back to New York this morning," said Julia. "He'd have been coming from downtown, right down Airways to the airport. I wonder if that's who he was waiting for."

"And if it was Gustafson, how'd he know he'd be coming this way? At this time?" Tagger asked.

"If he planned to take someone out, Forturello didn't have an exit strategy," Powers said. "No way he could have detonated that bomb and lived. I've seen too many of these. This was a suicide mission."

"A suicide mission?" said Julia.

Powers nodded. "I wonder if the second man is as desperate," he said. "Assuming there are only two bombers."

"Who's most likely to be the next victim?" asked Tagger. "Besides us?"

"I would've thought it'd be Sigforth," said Julia. "But maybe it's because he's the one I'd go after."

"He's got my vote, Lieutenant," Powers said.

* * *

Julia's cell rang. "Todd," she answered.

"This is Lindsey Barrington."

"Yes, Mr. Barrington. Thank you for calling. Did you find anything?"

"Yes."

"Tell me what you found?" asked Julia, trying to stay calm.

"I found the IP address of the computer that hacked into the human resources computers."

"Who owns the computer with that IP address?"

"It also hacked into the computers in security."

"Security?"

"And the CEO's computer."

"Who does the IP address belong to?"

"I don't know."

"Do you know where we can find that particular computer?"

"Yes."

"Mr. Barrington," said Julia, taking a deep breath. "How do I find this hacker's computer?"

"Snow Lake. Snow Lake, in Mississippi."

* * *

"Tag, I've called Diggs for a search warrant," said Julia. "He's coordinating with the Mississippi authorities. They'll meet you at this address at Snow Lake.

"Where the hell's Snow Lake?" asked Tagger.

"Don't have a clue. MapQuest it."

Chapter 95

Heading to the Casinos

feeling lucky...The Mercedes pulled into Conway's driveway. He came out rolling a suitcase with a laptop case stacked on top, *The Girl With The Dragon Tattoo* in his other hand.

"Good afternoon, sir," said Furman, standing beside the open door. "Let me take your bags." Conway climbed in the back seat on the driver's side. Furman closed the door. Sigforth was engrossed in a telephone conversation, looking out the side window. Furman stowed the bags in the trunk and returned to the driver's seat.

"Furman?" asked Conway.

"Sir?" Furman said.

"I've got this tickle in my throat. Can you stop somewhere on the way and get a small bottle of orange juice?"

"I believe there's some juice in the mini-fridge, sir. If not, I'll stop before we get on the highway."

"You're a good man, Furman."

Chapter 96

From the West Coast

Saturday afternoon…out of town for one day.

"Teresa, this is Marino."

"Hey, Sergeant. How you coping with all those gorgeous Hollywood women?"

"So far the sexiest women I've seen are really men."

Teresa couldn't stop laughing as she pictured Marino trying to pick up a Hollywood *woman*.

"Let me talk to the lieutenant," Marino said. "I'll call back later. Maybe I can talk to Jarvis."

"That would be great. I'll get her."

* * *

"Afternoon, Professor," Julia answered.

"Hey, Lieutenant. Good to hear your voice. Johnnie told me about you pole vaulting over a fence while holding a dog in your teeth."

"Remind me to have his eyes checked on his next physical," said Julia.

"Glad you're okay, Lieutenant."

"Thanks. Me, too. And for the record, the dog weighed seventy-five pounds if he was an ounce. And I didn't use a pole. It was a classic nineteen-sixties-style *western roll* type of high-jump."

Marino smiled. "I just finished talking to Trigger," he said.

"He doesn't know a lot more than we do. He said he was hired by a guy flashing a lot of money and driving a Lexus. Said he drove him to some lake in Mississippi."

"Snow Lake?"

"How'd you know?"

"Fill you in later. Go on with your story."

"Anyway, they met with another guy. Trigger built the pipe bombs for them."

"How many?" Julia asked.

"He says nine or ten."

"What about names?"

"Said nobody mentioned any names, and he didn't ask."

"Could he describe them?"

"Not much beyond white, average height, average weight, average yadda yadda."

"They arrange for him to leave town?"

"He had a sweet deal. A pre-paid rental cabin not far from the beach. And money from an

ATM—up to five hundred dollars a week. Said he got a call from one of the men a few nights ago."

"What about?"

"Seems the guy was upset about Powers jamming his bombs. Wanted to know how to get

around that."

"Did Trigger tell him?"

"More than that. He made arrangements for the man to pick up new receivers and cell phones calibrated to rarely used frequencies."

"Where'd he get those things?" she asked.

"Where we get everything in the midsouth—at our friendly neighborhood WalMart."

"WalMart. Damn."

"Turns out there's someone named Paul who hangs

around the gun section in the West
Memphis WalMart. Paul agreed to set them up for a price."

"So now the bombs can't be jammed?" Julia asked.

"Not unless Powers can figure out the new frequency."

"How'd LAPD find Trigger?"

"They picked him and his three girlfriends up for partying a little too hard. Unfortunately, he had rock cocaine on him. So they hauled him in," Marino said. "How'd you know about Snow Lake?"

"I asked Barrington to see if someone's been hacking into the Pharaoh Health human
resources computers."

"Barrington? How'd you swing that?"

"His attorney helped," said Julia. "She assured him we weren't after Charlie."

"I didn't think we were after Charlie anymore."

"You sitting down?"

"Yeah. Why?"

"Turns out Charlie really did build a bomb after all."

"What?"

"And Scotty planted it under his father's old truck."

"Scotty?" Marino said. "I don't believe it. Not Scotty."

"It was a dud," Julia said. "The Tuttle bomb went off before they could try again. They got scared and decided to keep their mouths shut."

"So why'd they fess up?"

"Scotty was feeling guilty. Needed to get it off his chest, didn't want Charlie getting in trouble."

"It must be the time change," said Marino. "I'm not following this."

"It's complicated," said Julia. "Short version is Scotty went to his attorney Collins, who came to me. We went to Diggs to get a plea agreement to keep the boys out of jail if Barrington would help us find the Pharaoh hacker."

"Barrington agreed? I'll be damned."

"He did. Found the whole place had been hacked— human services, security, and the CEO's office. The IP address was linked to a house on Snow Lake."

"Who owns it?"

"We don't know. I sent Tag down there to find out."

"Sounds like things are falling into place."

"We got one more puzzle piece. Sammie Forturello blew himself up a few hours ago."

"You shitting me? I leave town for one day and the case breaks open."

"As far as we can figure, Forturello had one last bomb. He was willing to die
to get Gustafson. But before he could pull it off, a young officer closed in on him. He blew himself up."

"I'll be…"

"We're still thinking there's only one more bomber. I hope so. Maybe we'll have him by
the time you return."

"I already told Johnnie to be extra careful. The same goes for you, Lieutenant I want you
both alive and well when I step off that plane."

"I want that too. I'll make arrangements for you to bring Trigger back to Memphis. You
may have to stay in LA a little longer."

"Don't wait too long. This is a dangerous city. A person could get killed here."

* * *

Marino called back to Union Station. Teresa answered the call.

"How's my boy?" asked Marino.

"Jarvis is acting funny," Teresa said. "He keeps looking at the door. I think he misses you."

"How does he do on the phone?"

"I don't know. You want to try?"

"Sure."

"I'll put you through to the conference room phone. Hold on, it'll be ringing till I pick it up."

* * *

"Here's Jarvis," Teresa said, handing him the phone. Jarvis looked at it. "Say hello, Jarvis."

No response.

"Hey, Jarvis. This is Sergeant Marino."

Jarvis held the receiver away, still looking at it.

Teresa moved it closer to his ear. "Say hello, Jarvis," she said.

"Hello, Jarvis," he repeated.

"Are you playing *Saints Row?*" asked Marino.

Jarvis nodded.

"You can't just nod, Jarvis," said Teresa. "You have to talk. Say yes."

"Yes," said Jarvis.

"I wanted to tell you that I'm in Los Angeles, California," said Marino. "And we just had a 4.2 quake."

Jarvis smiled.

* * *

"Well, that was a new experience," said Teresa.

"Yeah. Thanks for the help," said Marino.

"Must be something in that manual of yours about using a telephone."

"I don't remember seeing it. But I'll check with Mrs. Patterson when I get back. Maybe there's a volume two."

Chapter 97

The Snow Lake Manifesto

Organized till the very end... Tagger got directions from the regional Mississippi district attorney's office. He and Franklin drove southeast from midtown on Lamar, across the state line to Holly Springs, then east on Route 4 to Snow Lake. He eased over the spillway and around the lake, stopping when he saw the black pickup. Mississippi authorities waited on the back porch of the lake house. Tagger and Franklin walked to the group and introduced themselves.

"We need to break in?" asked Tagger. The Highway Patrol Officer pointed to a plastic bag nailed to the door. Tagger stepped forward, snapped on rubber gloves, and opened the bag. Inside were a key and a folded piece of paper. He opened the typewritten note.

Dear Officers,
If you are here it means our work is done, and we are probably dead. No need to break in. Please use the key. You will find a detailed accounting of our actions and the reasons for those actions.
We understand what we have done is murder. We accept the consequences. But we believe what Pharaoh Health Management Systems and so many other health insurance companies have done, and

continue to do, is also murder. Thousands of Americans have died because of greedy, selfish, and insensitive decisions made by the health insurance executives and staffs. But until now, none of those executives ever died because of their actions.

We hope we have sent a message in behalf of the American people who all deserve access to medical care, regardless of what the shareholders demand and politicians acquiesce to.

* * *

"Sergeant Tagger on one, Lieutenant," said Teresa.

"Tag, whatcha got?" said Julia.

"The mother lode, Lieutenant," said Tagger. "There's a ream of notes. This guy makes Scott Wallace look like a piker. No detail is too small to be included."

Chapter 98

The Last Bombs

No collateral damage...Furman's route to Tunica was almost all interstate. From Collierville he took the Bill Morris Parkway to I-240 west, then south on I-55 into Mississippi, and west on the new leg of I-69. They were five minutes from the Tunica exit. Sigforth remained on the phone.

Conway's cell rang. "Troy Conway," he answered.

"Mr. Conway, this is Lieutenant Todd."

"Good afternoon, Lieutenant."

"You with Mr. Sigforth?"

"He's sitting right beside me."

"Did you know two more bombs were exploded this morning?" asked Julia.

"I heard about one, and that no one was hurt. I haven't heard about the second."

"Sammie Forturello blew himself up at the fairgrounds. He was waiting for Dr. Gustafson's car to pass by on his way to the airport."

"No one else was...injured?" asked Conway. "Eric is okay?"

"He's okay. Had no idea he was almost killed."

"So the bomber killed himself. I suppose that's the end of it."

"I'm sure it's not."

"It's not?"

"No," Julia said.

"I gather you've been to Snow Lake."

"Yes sir. We found your manifesto."

"Then you know why I have to do what I'm going to do."

"It's over, Mr. Conway. You don't have to do this."

"Excuse me a second, Lieutenant," he said, calling to Furman. "I've still got a tickle in my throat. Would you be so kind as stop and buy me some cough drops?"

"No problem, sir," said Furman. "We'll be exiting onto Highway 61 just ahead. I'll stop at the first store we come to."

"I'm sorry, Lieutenant," said Conway. "I had to take care of a little business. Now, where were we?"

"It's over. Please don't do this. Believe me. I know Sigforth is the ultimate jerk, but that doesn't mean you have to kill him."

"I disagree, Lieutenant. And you have no idea how evil he is." He looked over at Sigforth who was getting animated. "He's been on the phone since I got in the car. He's working on some deal to increase his scandalously high income. He doesn't even know we're talking."

Furman took the Tunica exit south toward Casino Row.

"Furman is pulling into this store to get me some cough drops, Lieutenant," said Conway. "He's really a good person. John and I will be alone."

"Please, please don't do this."

"I have a call to make on my other phone. Oh, Lieutenant, I'm glad Sammie didn't kill you. You're a good person, too."

Julia's phone went dead. Conway opened a second cell phone and punched in Antonio's birthdate...6, 3, 9, 4.

Chapter 99

The Roll of the Dice

Saturday afternoon…craps. Julia and Powers took the I-240 loop south from Union Avenue, continuing on I-55 into Mississippi, following the path Furman had driven toward the Tunica casinos. Tagger and Franklin headed west from Snow Lake to meet them.

"The biggest blast radius yet," said Powers. "Looks like there were two pipe bombs in the trunk. He put all his remaining eggs in this basket."

"Another suicide mission, but he took out his target," said Julia.

"I've only read halfway through Conway's notes," said Tagger. "But I did read the part about his turnaround. According to him, Pharaoh Health routinely refused to cover medical treatment, and part of Conway's job was to protect the company by snowing subscribers and the media."

"Yeah," said Julia. "I read that on the OPRESSD blog."

"His conscience got the better of him," Tagger said. "He began siding with subscribers, trying to convince Sigforth to give in, but no dice. He took a personal interest in Pandora Wallace's denial. He called Wallace when Pharaoh refused to cover the treatment for his daughter despite his objections. After she died, he went to Wallace's house to talk with him. His notes say Wallace shot himself right in front of him. That would get anyone's attention. From what he says, that image was seared in his mind. He decided he had to do something."

Chapter 100

The Postmortem

Tuesday morning, May 5, 2009...that's a wrap. The atmosphere was relaxed—a combination of fatigue and emotional relief. The Memphis bombings were over.

"What kind of car you getting, Lieutenant?" asked Tagger.

"You considered an armor-plated one?" Powers asked.

"Or maybe just installing a mirror in your driveway," said Marino.

"Haven't decided," Julia said. "But I'll keep your suggestions in mind. In the meantime, I'll just drive my loaner."

"Tell us about California," Tagger said.

"Not much to tell," said Marino. "It ain't Kansas—smog, traffic, gang graffiti, crime, the smell of marijuana. I walked through three different gang-marked turfs on my trips to and from the police station."

"No beautiful people?" asked Powers.

"They must've been partying while I slept," Marino said. "It's good to be home."

"Trigger give you any trouble?" asked Julia.

"Nah," said Marino. "Like Doc said, that Iraqi IED slowed him down. He's just an easygoing guy, lacking in judgment."

"Having shrapnel in your brain'll do that," Powers said.

"Yeah. He set off the airport metal detector," Marino said. "The TSA guys went crazy trying to figure out what was activating their equipment. I'd never seen them wand anyone's head before."

"Speaking of Trigger, our guys found Paul in aisle five," said Powers. "Turns out he's been a very active entrepreneur, a key man in the explosives trade with lots of connections. He's a great find."

"Maybe we can all sleep easier," said Tagger.

"Fill me in on this manifesto you found," Marino said. "Never figured Conway for a bomber."

"Just a real talented guy who got caught up in the game of verbal manipulation," said Tagger. "The more he did, the more skilled he became. The greater his skill, the higher he rose in the company ranks, and the harder he chased the financial benefits."

"But something happened?" asked Marino.

"Yeah," said Julia. "For some reason he began to pay attention to the pleas for coverage from family members. He was moved by the individual subscribers' stories. He got personally involved."

"He got a conscience," said Tagger. "Started sticking up for the subscribers. Management wasn't happy with him. They didn't consider him a team player anymore. Sigforth in particular was upset with him. He figured his days with the company were numbered."

"For some reason he got really drawn to Pandora Wallace's case," Julia said. "He lobbied for the insurance coverage to be reinstated. But Sigforth wouldn't budge. When Pandora died Conway knew something had to change in his life. That's when he started talking to Pandora's father. Watching Wallace shoot himself was the proverbial straw."

"And the idea for car bombs?" asked Marino.

"It came from the Wynne, Arkansas car bombing," said Tagger.

"How'd he get hooked up with Trigger?" asked Marino.

"It was Forturello who'd run into Trigger," said Tagger. "According to Conway's journal, Forturello was in so much grief about his son Antonio's death that he'd see his kid everywhere. One day he thought he saw Antonio, but it was Trigger. They got to talking."

"Conway was a regular OPRESSD blog reader," said Julia. "He knew Forturello was angry. He approached him. After several meetings they agreed to work together to pay back Pharaoh Health. The idea of car bombs came up, and Forturello remembered Trigger."

"So it was Conway who got Allen's Mississippi address from human resources." Marino said.

"And he knew what Tankersly's security plans were—who'd be where, and when," said Tagger. "That's how Forturello knew Gustafson's route to the airport, and when he'd be leaving the Peabody."

"How'd it turn out for Charlie and Scotty?" asked Marino.

"Diggs didn't really have a case without a confession," Julia said. "If Scotty hadn't have come forward, we never would have known. Barrington was interested in getting beyond this thing, as long as Charlie wouldn't be arrested. Attorney Collins worked magic with her straw horse scenarios, and of course, we wanted help from Barrington. The punch line is the boys will be doing a lot of community service."

"What's the latest on Lyndale?" Marino asked.

"He's still in a coma," Tagger said. "The doctors are pessimistic. Pharaoh Health insisted on moving him to a less expensive hospice program."

"I don't know how I feel about that," said Marino. "All his chickens came home to roost, but still…"

No one spoke for several seconds.

Powers broke the silence. "I guess Conway was *pms*," he

said. "But I'm not getting the connection."

"All we have are guesses," said Julia. "I'm thinking it stands for Pharaoh Management Systems."

"That's a whole lot better than pinning that moniker on you, Lieutenant," said Tagger.

Julia rolled her eyes.

Chapter 101

Touching Base with the Boss

*Running the media gauntlet...*Julia sat in Major Williams' outer office at 201 Poplar. The door opened.

"Lieutenant, please come in," said Williams. "Thanks for stopping by."

"No problem, sir," Julia said.

"I know press conferences are a pain in the ass. I apologize for that. But I thought it went well, didn't you?"

"I don't think I'll ever get used to those things. I realize the public has a right to know, and I understand the department's need for positive news. I just wish it were somebody else doing it."

"I seem to recall making similar statements early on in my career. Tell me, Julia, how are you doing? You know, so many close calls."

"I'm hanging in there, sir. I've received good help from the psychologists—*all the psychologists*, she thought—and my team seems to be doing well."

"The Director received an outstanding letter from ATF. Seems you made quite an impression on...er..."

"Special Agent Powers, sir?"

"Yes, that's the name."

"He's a good man."

"Please accept my congratulations on a job well

done, Lieutenant."

"Thank you, sir."

"And convey my congratulations and gratitude to Sergeants Tagger and Marino, as well."

"I'll do it, sir. Thank you. They're good men, too."

Chapter 102

The Silver Lining

"Hello," answered Julia.

"Good news, dear," said Aunt Louise.

"I'm all ears."

"Beth's grandson Dana is going to have his heart surgeries after all."

"They find a new health insurance company?"

"Same company. Seems they had a change of heart, so to speak."

"Any chance Pharaoh Health had anything to do with that?" Julia asked.

"Beth said the Memphis car bombings made headlines for a week in their local paper. The public was outraged at their health insurance company's refusal to cover necessary medical costs of their subscribers. The company reversed dozens of denials."

"Glad to hear it."

"You made a real difference, my brave little guardian," said Aunt Louise. "Good has already come from it."

"That's sweet of you to say."

"Now, staying with good things, I'm hoping you'll bring Mark to Sunday dinner."

"I think that can be arranged."

"I got him with the photo albums, didn't I?"

"I think it was the eggplant."